NEVER GO FULL PAI

Jeffrey Eng

A NOVEL

Illustrations: Bruno Guerreiro
Layout: Jon Loudon

Title: Never Go Full Pai / A novel / Fiction
Never Go Full Pai Copyright © 2019 by Jeffrey Eng
ISBN: 978-1-7334112-0-2 (Hardcover)
ISBN: 978-1-7334112-1-9 (Paperback)
ISBN: 978-1-7334112-2-6 (Ebook)

www.jeffreyengbooks.com
Instagram: @jengajenga

To Mom, Dad, and Chris

On a brisk morning, in a warm bed, next to the woman he loved, he declared himself a writer. A hidden declaration in a foreign city he now called home.

But like most writers, he liked to drink, and unfortunately also like most writers, he became better at drinking than he was at writing...

JEFFREY ENG

PROLOGUE

The city was growing dark, as the sun began to hide behind the buildings and the trees. The expanding shadows were a much-welcomed arrival from the hot Southeast Asian sun. Ace and I had been at the bar for several hours while most of the other hostel occupants, those more prone to sightseeing, hadn't yet made it back from their daily excursions. Only the fresh new arrivals scattered meekly around the quiet bar. I was already drunk and slouched trying to keep up with Ace's drinking pace, while Ace sat tall and seemingly unaffected by the mass alcohol we had already consumed. A childish grin of excitement plastered across his face just like it did at the beginning of every night, before the drinks caught up with him, and before the sadness in his eyes arrived. But as we sat in the early moments of the night he was full of eagerness and hope as he began his routine of explaining a card game to new hostel arrivals.

"Can I use these cards?" the young woman asked, pointing to the cards on the table, confused, and, at the least, a bit drunk.

"No! No! No! You can't touch those cards until you finish discarding the cards in your hand," Ace said, smiling. I think he enjoyed seeing people struggle with the rules, and if you were drunk, then even better.

The game was called Shithead. The game started with each player holding three cards in their hands. On the table were three cards face down and, on top of that, three cards face up. This was a common card game played among backpackers in hostel bars. I'd played almost nightly since I had arrived in Asia. Ace had taught me the same way he was now teaching the new arrivals.

Ace took a large swig of his beer, emptying the remaining liquid into his mouth. He quickly put the empty beer down and exchanged it for a new one. The brief pause to fill his mouth with beer was the only time he took a break from talking. After a large swig from his fresh beer, he continued his explanation and shuffled the remaining cards in a Hindu shuffle that he had perfected over the years in backpacker hostels just like this one. The cards floated around his fingers with ease and moved with speed and efficiency. On most days it was actually quite entertaining to watch, but today I was annoyed with his antics.

I knew the rules. I knew Ace was going to keep talking. I knew how this night was going to go, as I had seen it night after night since I'd been traveling. And I knew that Ace would need another beer soon, so I excused myself to get everyone a fresh Tiger beer for the game. If I was lucky, I would be able to skip most of his performance as well.

When we started the game, the hostel bar was quiet. A few people milled about the room checking their phones or talking on FaceTime to someone back home. Others gathered in small groups having quiet conversations. The only other sound was Ace's loud voice that boomed around the hostel bar.

Two players at our table had just arrived and were fresh into their first week of a three-month travel stint in Southeast Asia. They were Ace's favorite kind of people to play with, not because he gained an advantage by knowing a winning strategy, but because it gave him a chance to explain the rules and be in control of the table. Every question and comment would go through him.

His speech continued, "The goal is to get rid of all your cards. The winner is the first person to do that, but no one gives a shit about winning this game. The real goal... is not to finish last! Because, you see, if

4

you finish last, you become the shithead, and if you are the shithead, you have to finish all the beer left in these beautiful Tiger bottles." He tapped his fingers gently against his almost full beer and took another large swig of it.

The basic rules of the game were simple. To start, you would flip a card over from the center pile, and then in a clockwise direction the next player would have to put a higher card down and so on. If you didn't have a higher card, you were forced to pick up the ever-growing pile of discarded cards.

"Seems easy enough," commented the other girl in our game.

"Yes! That part is easy!" Ace proclaimed. The next step is where everyone always got confused. Ace paused to survey the audience, like he was making a formal speech, making sure to look everyone in the eye.

"However," he paused—he always paused here, just long enough to add a bit of dramatic effect. I had seen him teach this game so many times that I had practically memorized his lines. Every time Ace taught the game, he made it a show, as if people had come to see him perform. I was sure he liked explaining the rules of the game more than actually playing.

"The twist of the game is there are four *magic* cards," he continued. That was true, but rules changed dramatically depending on who was playing. "The *magic* cards are... the 7, the 8, the 10, and the jack." He loved calling them magic cards and emphasizing the word "magic" to make it seem more mysterious. He went on to explain what each magic card did and how to use it in the game. "Everyone got it?" He looked around the table with a mischievous smile. No one ever did; new players always stared back at him with bewildered expressions.

"You will get the hang of it as we play," I chimed in, looking at the other two faces as they tried to remember all the rules they were just explained.

"Now, let's play!" Ace announced, and we all clanked our beers together.

The game moved fast, and cards were thrown down quickly, almost as quickly as we drank the beer from the bottles. Soon the empty beers and pile of cards in the center of the table grew and everyone became desperate, trying to avoid picking them up. But eventually, no matter what, someone would not possess a higher card and would be relegated to picking up the pile of discarded cards. That was, unless they had one of the specified magic cards that could be used at any time. This is where strategy diverged, and each person developed their own style to either win or become the shithead.

Ace always threw down his magic cards as quickly as possible, trying at all costs to avoid picking up the discarded middle pile, no matter how big or how small that pile was, and making everyone react to his play. It was carefree and loose and was almost spontaneous to a fault, as if he had gained no knowledge from past mistakes. I, on the other hand, waited patiently and opted for a more conservative strategy. I tended to hoard magic cards, and would wait for just the right moment, for the perfect opportunity to strike. Sometimes, though, that opportunity sailed past me and I would watch someone else glide into victory as I stared passively at a handful of unused cards that were now no benefit to me in future games.

As suspected, the two other players picked up the rules quickly, and after they had played a few rounds, the game flowed beautifully. Cards were placed down fast, and reactions to smart plays were congratulated. The empty Tiger bottles piled across the table, and it looked like a streak of tigers resting in the jungle. We grew louder, and everyone became more animated, the more we drank. Soon the quiet bar was no longer quiet, and other travelers who were checking their social media pages were now drawn to our table. In Ace's eyes, that would usually deem the night a success. We would open up the game to new players, and, once again, Ace could run through his spiel of the rules.

After several games, and with everyone in the hostel now participating, the night had truly sprung to life. Soon enough we would all be drunk and stumble our way through the bars, where we'd sing and dance to American pop songs. The beautiful people from around the world would try to hook up with other beautiful people. If you were unlucky in that department, you would find yourself happily stuffing your face with the delicious street food from vendors who made a killing on the loose pockets of drunk Western travelers. This was the hostel life I had come to know, but I was waiting and hoping that, in all this, there was something more. Something other than the bars and parties and the long drunken nights.

1

It was eleven o'clock in the morning and I limped my way through the large airport. After the long flight, my ankles had swelled, and my skin pushed against the brace on my right ankle, causing severe pain with each step. I followed the signs to immigration as I clenched my blue passport with my fingers, my knuckles turning white from the pressure.

Passing the time in the immigration line, I flipped through my passport and I read and re-read the inspirational quotes and stared at the pictures that covered the blank pages. Roaming buffaloes. Steam engine trains. Farmers tending to their land. Nostalgic images of an old America.

I soon reached the front of the line and answered the questions nervously from the immigration officer, smiling awkwardly. Giving me a quick look, he turned to the empty first page of my passport and aggressively stamped it, passing me through. I stared at the new marking that now appeared in my passport. That small stamp made it official; I was no longer in a place of familiarity. Gone were the comforts of my city, my room, of everything I knew. I was now somewhere completely new. Somewhere completely and utterly foreign to me.

I continued to limp my way through the airport to baggage claim. The conveyor belt rolled and the carousel turned. I wiped my sweaty palms against my sweater as I watched bag after bag slide down and crash against the sidewall. With each loud thump I cringed with the thought that my belongings were going to arrive broken and shattered. Those belongings that I so safely tried to pack made me think about my family, especially my dad, and I took a shallow breath. I hope he was right.

Then I saw it emerge. A giant blue backpack peeked over the horizon of the churning machine and slid down and landed safely into my awaiting hands. I lifted it up, it felt heavier than it had just one day ago. I hoisted it on my back and slowly limped away. I was used to the pain and the limp, so I continued and followed the path to the exit signs. I passed a large sign. It was written in several languages; I could only read one: "Welcome to Vietnam."

2

The ride from the airport was long, and the traffic was thick. The cab drifted from side to side as we made our way through the large highways that were filled mostly with cars leaving the airport. The cab driver caught my eye as I shifted in the backseat, trying to gently massage my ankles trying to relieve my achy legs. It wasn't working, so I decided to forget my ankle and instead stared out the window at my new surroundings.

As we approached the city, the large highways shrank to smaller and busier streets. A heavy rain began to fall, soaking the cars and streets and everything else outside my window. No one outside seemed to notice as life continued. The traffic continued just as heavy with cars and motorbikes, seemingly floating on the water-soaked ground. I again caught the cab driver's eyes in the rearview mirror as he squinted and smiled. I could tell when he smiled, as the wrinkles on his weathered face curled up around his eyes as he stared at me. He seemed more interested in me than the road, but his eyes were calming, and I was able to relax as I stared out into this foreign land.

My heavy blue backpack occupied the seat next to me. It was huge and packed to the brim with my possessions. I wasn't particularly looking forward to carrying it on the trip, and I had already struggled with its size and weight when I had limped my way from baggage claim to the taxi pickup line. I thought, *How am I supposed to carry this thing across Asia for the next two months?* I pushed the bag aside and continued watching the rain fall hard outside as quarter-size droplets fell on the windshield of the taxi.

My eyes once again met the taxi driver's eyes, and his eyes squinted from his grin.

"American?" he said, almost turning completely around, and proving his smile was large and happy.

"Yes!" I shouted, hoping to be heard over the noise of the traffic that surrounded us.

"First time in Saigon?"

"Yes!" I said, almost yelling.

"Sun Always Rises Backpacker? Yes? Party party. Very beautiful girls. I take there." The driver again turned around and smiled that big smile. "We very close now. Lot of people here in Saigon. Traffic crazy."

Just as quickly as the rain had started, the raindrops instantaneously stopped as we inched our way deeper into the city. Here, small motorbikes began to quickly outnumber the cars, and they zipped around the slow-moving traffic and created an ever-present buzzing noise. My face was pressed against the window, trying to take it all in. We passed wide tree-lined streets and chaotic roundabouts that somehow kept the traffic moving, albeit slowly. The streets and sidewalks were full of action, and I tried to follow it with my eyes and absorb my new surroundings. Suddenly, the car stopped.

"We here. Sun Always Rises Backpackers," the taxi driver announced, pointing across the street to a large truck.

"Where?" I questioned.

"Sorry, truck blocking road. I can drop off here. You... walk across. Hostel is behind truck." He made a walking motion with his fingers and continued to smile.

I stepped out onto the sidewalk and noticed that the sun was beginning to show through the thinning dark clouds. The warmth of the morning immediately caused my upper brow to release a few drops of sweat. The sweater I wore had felt thin and cold only one day ago but was now hot and suffocating in the Southeast Asian heat. I dragged my heavy backpack from the back seat and paid the taxi driver with my fresh new Vietnamese dong. The taxi driver smiled, got into his car and vanished into the sea of traffic.

The streets and sidewalks were bustling like a wild circus. Men and women walked through the busy streets and in between the traffic like magicians. Small motorbikes, some with three to four passengers, wiggled down the streets like a well-rehearsed juggling act. Men and women on old rickety pedal bikes crept down the street carrying unknown parcels with a weight that seemed impossibly heavy. Swarms of people walked around the streets screaming and yelling, like ringmasters selling an assortment of goodies. In all the chaos, however, everyone seemed to be in sync.

I, on the other hand, stood like a statue, trapped in my stillness. An almost overflowing feeling of disorientation swept over me. I could now see the small hostel sign that read The Sun Always Rises Hostel across the street, but how was I supposed to get there? The street in front of me was like a fast-flowing rapid river after a winters melt. I looked to the left and to the right for some type of crosswalk. There was nothing. I tried to step forward, but every time I did, a taxi or a motorbike would zoom past me, missing me by inches. My heart was pounding in my chest, and I could feel the sweat build on my body. The heat began to feel suffocating, and my heavy backpack made my legs quiver and ache with pain. My eyes darted from one direction to another. All of my senses seemed to be working to exhaustion as I tried to wrap my head around the scene that I had been thrust into.

My breath was rapid and shallow. The panic inside began to rise. I felt my pulse pick up even more with every car and motorbike that passed. The doubts I had had before the trip burned inside me like a wildfire. How could I travel in Asia by myself when I couldn't even cross the street? What was I doing here? Why did I think I could do a trip like this? A wave of regret suddenly rushed over me. My fingers began digging into my pockets, searching for an escape route to more comfortable surroundings. I felt dizzy, and my body swayed back and forth like a fighter that was a punch away from being knocked out. I tried to close my eyes and breathe, but that only seemed to heighten my anxiety.

There on the sidewalk of Phạm Ngũ Lão, on the first day of my first adventure away from home, I stood like a deer in headlights. I could feel bodies passing me in every direction and at great speed. Some missed me, some gently nudged me, and some walloped me like I was invisible. As the anxiety kept me frozen, a man appeared in front of me. He was talking to me, but I couldn't hear a word he was saying. My ears could hear only the buzz of thousands of motorbikes racing past. The man moved closer, and still, I stood there, frozen. My legs wouldn't move, and my ears wouldn't listen. A drop of sweat dripped down my forehead, and I watched as it fell from my face in slow motion, descending through the air and down to the ground, where it splattered on the warm sidewalk. As I looked up, the man was now inches from my face.

"Hey kid! HEY MATE! Are you ok?"

I could now hear him, as he was yelling inches from my face, but still didn't react. *Snap out of it*, I repeated inside my spinning head. I shook my head, and my tunnel vision widened, and the blood seemed to rush back into my brain.

"Ummmm... yes. Umm, yes... Yes, I'm ok," I sheepishly whispered.

"That's a relief, mate. I thought I was going to have to call a bloody ambulance. You are probably suffering from heat exhaustion from wearing those trousers and that jumper. Bro, you know it's bloody hot today. Where are you staying?"

The man who faced me was older than me but had a young face. He had an American accent, but he used a mix of slang that resembled a blended version of other English-speaking countries. He stood tall and tanned and had an athletic build that impressively filled out his tank top. His face was a wonderful combination of ruggedness and handsomeness.

"You got a monster of a backpack on. Are you coming from a trek?" Unsure of what that meant, I didn't say anything. "Well, hmmm . . ." He looked around several times, probably hoping someone would soon claim me. "You must be in the right place. What backpacker's hostel are you staying in?" he asked.

"The Sun Always Rises Backpackers," I murmured, as I pulled out the piece of paper with my confirmation on it. The paper was moist from the sweat on my palms.

"Brilliant! You only have a few more steps, and you are home. Let's hit it." He waved emphatically from just outside the chaos that was the road that blocked my passage. "I'll show you where you need to check-in." He looked at me and smiled a big smile and stuck his hand out.

I didn't move, as if I were on the edge of a cliff and one wrong step would send me plummeting to my death.

Without saying anything, I gave him another piece of paper that was equally wet. He took the letter, and I could see him mouthing the words over and over again in disbelief. He looked quizzically at me as if he were assessing me. His eyes moved up and down, and I tried to stand up straight, but with my large backpack I looked at best like a lost puppy and at worst like someone who definitely didn't belong there. The man shook his head playfully and smiled.

"Well then, Charlie. I'm Ace. It looks like we'll be working together, and this time I expect a proper colleague handshake." He reached out his hand again, grabbed my hand and shook it so hard I thought my bones were going to break. "I work at that this ol' backpacker's hostel too. Only for a few more weeks, though, and then I'm off to Myanmar. After that, I'll make my way up to Central Asia, maybe Uzbekistan or Kyrgyzstan. The Silk Road is supposed to be unreal, and I need to get there before it gets too touristy. You know what I mean?" Ace got all this out while still shaking my hand. I didn't have the slightest clue what he was talking about.

"Enough ideal chitchat. Let's get inside. Fucking hot out today. I'll show you around quickly, and then I need to work my shift. We run a tight ship here, mate. No time for hanging about," he added.

I stood frozen, and sensing my hesitation with crossing the road, Ace yanked my hand and pulled me into the street, right into the heart of the rapid river. He was talking to me as we pushed ourselves into the streets, but I couldn't hear a word he said. My legs could barely keep up with my upper body as Ace held his firm grip on my wrist. The cars and motorbikes whooshed passed us, and several times I closed my eyes, thinking I was on the brink of being smashed to bits, but soon enough we stood safely on the other side. I looked back and forth in shock at what had just happened, checking my body with my hands to make sure nothing had been ripped off.

"Sorry about dragging ya, but the key to crossing the street here is to keep walking. You just have to walk confidently, and all the cars and bikes, and whatever else is in those crazy streets, will simply go around you." He pantomimed a Spanish matador avoiding a charging bull. "But... if ya hesitate walking on the street, you will end up on the street. You know what I mean?"

Again, I had no idea, but before I could answer, Ace was already on the move, and soon he vanished under the large sign spray-painted in bright red and yellow letters: The Sun Always Rises Hostel.

3

Every inch of the lobby was painted in vibrant colors. It was in a large rectangular shape, and there were people either milling around or sitting on large beanbags, staring at their phones. The wall on the left featured a large map of Vietnam, and a big painting of the Vietnamese flag covered a sizable portion of the right wall. From the ceiling, two large pens hung where people could write on the flag and leave quotes, jokes or heartfelt messages. Mostly it was filled with people's Instagram handles, along with desperate pleas such as "FOLLOW ME @notlostjusttraveling95."

Directly in front of us at the opposite end of the room was a large desk and behind it a wall covered with a daily schedule of day and night activities. Ace was there and waving me over.

"This is her! The best hostel in Saigon! And home to the world-famous The Sun Always Drinks Pub Crawl," Ace boomed with pride as if he were introducing the hostel for entry into a royal party. His arms were splayed out wide as he turned in a circle.

"I've been here off and on for the past few years. I'll check you in and show you to your room. I saw your letter; now let's see that passport and visa, and then we are good to go." Ace took the items from me and quickly raced around the desk where a woman with her back turned to me was working. I looked up and saw tonight's schedule, and it read "Sun Always Drinks Bar Crawl—8 p.m. to... Sun Rise."

"Hey, Charlie boy. I need you," Ace yelled, his back turned to me as he continued talking to the person at the front desk.

I hoisted my backpack that weighed my shoulders down and walked over to Ace. Instantly the muscles in my shoulder began to burn again under the weight of my pack. The waist strap tugged at my hips as I walked to the desk in a penguin motion as the momentum of the bag swayed me side to side.

"Mr. Charlie, let me introduce you to another member of our respected team. This here is Margarita or, as I call her, Magaroni. She has the best smile in Vietnam and the biggest heart. Right, love?"

Ace reached his head across the counter and kissed her on the cheek. When Ace moved his head, it revealed one of the most beautiful girls I had ever seen. Her tanned complexion was smooth and soft, and she had a radiant smile so contagious that even I began to smile. She had long dark hair that fell loosely over her bare shoulders, and she wore a tank top that read "The Sun Always Drinks Pub Crawl."

"Oh, thanks for the intro, Ace. Hello, I'm Margarita, but everyone, except Ace, calls me Maggie," she said.

"Hi, I'm Charlie," I responded, still smiling.

"Where are you coming from? You are making me feel hot in that sweater," she said.

"Ummm, Philadelphia, Margarita... I mean Maggie. It's winter there."

"Well, it's always summer here, mate. I hope you got some jerseys in that Mount Everest bag," Ace said, still looking at Maggie.

Maggie replied, "Stop being a dick, Ace. Welcome to Vietnam, Charlie. You've met Ace, the biggest asshole in Vietnam," she added with such a big smile that it was hard to take the insult seriously, and Ace obviously didn't, as he went in for another kiss on her cheek.

"So, what room is Mr. Dickens staying in?" Ace asked.

Maggie looked down at the computer screen and then looked back up, still smiling. "Looks like we got Charlie in The Pilar Room."

"Perfect! Great room. Let's go, mate. I got to come back down here and help Miss Magaroni." He winked at her as he reached down and lifted my pack up with ease and carried it to the elevators.

"No rush! You don't do any work anyway!" she yelled as we headed into the elevator.

"Floor two. Room 204—The Pilar Room," Ace said. "I have a private room, perks of being a veteran here on the road." He elbowed me softly with a big mischievous smile.

"Where is she from?" I responded.

"Who? Oh, Magaroni? She's from Mexico. Beautiful lass. And, hey, I've been helping you for the past 15 minutes, and you can't string two words together, but then a beautiful girl appears and you finally find your tongue? Oh, Charlie, you are in trouble here, mate."

The doors of the elevator opened, and Ace led the way down the long, narrow hallway.

201: A Moveable Feast

202: The Torrents of Spring

203: The Cuba Room

"And here we are, 204. The Pilar Room. Little history, my young Charlie. This room was named after Mr. Ernest Hemingway's infamous boat *Pilar* that he used while living in Cuba. She is a lovely room, full of beauty and mystery, but don't get any wild thoughts. She may get wet in seas, but only a select few will get lucky in her." Ace laughed hysterically at his own joke.

"Geez, mate, that was one of my better jokes," Ace laughed again when I didn't respond.

"Sorry, I think I'm a bit jet-lagged," I said, trying to smile.

"Well, I guess you only react to beautiful girls," Ace said and shrugged.

I stood at the door. Ace put the key into the lock—*click click click*— and opened the door to the room.

The room was small and hot. It might have been even warmer in here than outside. A small fan churned on the ceiling, but its best attempts of providing any cooling were defeated by the Saigon heat. There were two bunk beds that sat on adjacent sides of the room. Two of the beds had large packs placed on them, and each of them was covered with flags badly sewn on. The packs were open, with clothes pouring out of them and onto the floor. Half-empty water bottles lay scattered on the beds, and dirty towels slumped half on the beds and half on the floor.

Ace, still holding my pack, looked around.

"Fucking savages in here, Charlie," he said, surveying the mess on the beds.

"Bad luck today getting a top bunk. Remember, always get the bottom bunk. You won't believe the times I have drunkenly fallen off the top bunk. The good news is I think your roommates are checking out tomorrow, so you should move your stuff down here after they leave." As Ace kept talking, I began carefully pulling my belongings out of my pack, starting with a large case that sat on my pile of clothes.

"Mate, what the fuck do you have in there?" Ace asked.

"My camera," I said, a little embarrassed.

"Oh, so are you some travel photographer on Instagram?" Ace said in a dismissive, sarcastic tone.

"Oh no, I don't have Instagram," I said, not looking up as I began unzipping the top compartment and pulling out my camera, making sure that everything had made it through the journey in one piece.

Ace was now standing over me as I removed the camera from the soft material of its casing.

"Film?" he asked in a completely different tone than his last question. I was always a bit hesitant of answering that question because it was usually followed up with a hipster comment, but Ace didn't say anything after I nodded; he just continued to stare as I inspected the camera. Everything looked to be in order, and my camera seemed to have survived the journey in one piece.

"May I?" Ace asked very politely in a more subdued voice as he reached his arms out like he was going to pick up a newborn baby. I handed the camera over to him, and he held it gently in his hands as he examined it. The smile that had been plastered all over his face since I had met him vanished and a look of sadness replaced it as he quietly ran his fingers over the body of the camera.

"What camera do you have?" I asked, assuming that because of his interest in my camera, he must have one of his own.

"This one." He pulled out his phone. "I'm no photographer, but I once knew someone who was an amazing talent behind the lens." He paused, and his face turned white and his voice softened "She used a film camera, just like this one." He stared at the camera in a daze, his eyes not blinking, as if he were seeing a ghost.

"It's a nice camera," Ace said softly as he handed it slowly back to me.

I held the camera in my hands like I was seeing an old friend.

* * *

He can't describe the bones cracking or his mother's screams as the car catapulted into him, but he has lived ever since with the results. The mangled ankle bones that healed like the pieces of a jigsaw puzzle wrongly forced together and a nerve that was too far severed to repair left his disfigured foot limp and unusable. To keep him mobile he was given a large brace. He hated that brace. He hated the bulkiness of it. He hated the way it made his shoes look as it bulged and stretched out the sides. He hated catching his toe on curbs and the limp that he was sure everyone laughed at. He hated the jeans he always wore in the peak of the Philadelphia summers so that his brace wouldn't show. He hated how his life was so stagnant while other kids ran and jumped and explored.

The injury may have made him limp, but nothing physical caused him to slump the way he did when he walked. To stare out at the ground. To constantly look at that shoe with the worn-out toe box from striking too many curbs. To walk chin down, staring at the inefficient gait and the hard plastic that pushed on his skin and out against his shoes, causing a permanent mass of ugliness. Nothing made him do it, but that is what happened, and for most of his childhood, he lived with a self-imposed restriction on where and how far he would walk. Eventually, he found solace in the stillness that came with being by himself.

Stillness, however, lent him plenty of time for observation. Staring at the kids from his window as they sped up and down the streets on their bikes. Peeking his eyes over the counter at his favorite pizza restaurant as the pizza maker flung the dough high into the air. Watching his mom and dad dance to old records in the living room. And on the best of weekends, watching his dad take photographs. He had grown up silently observing his dad operate that camera. He would watch him, study him, idolize him. Often, they would leave their neighborhood together and venture out to the park benches in Fairmount Park or Rittenhouse

Square. As long as the camera was there, Charlie would follow.

The camera was a Nikon FM2. His dad had bought it sometime in the early 1980s. Now, you could probably find it online for a cheap price, but it was his father's prized possession, and Charlie loved watching what those little clicks would turn into.

If Charlie was static, his dad was dynamic. He was always moving and always with his camera in hand. He walked everywhere he could. From the tree-lined neighborhoods of Society Hill to the narrow alleyways of South Philly. Through the cobblestone streets of Old City and up and around the gentrifying streets of Northern Liberties.

His dad was a United States Postal Services employee, one of the few mailmen who still walked their beat every day. He walked in the cold winters with snow up to his knees and walked in the hot summers as sweat soaked his shirt. A person invisible to everyone except for the occasional head nod or silent wave. But he loved his job and loved the streets he walked.

When he came home after a long shift, he always wore a big smile, like he had just had the best day of his life, with his camera dangling behind him. Charlie would sometimes ask him, "Why do you smile so much after work? Do you really like walking the same streets every day?"

"Sometimes you can find beauty in the ordinary," his dad always responded.

"But every day is the same. When I'm older, I want something more exciting for my job," Charlie rebutted once, in a regrettable voice full of teenage angst.

"Well, what job would that be?" his dad asked, smiling down at him.

Charlie shook his head and shifted his eyes downwards. He had no idea what he wanted to do. Up to that point, all he knew was what he couldn't do.

"If you think every day you are going to find a pot of gold, then you will always be chasing rainbows. But for me, I find small pieces of gold every time I step out onto the streets. Go get my camera; let me show you!"

It was the first time his dad had let him use the camera, and when Charlie peered through the lens, something lit up inside him. A whole new world opened up before him, all through that narrow opening of the camera. His dad showed him little subtleties of life on the streets that he had never noticed before. All the little pieces of gold that could be found when looking through the right lens. Charlie's fingers were anxious and wanted to quickly take photos. "Be patient. Study the subject. Do not rush," Charlie's dad repeated. But Charlie couldn't help himself. He clicked away fast and free. His eyes and camera darted quickly around the streets.

"Charlie! What are you shooting?" his dad questioned softly.

Charlie shrugged. The momentum of the camera in constant motion had now swung him almost dizzy.

"Listen, Charlie. Digital cameras are about capturing all of the moments. Film cameras like the one you are holding is about capturing that one moment—that one moment in which you can catch a singular emotion. That singular time in a person's life. Being able to wait for that moment is what will make your pictures breathe. Remember... be patient. Study the subject. Do not rush."

More camera lessons soon followed, and Charlie's dad taught him about depth of field and shutter speed, and how to work with different lighting and shadows. That is when Charlie began truly seeing the world for the first time, on a no-name street with his head up and a camera in his hand. He was soon obsessed.

While other children asked for bikes for their birthday, he asked for a subscription to *National Geographic*. He was mesmerized by the photographs that spread across the glossy sheets of paper. In that magazine and with those images, he could travel anywhere. The deserts of Morocco. The markets of India. The city streets of London. The mountaintops of the Himalayas. He spent hours combing through the pages, and late at night, with a flashlight illuminating the pages, he imagined himself in exotic lands where he would take photographs and have adventures far beyond Philadelphia.

Soon Charlie no longer had to be coerced into taking walking trips through the city. The weight of the camera around his neck felt like a shield of armor, and he didn't care how he limped. Charlie and his dad would walk through Reading Terminal and the Ninth Street Italian markets in South Philly. They would take photographs of the vendors with their produce and women with the flowers and his dad would give him tips on how to focus the camera and how to frame a great picture. On Friday nights, his parents would order pizza, and then his dad would drop the freshly developed prints on the table, and they would all relive the beautiful sights of the city. His dad would always say how Charlie's photos were better than his, but Charlie never believed him.

Soon, he was taking after-school classes in photography, and when he went away to college, he studied photography there too. He excelled in his classes, but he still didn't think anyone would ever want to see his photographs.

Charlie assumed anyone could take a photo like his. All someone had to do was take a class or two. Learn the basics of aperture, shutter speed, and ISO, and you would instantly become a photographer. He always thought his talent was blown out of proportion, that maybe his parents just felt so sorry for him and his disability that they overcompensated and praised his photographs more than they deserved. But what he didn't understand, what he didn't realize, was that what separated him from others wasn't necessarily his great ability to manipulate buttons on a camera. It was something more, something you couldn't teach, something you couldn't learn from a diagram or an exposure triangle. Charlie's unseen talent was his ability to set a scene and allow the characters to act naturally and move as if he wasn't there. His presence was calm and put all of his subjects at ease. His camera pointed in their direction evoked no fake smiles, pouted faces or the simulated gestures that often result when a stranger's camera is shoved in someone's face. Charlie was able to connect with someone whom he had never met and allow them to be vulnerable, and in return he was able to capture a true emotion. A truth that only a photograph taken at the right time could reveal. When it was time to develop his photographs, his pictures would leap off the page with vibrance and energy while his classmates' photos stayed flat and still. During critiques, teachers and students alike praised and raved, but Charlie would just nod and repeat his favorite line: "It's just finding beauty in the ordinary. Well, at least that's what my dad would say."

After he graduated from college, he returned home. Waiting for him in his room was a small box that was wrapped perfectly with a card. His parents stood just outside the door. His dad seemed nervous as he began speaking:

"Charlie, your mother and I are so proud of you and everything you've accomplished. We don't have a lot, but we are so thankful for you. Happy graduation, my boy!" On top of the package, a small card with his mother's beautiful handwriting read, simply:

> *Dear Charlie,*
> *To the only person who can do this camera justice.*
> *Love, Mom and Dad*

Two months later, Charlie's dad died. If that sounds abrupt, it was. He had been diagnosed with leukemia 10 years earlier. His parents had held that information from him to avoid any undue stress. Instead, the world crashed down on him all in one go. With his dad gone and feeling lost and empty, he resorted to staying mostly in his room, and his eyes drifted back to the ground. His dad's old camera, Charlie was still unable to call it his, hung untouched, along with a sealed envelope from him that sat unread.

Months passed, and soon winter and the snow hugged against his window. One day, his mom burst into his room.

"If you're not going to open this, I will!" She held the envelope in her hand. He didn't want to read his dad's handwriting. He didn't want to get that close to him again and then realize he was gone. "Open it!" She threw it at him as he lay on the bed. Charlie's hands shook as he ripped open the edges. One small piece of paper was inside.

> *I know you were upset that we didn't tell you I was sick.*
> *Your mother and I have our reasoning that you may or*
> *may not ever understand, but we thought it was for the*
> *best. Thank you for being such a wonderful son. Trust me,*
> *I had a great life, and I don't have many regrets, but if I*
> *have one, it was that I never took a risk. I don't want you*
> *to have the same regret. Look up and follow your dreams.*
> *Go find that pot of gold.*

Enclosed was a check with an amount that made Charlie's jaw drop. On the memo it read *"National Geographic* photo shoot." He looked at his mom, and they hugged and cried until they couldn't cry anymore. One month later, Charlie was on a plane to the other side of the world.

* * *

It was just an old Nikon, but I was happy it was here with me. I placed the camera back into the case and zipped it up and placed it back in my pack.

"Alright, Charlie, you probably want to get things sorted. How about we meet down in the lobby around six, and I'll take you out for your first proper Vietnamese dinner."

"That would be wonderful. I think I'd get lost in this city if I went by myself."

"You will get used to it. Alright, here is your key. And, Charlie, take off that fucking jumper."

4

My eyes slowly blinked open, my neck wet with sweat, and for a moment I was confused about where I was. All I could feel was the heat of the room. I quickly popped up to find myself staring at the ceiling fan that spun indolently as I sat on a thin mattress on the top bunk. I was still here. Still in Vietnam.

My eyes slowly adjusted to the new familiarity of the room. The two empty beds that had lain silent before were now occupied by two men talking loudly.

"Sorry, mate. Hope we didn't wake you," a man with light-brown hair said, looking up at me as I rubbed my eyes awake.

"It's ok. I didn't hear you until I woke up," I replied. It was true; I hadn't heard a thing in my deep sleep.

"But we heard you, mate. You sounded like you were sawing off redwoods," said the larger man. His hair was bright red, and he laughed obnoxiously at his own joke. Both had an English accent.

"Ohhhh, sorry. I snore when I'm really tired," I said, embarrassed.

"It's ok; this little wanker snores too." The redhead laughed again at his own joke and this time threw an empty water bottle at his friend, who was lying down opposite him.

"Fuck off! I don't snore. At least I don't think so," his friend said with a smile and a shrug.

"I know I don't. With all the girls I've shagged, none have reported any snoring from me," the redhead responded as he threw another empty bottle at his friend.

His attempt again was blocked. "Mate, where do you keep getting these water bottles? I guess that's one of the benefits of having a messy bag. You always have trash to throw around," the brown-haired man laughed, and I had a bit of a smile on my face too.

The red-haired man ignored the comment and continued talking: "So, where are you from?" he asked me.

"Philadelphia," I answered.

"Philadelphia?! USA, USA, USA! Cheesesteaks and Rocky!" He sounded excited.

"Have you been there?"

"Nope, never been there. Was in New York a few years ago. Fittest birds I'd ever seen and horny as shit. They loved my little accent too. Played it up a bit, and they went crazy for it."

"How long are you traveling?" the two men simultaneously asked as they continued to pepper me with questions.

"Two months. I just arrived today. I'm working here for a month and then traveling for a month after that. I . . ."

The red-haired man interrupted me before I could finish, "Oh mate, your first day here?! This place is great. Henry and I—oh yeah, that little runt is Henry and I'm Rhys—been here for about a week, but we're leaving tomorrow. We're heading up to Cambodia. Angkor Whhhhh-haaaaaat. I can't wait to party on pub streets, but let me tell you, this hostel is crazy too. The girls here are always fit, and everyone is keen for a good time. Just fair warning, I might bring home a girl tonight and keep you up."

"Trust me, no need to worry about that because he won't!" Henry said jokingly.

"Don't listen to him. We've been traveling for six months now, and he's been jealous of me and all my glorious conquests. Sadly, we will be heading home in a few weeks, so I need to get me some more before I go back to cold and rainy England."

"Yeah, before you are back home living with your mum," Henry shouted.

"Boot off, mate!" Rhys yelled back. "When I get back home, I will be tanned and all the local fitties will love it." He looked down and admired his bare shoulders.

"Tanned?! Mate, you'd win first prize in the English contest with those pasty-looking arms," Henry responded.

Rhys searched for anything to throw but was out of ammunition.

"That's fine. I obviously sleep heavy, so I hope my snoring doesn't interrupt you," I said, and turned to look at my phone. It was six thirty p.m.

"I'm late!" Just as I said that Ace walked through the slightly ajar door. Rhys immediately sprung to his feet like a commanding officer had just walked in.

"Ace! Legend. What a night last night, eh? Oh man, Maggie is a stunner." Rhys clambered over and gave him a handshake.

"Hey Rhys. How was your night? Saw you talking to Swedes? How'd that go?" Ace asked.

"Ahhh, Ace, you know how it goes sometimes. They were complaining about catching an early bus to the Củ Chi Tunnels. But they are here one more night. I'm sure one of them will be keen as a bean tonight," Rhys answered confidently.

"Good luck with that," Ace said with a dismissive smile and waved to Henry. "Hey Henry, how are you feeling today? You are quite the card player."

"Thanks, Ace," Henry replied. "Luck of the draw last night. I feel a bit rough today, but I will be ready to get on it again tonight."

"Sounds good. And it looks like you've met Charles here, the new head of the party planning committee." Ace walked over to me and looked at the other belongings on my bed. He began picking them up and examining them like he was investigating a crime scene.

"A film camera and actual books? Aren't you quite the Renaissance man! I'll need to take you to my favorite place in the city. It's a great little hole-in-the-wall bookstore. But right now I'm hungry. How about we get some food? You don't want to do your first pub crawl on an empty stomach—right, boys?"

"No way. You got to get some food, Charlie. We will be getting food soon too. Where are you going, Ace?" Rhys asked.

"Perfect. Alright, see you boys later, eh? Charlie meet me downstairs in a few," Ace replied, walking out the door without responding to Rhys's question.

"Mate, that Ace is living the dream. Been traveling for years and has been everywhere. Lucky bloke," Henry said.

Rhys agreed. "Can you imagine that? Just traveling and drinking and partying with all these beautiful girls. Ohhhh, what a life." I nodded and stayed silent.

5

Together we both stood outside the hostel on Phạm Ngũ Lão street. It was still as noisy and just as busy as it had been a few hours ago.

Phạm Ngũ Lão street was the main artery of District 1 and the center for all things backpacker. Fast food restaurants, bars, coffee shops and a host of massage stores lined the avenue. Hostels were in abundance and dotted the streets in both directions. Tour companies had their doors open with posters plastered on their windows selling bus tickets and tour packages. Everywhere you looked, someone was going somewhere, or someone was selling something. As I gazed across the streets, I observed the fashion of most backpackers. I was the only one wearing jeans, except for the locals, who all wore long dress slacks. All the other backpackers in this district wore either rolled-up or cutoff jean shorts and tank tops that displayed Vietnam-specific slogans such as "Got pho?" or the word "Vietnam" written in Run-DMC type. It was like a uniform that I didn't know about it. I immediately felt self-conscious. I had only just arrived and already felt out of place. For a brief moment, I thought about returning upstairs to put on the one pair of shorts I had brought with me. But I hated wearing shorts. I hated the way my skinny legs looked and how my brace stuck out of my shoe. I decided to stay in my jeans and watched the people on the streets move at a rapid pace.

In District 1 near all the hostels and backpackers, it seemed more common to hear English than Vietnamese. Wide-eyed men and women scattered in different directions as they exited taxis and buses with their large bags in search of their accommodations. Nothing stood still. Nothing stopped.

Ace stood next to me with wide foggy eyes and glared out into the busyness of the city. He seemed in a sort of trance. His hands, however, moved rhythmically over one another as he rolled a cigarette. Sensing we were not in a rush, I watched four men who were standing next to a line of motorbikes that were neatly parked on the sidewalk. Each of the bikes looked freshly painted in either a matte black or a camouflage green. While the bikes sat idle, the men were in heavy conversation. Two of them were discussing the manual transmission on the bikes. One of them was instructing the other on bike mechanics and how to shift. The other two were reviewing their route on a large map and taking turns photographing each other straddling their bikes.

When I glanced at Ace again, I saw that his eyes had come back to reality and he was now performing a series of stretches. They looked like a watered-down version of yoga. He stretched his arms overhead and bent forwards and touched his toes all while his freshly rolled cigarette rested unlit in his mouth. He then did another series of stretching and twisting his body, and I watched with amusement as the cigarette dangled and danced on the tip of his lips. As he rose from bending forward, he reached overhead and yelled, "Ugh! I need a light... but what a day, eh, Charlie?"

Without letting me answer, he asked another question, "You don't smoke, do ya?"

"Umm no," I said. Without waiting for my answer, he walked over and greeted the four men who were discussing their bikes and greeted them with large hugs and even larger laughs. He borrowed a lighter from one of the men, lit his cigarette and took a deep inhale and exhale as a large puff of smoke lifted into the air. He pointed to some things on a map, made a few hand gestures and said something that was inaudible to me, but the four men around the bikes all erupted in laughter. He shared another big hug with the men and walked back over to me.

"Ok. Ready to go?" Ace asked.

"Where are they going?" I asked, as I nodded my head toward the men with the bikes.

"Those lads? I think they are heading to Hanoi and stopping at Hoi An and Hue and probably a couple other places, if they don't kill themselves first. First-timers on bikes are always risky," Ace replied.

"It's their first time riding a motorbike? And they're going to ride on these streets?" I said in complete bewilderment. My eyes veered to the craziness of the streets in front of me. It was chaotic to say the least. I knew I could never do it.

"Yup, I see it all the time. Backpackers as green as spinach rent bikes and want to act like Che in *Motorcycle Diaries*. You either figure it out or you don't. You know the most common injuries for backpackers are from those bloody things. I was once in Indonesia with this girl, and everything was fine until we were almost back to the hostel. She took her eyes off the road for one second, and she nearly flew off the side of a mountain. *Boom*, broken clavicle," Ace laughed.

He nudged me and pointed to a young woman walking down the street, limping, with bandages on her lower leg. "One hundred P a motorbike accident. Fucking rookies."

"One hundred P?" I asked.

"Oh. One hundred P. It means one hundred percent. I stole it from Maggie. Everyone here talks in slang. Backpackers almost have their own language of slang. Mashed-up English from all over the entire world. You'll learn, mate."

"I'll try. One hundred P," I said awkwardly.

"Umm, yeah. Something like that." Ace smiled kindly, but I knew I didn't sound like a backpacker.

"Don't you need a license? Insurance?" I said, revisiting my fascination with the motorbikes.

"Mate, this isn't America. This is Southeast Asia. This... is... Vietnam. You buy those bikes for cash, and then that's it. It's yours, and you're off. You might be hassled by a local police officer, but if you have a bit of cash, you're pretty safe. It's the beauty of Asia. If you want something, it's yours, and, boom, you are sitting on a bike on the open road. And when you need to, you sell it back to some other excited backpacker. Or you can just rent one for a few dollars and off you go. It's pretty flawless if you don't kill yourself."

I glanced again at the chaos in front of us as the road moved dizzyingly fast and then back to the four men who were teaching each other how to shift gears. It was crazy, but I was fascinated.

"They will be fine. Once they are out of the city, they only have miles and miles of smooth country roads filled with endless rice paddies, and they will have stories to tell everyone back home, and, by the looks of it, they will have plenty of Instagram shots too." The men were now posing on their bikes, smiling from ear to ear.

"But how do they get out of the city?" I was still mystified that anyone could learn how to ride a motorbike on streets like these.

"Carefully, mate. Carefully. Ok, enough talking; I'm bloody hungry. Enough talking—let's get food," Ace said, abruptly ending our conversation.

I looked at the bikes once more as we walked away. The men strapped their packs on their backs, and each of them climbed onto one of the bikes and put his hands on the handlebars. I had so many more questions, but Ace was already walking.

Ace walked as gracefully as I had ever seen anybody walk. He glided in the busy streets with long, smooth strides, which was the complete opposite of me as I limped my way forward, trying my best to keep up with him.

Ace looked back after a bit. "You ok? You look like you have a bit of an injury? Or is that just your swag walk?" It had taken only a few minutes for him to notice my limp. The jeans didn't mask much.

"Yes. I'm fine. I have a bit of a foot drop," I said.

"A what?"

"I had an accident when I was younger, and I severed a nerve in my leg, so now I have to wear a brace." I lifted up my jeans and showed him my brace and my scars.

"Must have been a gnarly accident," Ace said, sounding almost sympathetic.

"I was young; I don't really remember. I'm fine. I just can't walk that fast."

Ace nodded and smiled. "Ok, then we must race sometime. I'm always looking for ways to increase my self-esteem." This time I laughed and Ace seemed pleased with himself.

Ace walked fast, and he moved right through the crowd. While street vendors ignored him, I seemed to catch the eye of everyone selling something. It was as if they could smell new tourist blood. An easy target. I stopped and apologized to everyone and politely declined whatever they were selling. Periodically, Ace would stop and wait, but just before I caught up with him, he was off again.

This happened for several blocks until in the far distance I saw Ace standing perpendicular to the busy Phạm Ngũ Lão street. He stepped onto the street as the traffic hurled in his direction. Motorbikes and taxicabs weaved around him, and in less than a few seconds, Ace was across the street and smiling like he had just performed a magic trick. Something told me he did this often to impress new travelers.

By the time I caught up to his location, he was facing me across the street and smiling. Between us was only about 20 feet, but it could have been a mile as the hectic traffic roared between us.

Across the busy road, Ace yelled, "Charlie boy! Let's move. I'm hungry," all the while giggling and thoroughly enjoying himself.

I stood silent. How do you cross such a road? The traffic was like a puzzle with no pattern, and it shifted and moved and never stopped or allowed me time to see a clear path to cross.

"One step and then another," Ace yelled again, sensing my nervousness. "Remember, just keep walking and do NOT stop!"

The traffic somehow seemed to speed up as I briefly attempted to cross. My eyes moved left and right at a rapid pace. I was unable to move and unable to find an opening. My palms began to feel moist, and my heart once again pumped with a flurry that felt as chaotic as the traffic. The movement in front of me was now one big blur. My only clear vision was Ace standing on the other side of the chaos, shouting encouragements.

"One step at a time!" Ace hollered over the sea of cars.

What was I supposed to do? Walk and get hit by a taxi or stay here all night? "Fuck it," I said loudly. Eyes closed and legs steady, I stepped forward and off the low curb. My foot slammed on the asphalt below and then my back foot rose and swung forward. One foot followed the other. I could feel the motorbikes slow and move around me. The road fell silent as my feet moved. I felt the whisking of heavy death machines breeze past. I couldn't bear to look anywhere but straight ahead, right at Ace. He was jumping and hollering like he was watching a miracle. He waved his hands furiously towards him, like he was somehow pulling me in. Maybe he was watching a miracle, because, miraculously, I wasn't being crushed by the swell of traffic and I was still moving. And, just like that, I was standing next to Ace. I looked back at the road I had just crossed, almost unsure that I had actually done it.

Ace seemed more surprised than me and yelled, "HAHA! My man! That was incredible!" He laughed enthusiastically and slapped me on the back.

"You just passed the first test of a true backpacker. Foot drop be damned. Usually it takes people a few tries to get across, but you, my friend, were like Jesus walking on bloody water! You didn't even look. Good on ya, Charlie. Dinner is on me. Vamos!"

6

The city was something I had never seen before. Even the busy streets of New York City didn't compare to the streets here in Saigon. So much action in one place. Ace had slowed down after my brief miracle of crossing the street, but now I was slowed down by the chaos around me. My head was on a consistent swirl, looking at the mad circus. It felt like any moment the streets would explode, but the chaos continued without interruption.

"Organized chaos. Organized chaos," Ace would repeat as we passed busy markets or streets.

While we walked, Ace talked the entire time. His words came out fast like they'd been shot out by a machine gun. He stopped talking only to reload with a short quick breath, and then he'd fire away again. I didn't mind listening. He told wonderful stories. Stories about past travels and past adventures. I wasn't sure if any of them were true, but they were entertaining. Then out of nowhere he stopped and paused just long enough to signal that whatever was coming out of his mouth next was the most important.

He began slowly and methodically by saying, "Now, Charlie. There are rules on how to be a true backpacker and certain things you should and shouldn't do."

"There are rules?" I asked, confused. Another thing I didn't know.

"Well, not really rules. Just things you should know so you don't look like a twat."

He held out his hands and looked me earnestly in the eye as he began counting and explaining his guidelines for backpacking.

"One," he said, pulling down his left forefinger and holding it there with his right thumb. "Do not wear any bracelets on your arms. No one cares about the 10 festivals you've been to and how awesome they were.

"Two," he said, pulling down his middle finger and forefinger. "Never sew stupid flags onto your bag. No one gives a shit about how many countries you've been to, and it makes you look like a noob.

"Three"—pulling down his ring finger—"Never book your return flight until you are certain you are ready to go home. You never know if an adventure will arise that you can't pass up.

"Number four." His left fingers were now almost completely in his right hand. "Never ever fall in love. Girls are important, and there will be some beautiful ones you will meet. It's great to travel with one, and sometimes you may get lucky, but if you do, don't be that asshole that has sex in a shared hostel room. No one likes that guy. But most importantly, never fall in love. It will end badly. Trust me."

"And number five!" He stopped, and you could see his mind thinking as he stayed quiet for a moment. "I guess I'm too hungry to remember, probably something about god-awful Instagram travelers."

"That sounds a lot like rules," I said, confused, and also trying to remember at the same time what the rules were.

"They are not rules! You can do whatever you want out here. I'm just trying to make sure you don't annoy me!" he laughed. "Ha, only kidding, Charlie." Ace half smiled, and I wasn't sure if he was joking. Little did I know that more and more rules would be explained to me over the next few weeks.

Then, with a snap of a finger, Ace moved on to a different topic, and the previous thought was quickly deleted. He was now playing tour guide and pointing out landmarks as we moved across the city. He would shout "Go here!" or "Don't go there." I had done a bit of research myself before my trip, and most of his explanations of landmarks were half correct, but just as I was about to question him, he would abruptly change the subject and would start ranting on another topic. He would inhale fast, abbreviated breaths, and then boom, his machine-gun voice would roar off again onto some half-baked explanation of history.

"You know what beat communism? Not war. Not soldiers. Corporations and businessmen with money. People with too much money, if you ask me. Those are the new weapons of our era, and they are way more effective. Nixon and the rest of them were so afraid of communism they sent thousands of kids here to die. And when those kids died, they sent thousands more. And when they died? You get my point. You know what we should have sent over instead? Big Macs. Because look at this place now. Like, ummm, right over there. You see that?" Ace pointed up at the communist hammer and sickle flag waving high above the street. "Look how proud they are still waving that flag up high, but then follow the flagpole down, and what do you see on the street?"

"McDonald's?" I asked.

"You are goddamn right, Charlie. Big Macs defeated communism, not machine guns. America's biggest weapon wasn't the millions of bullets and bombs but a Big Mac. A goddamn Big Mac took down communism. No blood spilled. No Americans protesting. Just good old-fashioned American obesity and waste. You look at North Korea. You know how you solve it? Send a big bomber jet over North Korea and instead of dropping bombs, drop thousands of Big Macs on that poor little country. Once those poor and starving farmers get some of that American capitalism, that whole country will revolt against Kim Jong-un. And now all Americans want is to stop global warming and become minimalist and save the world. Well, good luck. These people here are just getting a taste of consumerism, and they bloody love it. Capitalism isn't broken. It just works too damn well. Everyone here wants the house with the garage and the car. The smartphone with the selfies. They want the American dream that no longer exists in America. You know what I mean?"

I nodded, trying to understand, but I wasn't completely sure I did. He bounced back and forth from history to economics to geopolitics like a Ping-Pong ball. I think even he often didn't know exactly what he was trying to say, and instead of trying to figure it out, off he'd go, without any transition, to the next stream of thought. He seemed to start most stories without a map, without knowing where they would end up, hoping if he talked long enough and fast enough, they would eventually make sense. I could barely keep up and was confused most of the time he talked, but Ace didn't seem to care one way or another as he kept right on talking. And talking. Soon I was hearing stories about Eastern Europe. Then South America. Then Asia. Stories that wandered into his past adventures. Those stories set in distant lands he had traveled to. Lands that I had only seen in maps and in magazines. Those were his best stories: the stories about travel and friendship and love were clear and organized and filled with color and drama. When he told those stories that were true and honest, I would listen with amazement, as if they were happening in real-time, and I would get lost in his words. Just as he finished a story, I glanced up and realized I was actually indeed lost. I had no idea where we had walked to, as the scenery had dramatically shifted from District 1 to wherever we were now.

Ace informed me that we were now in District 6. Here the large streets narrowed but were just as busy. Instead of people yelling and selling us glossy tour packages, bike mechanics in tiny garages watched us pass by. I watched their greasy and stained black fingers work with some unknown bike part as their stoic faces looked me and up and down, and they would smile as we passed. I hoped that meant we were welcomed.

Above the garages, large apartment buildings rose from the narrow streets, and every window was left wide open as clothes dangled, drying in the warm evening air. Children on motorbikes zipped through the tiny streets, and they laughed and giggled as I jumped out of the way with fear when they zoomed by. As we walked the streets, we turned left, then right, then left and then right again. Each passing street and block looked identical to the one before, and I was completely turned around and utterly lost.

Unlike District 1, there was no English being spoken here. No backpackers. No one selling sunglasses or tour packages. I liked it here and told myself I would bring my camera next time even though I didn't have the slightest idea how to get back here. Then we made one last left turn and emerged onto a larger street.

On the sidewalks, small plastic chairs and tables were laid out. Tiny ovens burned bright over large pots. The women who hovered over the pots played host, server and chef in these tiny makeshift restaurants.

The smell on the street was intoxicating. It permeated its way through my skin and into my stomach. I was exhausted from the walk and famished from my long journey and in desperate need of food.

"We are here!" Ace announced.

Ace pointed down to tiny little chairs on the sidewalk. They were bright red and made of shiny plastic, like ones used in a kindergarten. I had been expecting a formal sit-down restaurant, but this seemed more authentic—well, at least I thought so—and mostly all I thought about was how happy I was to be about to eat.

I took a seat, my knees hugged closely into my chest, and for the first time was thankful for being short, because when Ace plopped his large body down into the chair, he looked like an uncomfortable giant.

"You like Phở?" he asked, as he shimmied around the chair, trying to get into a comfortable position.

"I don't know. Don't think I've ever had it, but I've been seeing a lot of people wearing shirts with it on, so I assume it's good."

"HAHA yeah. Part of the backpacker uniform. Again, American capitalism at work, but, my boy, you are in for a treat. Your first day in Vietnam and your first bowl of Phở. Your whole life is about to change." Ace wandered over to the women cooking. I watched Ace pay one of the women and come back with two large bowls and two sets of chopsticks.

I looked down and felt the warm steam rise from the bowl. The smell engulfed my nose, and my mouth began to water. I stirred the soup with my chopsticks, moving them around the thin noodles, pork and green vegetables that floated in the warm broth. I took my chopsticks and lifted the hot noodles out of the broth and up to my mouth. The noodles melted in my mouth, and the broth warmed my empty belly. Not much talking occurred for a while as Ace and I were both quiet and fully consumed with our delicious dinner.

Several moments of furious eating passed as I tried to fill my empty stomach as quickly as possible. I ate hurriedly and rushed like someone would take our bowls away if we didn't eat fast enough. When I was able to take a breath from my intoxicating food, I took a look around. On either side of us sat locals eating, talking and laughing. The sidewalk bustled with several other makeshift restaurants just like this one. Hundreds of patrons crowded the streets as I finally slowed down and began to enjoy the deliciousness of my new favorite food, a bowl of Phở.

Ace continued with his eating method of choice and used a technique that resembled speed eating. He aggressively plunged his chopsticks into the broth, grabbed large quantities of noodles with them and proceeded to launch and shovel the thin juicy strands into his mouth at a sprinter's pace. His face was buried in his bowl, only coming up for the occasional smile with noodles dangling from his mouth. After my own feverish start, I began to eat much more slowly. Slowly sipped on the warm broth. Slowly lifted the noodles and slowly chewed them, attempting to taste and absorb every ounce of flavor. It tasted delightful and felt remarkably refreshing even on a hot evening. Ace finished minutes before me, and he went right along talking as I enjoyed the broth to the very last drop. Finished, I sat back in the small chair, feeling full and happy while Ace obviously not as satisfied continued talking.

"Do you see how different this area is than the area where the hostel is located? This area used to be super dodgy. Rumor has it, it was where the Vietnamese gangs and mafia were located, but now it's the best area to get great, cheap street food," he said. I nodded, fully agreeing about the quality of the food.

"But like everything nowadays, nothing stays a secret for long. All it takes is one social media post, one hashtag or some TV personality like Anthony Bourdain to turn this place into a tourist trap. See, look over there!" Ace pointed at a collection of tourists who were gathering. "They're now doing food tours out here, 'The Adventurous Travelers Tour' or some bullshit name like that. It's crazy."

"Can't blame them, can we? It is good food," I said.

"I suppose you are right, but this place is changing too fast. This city is at a point where things have drastically become safer and more accessible. It isn't Thailand yet, but I'm afraid that it soon will be. Anyways, what brings you here, Charlie boy? What brings you to Vietnam?"

"I saw it on an Anthony Bourdain show," I said.

Ace paused, then noticed my smile growing. "Crossing the street and now jokes! You are surprising me, young Charlie."

"It wasn't Anthony Bourdain, but maybe you won't like this either. What brought me here was *National Geographic*."

"The magazine?" Ace asked.

"Well, kinda. I loved *National Geographic* as a kid. The big glossy pages of exotic places and the beautiful photographs that splashed on each page. My dad taught me how to use a camera and thought I would have the potential of becoming a *National Geographic* photographer, or something like that," I trailed off. "I don't even know if I'm any good."

"Where's the confidence, Charlie!"

"Yeah, my dad thought I was great. Sometimes I think it was just a dad thing. You know, to think his son is good at something."

"My dad's an asshole," Ace said. He then turned to me. "Don't worry about potential. If you want to do it, then do it. I know you will be a great photographer. Better than all those Instagrammers out there."

"Yeah... I guess... but you haven't seen—" Not letting me finish, Ace interrupted.

"Doesn't that bother you that everyone with a smartphone thinks they are a photographer? With Instagram and the million filters they use? You with a film camera have to be more selective and have to think about every shot. You only get that one chance to take the exact picture you can see in front of you. You are the real artist," he said.

"HAHA. I'm not an artist, and it honestly doesn't bother me. I think the more access people have to a camera the better."

"Yeah, but these kids don't know anything about photography. I bet most of them don't even know what an aperture is."

"That might be true, but one person who starts using a camera phone may find a passion for it, and they might turn into a great photographer, and the world will be thankful that a smartphone got them started," I said. I could tell that he didn't like my response, and without offering any continuation of the subject, he quickly moved on.

"What kinds of things do you like to shoot?" Ace asked.

"Normal life stuff mostly. I guess people would call it street photography; I don't really classify it, though. But I do have a rehearsed line that I stole from my father. He always said, 'Try to find beauty in the ordinary.'"

"I like that. I may steal it," Ace said.

"Like that over there." I pointed across the street. The woman cooking was holding a small baby in one hand and stirring the pot with the other as a streetlight lit her up enough to see her face.

"Yes, I can see that in Nat Geo!" Ace said. "Well, I can tell you got a great eye. Maybe you will become a world-famous travel photographer and travel the world," he added.

"I would love to travel the world like you! Got any suggestions? Seems you've been everywhere. Where should I go to take photographs? Does your friend that used a film camera still shoot with it?" I said, trying my chance at a conversation that Ace would want to continue.

Ace never seemed to hear what I said as he sat silent for a few moments. Only his fingers moved as he feverishly began rolling a cigarette. The light in his eyes, usually so full of life, dwindled, and a blankness fell over him as if a strong wind had blown out a candle, leaving the room dark and cold. He seemed to stare off to some distant past memory as I sat there dumbfounded. A moment later, his eyes blinked rapidly as if something had pulled him back to reality. With a perfectly rolled cigarette between his fingers, he glanced at his watch. His eyes widened, and he yelled, "Shit, we are late! Magaroni is going to have my nuts. We got to go!"

7

Adam Clark Edwards—everyone called him Ace—had been told since he was a young boy that he had inherited every trait from his father. He was athletic, charming and good looking. He hated his father.

Ace's father was born into a wealthy and prestigious family. An only child, he was born into excessive privilege and demonstrated the negative stereotypical characteristics that came with it: entitlement and laziness. The only concerns of his life revolved around his appearance. He always dressed well and had a handsome face. Women flocked to him, and he lived the life of a wealthy bachelor for several years until his parents died younger than expected. Reluctantly, he assumed his family duties and was put in charge of the family business.

The family company his father had inherited ran so smoothly due to the diligence and hard work of past generations that, when he took over, there was not much he had to do except slide right into his comfy office. He showed no desire to learn the details about the inner workings of the company and instead got by with enough surface-level knowledge and charm to keep things on track, at least for a little while.

Ace's father enjoyed the idea of running a business and the power and prestige that came with it, more than actually running a business. During his tenure at the helm, he took full advantage of all the perks that came with the title. He would parade about the office, usually half hungover, but always dressed immaculately, without a sliver of his dark black hair out of place. He would attend meetings and nod appropriately and head off before having to make any decisions about the daily operations. Usually awaiting him were drinks and his choice of women.

Despite his love of drinks and his ever-growing number of sexual conquests, he felt obligated to get married and become what he thought his life should look like: the successful businessman with a pretty wife attached to his arm and a few young children jumping about. It didn't take long before he married the most beautiful woman in town. That completed the look that, if he were to be honest with himself, he never wanted any actual part in.

The woman he married was gorgeous and extremely intelligent. At the ripe young age of twenty-three, she was full of energy and life. But she was young and unsure of herself when she fell in love with him. She was initially won over by his endless charm and family prestige. After a whirlwind relationship, they were quickly engaged and even quicker to the wedding chapel. During an extravagantly over-the-top wedding in which her new husband seemed to be more interested in drinking and having everyone laugh at his jokes than being with her, she immediately began to regret her decision. This pattern continued into their marriage, and she quickly fell into a sort of a purgatory way of life. Her ideas and dreams were too big for the conservative town, yet she was too insecure to completely depart from the comfortable routine her husband's lifestyle afforded her.

During the early stages of the marriage, she tried to spend time at parties with the other wives. With these women, gossip and rumors flew about almost as quickly as drinks were consumed. She found her husband's friends petty and vulgar and lacking in any sort of redeeming qualities. Skipping social events became the norm, and soon she would spend more days at home, away from her husband and alone in a big house she hated.

When Ace was born, she immediately fell in love with the idea of being a mother, while Ace's father found more reasons to be absent from the home. Her boundless energy returned, and she loved being playful with Ace. As a young child, Ace and his mother bonded during hikes just outside of town, and late at night she would recite poetry to him as he fell asleep in her arms. When she was able to sit down for a free moment, her head was buried in books. She loved reading books about adventures in far-off exotic lands. In their house, there was a room filled from floor to ceiling with books. She would spend hours in there buried in the words and stories, and she would often read to Ace. They would both fantasize about distant adventures, far away from their sleepy town.

His mother had always longed to travel, but his father had always made up excuses about how he was too busy with work, a lie, everyone knew, but no one argued. She would have to settle for her own adventures with Ace in the woods and the adventures she found in the books she loved.

But as Ace grew tall and has face began to resemble his father's he soon spent more time away from home either at school or with friends, and his mother was left in a big house all to herself. When Ace would return home, he would always find her in that little room filled with books. Sometimes she would be reading, but many times he would catch her staring blankly out the window, unmoved and unaware of Ace's presence. She looked like a statue with sad, glossed-over eyes. It would scare Ace, though he didn't know why, and he would wonder how much of the day she had spent like that. When she did finally take notice of Ace, she would leap up and smile and return to being full of energy and happiness.

Despite his father's absence, Ace seemingly enjoyed a fine childhood with his doting mother by his side. From the outset, everything seemed to be easy for Ace. He was a talented athlete and flourished in school. Being smart and good at school was one thing, but being a great athlete is what Ace really enjoyed.

He performed well in all physical activities, and was gifted with both size and agility, and people were in awe of what he could do on the field. Admiration and praise followed, and he loved the attention that performing well on the field garnered. However, due to such natural skill, Ace rarely worked hard at anything. Everything just came so easy for him. He hated practice. He hated trying to be patient and would quit any task that he deemed challenging. One thing that was never a challenge were the girls he so easily charmed. Ace was very handsome, and girls from school fawned over him; he took every advantage of their admiration. At this moment his potential seemed limitless, and most assumed the blessed child would grow into an even more blessed adult.

Then at seventeen, right before he was about to start his senior year of high school, something happened. A pickup basketball game. A soaring leap. An awkward landing. A knee that twisted and bent and popped in such a vulgar and grotesque way that the pain Ace felt as he writhed on the ground could be felt in every player and bystander watching with gaping mouths. Surgery and rehabilitation followed, and his once-pristine body was now mangled and atrophied.

At the same time, without anyone's knowledge, the family business that had run so smoothly for years began to show signs of cracks and fractures, as do all businesses when the owner is incompetent. Despite his dwindling income, Ace's father never changed his lifestyle as he continued to live in the only way he'd ever known: selfishly. His drinks still strong and plenty. His suits still fancy. And his eyes still wandering. It was no surprise to Ace when his father decided to fall in love with someone other than his mother—a woman younger and more willing to drink and gossip at parties but, more importantly, also unabashedly rich.

Driven by the fear of a company that was failing and losing a bank account that made him happy, Ace's father quickly divorced and remarried, saving himself and maintaining his own status quo while leaving Ace and his mother banished from their previous life. They were relegated to a tiny two-bedroom home just on the edge of town. In this new home, his mother's blank stares became more prevalent, and soon even the two of them began to drift apart.

A life that was once smooth and frictionless had now ground down to a quick and abrupt halt. Ace was hardly devastated by his father's infidelity because he had never truly believed that his father and mother were in love. But his mother was now a stranger to him, and a slow, mounting boredom grew in him. To fill his time as he recovered from his injury, Ace spent hours dusting off the books that had been crammed into moving boxes. They had lain silent and untouched for months after their exile from Ace's father's house. Ace, who had never enjoyed reading like his mother did, soon began to devour books like an animal who has come upon an oasis after a long summer drought. He soon got lost in the classic novels his mother had once loved: Hemingway. Kafka. Faulkner. Kerouac. Fitzgerald. Those books and those dead authors filled up the space in Ace and his mother's otherwise silent home.

Ace's senior year, which had once held such promise, came and went. College applications went uncompleted. Friends rarely came around. When he wasn't reading words by dead writers, Ace would find himself staring out the window, just like his mother did. Stuck in a moment that he couldn't get out of, a life that was moving fast as he stood still.

Then one day after returning from a night out, Ace found the quiet house even quieter. It was the type of quiet that made everything sound louder. The *clink clink* of the keys. The creaking of an old door as it opened, announcing his arrival. The noises never noticed before of an old house that seemed to moan and groan with each step as if warning of some impending doom. And loudest of all was the deafening silence that he heard when he called for his mom. He didn't know how he knew, but he knew. He knew before he opened her door. He knew before he saw her floating eyes in the middle of the room as her body swung above a turned-over chair.

Having one instinct —a burning desire to run—Ace escaped to the one place that he felt would not let him down. He booked a one-way ticket to the place where all of his dead friends had lived and written. Soon he and his backpack were off to Europe.

8

The train pulled up early at St. Pancras Station. Ace sat against a chair in the station with his large bag slung against his back. He was trying not to move too much, as a headache was beginning to manifest and grow. He had arrived in London about a week ago and had been drinking every day since. Today he sat, still drunk, with his mouth tasting of dry, rancid liquor and watched the train pull loudly into the station. The night before had been meant to be a quiet one. Only a few drinks and then off to bed to catch the early train. Instead, when Ace had been unable to say no to a party, the drinks had soon piled up, and he had soon found himself drunk yet again and even sooner had found himself back at the flat of a girl whom he had just met. He had gotten back to the hostel with only enough time to grab his bag and get into a taxi and arrive at the station for his 8:35 a.m. train to Brussels. The girl's name now escaped him as his brain rattled around inside his skull like a jackhammer. The train doors opened, and Ace found his seat next to the window and quickly fell asleep.

The next few months ticked away as the backpacker way of life became ingrained in him. England to Belgium. Belgium to the Netherlands. Short trips on sleepy trains. The Netherlands to Germany. Germany to Austria. Club nights that stretched into the early mornings. Austria to Hungary. Hungary to the Czech Republic. Drunken escapades with beautiful girls. Austria to Italy. Italy to Spain. Trips to visit the art gods in large museums that scattered around Europe. Spain to Portugal. Portugal to France. Carpe Noctem Hostel. Backpackers Hostel. The Yellow Hostel. The Naughty Squirrel Hostel. He sometimes made it to the walking tours, and often he would learn a small detail about the country he was in, and every now and then he would learn a word or two of the local language. Did they speak Magyar in Hungary or the Czech Republic? He wondered as he left Eastern Europe.

What he did learn during those first few months of backpacking around Europe were drinking and card games and finding precarious places in busy hostels where he could make love to other backpackers he had just met.

He circled Western and Eastern Europe, and on this particular route, he found himself in Nice, France. He had made the extra trip to the sleepy beach town on the southern coast of France to meet up with a girl he had met in Rome a few weeks before. She was a lovely and beautiful girl from Melbourne, Australia. She had been on his mind for the past few weeks. Mostly because he hadn't slept with her because of the annoying friend she had been with, but he had received word that the friend had returned back home to Australia and he had jumped at the idea of spending a few days in this coastal town with the Australian blonde-haired beauty, just the two of them.

It was late October, and together they celebrated Halloween. The hostel was throwing a large Halloween party, despite the rest of the town's being completely unaware of the holiday. His new friend was dressed up with three other girls. They were cats. Ace was a dog. The girls had painted his nose black and used an old T-shirt to fashion into large, floppy ears. The hostel inhabitants partied into the early morning hours, and several of them walked to the beach for sunrise.

"Ace, isn't Nice... Nice?" punned the girl.

"Yeah, it's not bad." He hated when people said Nice is Nice. To the point, he probably made a face of utter disgust.

"Are you sure you want to go to Paris?" she asked. He looked at her. She was very drunk, and her makeup was smeared from dancing all night. She looked like the saddest cat he had ever seen.

"I have to, darling. I fly home from there in a week," he lied. He didn't really have any plans on going anywhere, especially not home. Unlike most travelers, Ace was not constrained by a budget. He continued to receive monthly deposits into his bank account from his father, to whom he had not spoken in months. He sometimes jokingly told people that he might stay on the road forever.

"I wish you could come with me to Italy. We could rent a car and get out of these hostels and drive down the Amalfi Coast!" the girl said hopefully as if that would somehow convince Ace to stay.

But Ace was always ready with a response. "I was just there! It's a shame we didn't meet earlier." Ace smiled and kissed her softly on the cheek. He didn't really mean it, and he guessed she knew that too. Honestly, he was excited to leave Nice and head to Paris to be on his own again. Three days with her, despite her being absolutely stunning and fun, was beginning to make him feel constricted.

The next morning, she woke him up. "I almost didn't want to wake you, but you might miss your train," she half smiled.

"Shit—what time is it?" Ace yelled as he sprang up in bed.

"Your train leaves in 30 minutes."

As he had done in several cities before, Ace jumped out of bed and began stuffing his messy belongings into his bag before running to the train station just minutes later.

Nice to Gare du Nord: 11:35 a.m. His eyes shut as he plunked himself down in a seat. The train pulled away from the station, and Ace realized that he had never said good-bye to the girl as he had hurried out of the hostel. He soon nodded off without a worry.

9

Autumn was in full swing when Ace arrived in Paris. The leaves that clung desperately to the nakedness of the tree branches were a mixture of light browns and dark reds, but most had already fallen and blanketed the ground. He walked the streets just outside Gare du Nord and a light rain began to fall. The rain kept the streets quiet as most people moved on to seek drier conditions. Ace, however, liked the rain and walked alone as he made his way up to Montmartre.

Paris had always been the city Ace was mostly looking forward to visiting. It was one of the few happy memories he had from his adolescence. Not because he had been there, but because this was the city his mom loved the most. She had always dreamed of visiting but had never been able to, and now Ace was here, and he thought that counted for something. Paris was where the writers she had loved had written the novels she had read. She would always talk about how great it would be to walk the streets and sit in the cafés of Paris as if it were a fantasy place.

The hostel he booked was called Le Village, and it was quiet and relaxed. It had a balcony that directly faced the Sacré-Coeur basilica, providing a wonderful view of that fantastic white building that marched up to the clouds. On the corner attached to the hostel was a small hostel bar called On the Road Pub. Like most hostel bars, it was where you could meet fellow travelers and drink cheap beer. It was there that drunk backpackers retold the same stories with the same embellished lies about the best times of their lives. The stories were like footsteps in the snow; they all blended together as everyone seemed to be walking in the same circles.

Most nights he would go down to the hostel bar. During the first few days in Paris, he had been trying not to drink to excess and then waste the next day sleeping away a hangover. Before he got to the bar, he would promise himself, *Tonight I will one have a beer or two*, but he was never one to stick to a plan, especially once girls had arrived. If he thought there was a chance with one of them, the rule of *one or two* would vanish like the beers in his pint. There were always new ways to get the same drunk.

Most of the nights at the On the Road Pub started with Ace talking to the hostel bartender. He was Australian and had been living in France for three months. He had been traveling on and off for several years—a former art school grad who was spending his winter living at the hostel and then planning to be off traveling somewhere new in the spring. He was loud and obnoxious but was also funny and had great stories. His stories seemed more authentic than those of the casual backpackers, who all repeated tales of the same story. His stories were wild and included many adventures in lands beyond the safe and comfortable confines of Europe. The bartender intrigued Ace, and he also made strong cheap drinks. On slower nights, Ace would jump behind the bar, and the Australian would tell stories of his past adventures while teaching Ace how to make a few cocktails.

"Hey, dude, where do the local French girls go? I'm dying to meet some of these beautiful Parisian women," Ace said to the bartender.

"Parlez-vous Français, mate?" the bartender asked.

Ace finished his beer and shouted, "Parlor who!?"

"Ahh, mate, do you not speak any French? How long have you been in France now?"

Ace laughed, "Only three weeks!"

"Mate, you need to get out of this hostel and learn a bit before any of these French girls will want any part of you."

"I haven't had a problem with girls yet," Ace said smugly.

"You cocky bastard!" the Australian said, shaking his head but smiling. "You think because you got lucky at a few hostel parties you will be able to snog any girl walking around Paris? You are misled, my friend."

Ace, who never took criticism well, poured himself a few beers and a few shots and went to chat up some girls from the Netherlands who had just arrived.

What does he know, he thought as he introduced himself to the group of girls and presented them with drinks. One of the girls caught his eye, and what eyes she had, light green that seemed to glow in the dark bar. He could tell by how she looked up at him that he had a fair chance with her.

After several more beers and shots Ace's was in the back of the bar kissing the Dutch girl with the green eyes. Soon he was leading her up to his room. At that hour of the night the room was full, and everyone was sleeping. Drunk and horny, Ace couldn't have cared less and he tried to get her to come to the bunk where his belongings were scattered messily around.

"We are not going to have sex in this room with all these people if that's what you think!" she said adamantly.

"We can be quiet," Ace tried to whisper but already sensed annoyed eyes peering at him like raccoons in the night. "Hmmmm, follow me." Ace took her by the hand, and they left the room.

"Where are we going?" asked the Dutch girl.

"No one is on the balcony now. I promise we can just talk," Ace said, walking fast up the two flights of stairs.

"Talk? You are quite the talker. I'm afraid to let you talk anymore," she said, but still she followed him up.

Moments later, under the dim lights that lit up the Sacré-Coeur basilica, he and the Dutch girl fucked loudly and probably still woke up most of the people in the hostel. He didn't care when he was drunk. When they were finished, he repeated an almost memorized collection of sentences: "It would probably be best to sleep in different rooms. I don't want to be rude and wake up my roommates." The Dutch girl gave him the same sad nod full of regret that he had seen several times before with other girls after similar sexual conquests. Promptly, trying not to get into any discussion, he kissed her goodnight and quickly made his way to his bunk. There, without a second thought, he fell into a drunken night's sleep.

The next morning, Ace rushed downstairs to get the free hostel breakfast. He was planning on eating his weight in white bread and Nutella, but as he made his way down the stairs and into the lobby, he saw the Dutch girl eating with her friends. Not wanting any part of that conversation, he turned quickly and left the hostel before they had a chance to see him.

The tourists were already gathering around outside, and the street vendors were serving fresh warm crêpes to the cold backpackers who were getting ready to climb the white stairs up to the white church that overlooked all of Paris. Ace had yet to see that view, and he turned away quickly from the building. He walked aimlessly up the narrow and twisted streets of Montmartre. Just as the cold was getting to him, he stumbled upon an unassuming café named Café Lavender.

He walked in, and he saw her.

10

The sun had finally retreated, but the air still felt hot and sticky. I wasn't sure if I'd ever get used to Vietnam weather. With the sun gone the streets and alleyways were dark with only a slight illumination from the dim streetlights. The garages that had previously been motorbike repair shops were now makeshift karaoke bars. Men sat around drinking beers in one hand and holding microphones in the other. Small amplifiers belted out songs at a volume loud enough for large concert arenas. Children still sped up and down the alleyways on their motorbikes, but this time I didn't jump with fear but instead watched with amusement as I let them zoom past.

Ace turned and said, "You are in for a treat, Charlie boy. Asian cities only truly come alive at night."

"You mean, this city was sleeping before?" I asked, looking around astonished.

We now moved quickly through District 6, making our way back to

District 1. This time I didn't slow Ace down. I easily dodged sidewalk salesmen. I didn't freeze at the sight of a family of five on a motorbike. And I walked across busy streets like there was a bridge made for my feet. I may not have been adapting to the weather but I found myself becoming comfortable in the streets.

We reached the hostel, and Ace went in first. I barely recognized the lobby from a few hours before. Gone was the general haze of sleepy people checking their phones and napping. The lobby now was loud and congested with everyone funneling into the bar next door.

I paused to take in the new atmosphere when I felt a warm hand tap my shoulder. When I turned around, it was Maggie. She was standing there looking on the verge of stress, but when she smiled, she exuded a sense of calmness that demonstrated otherwise.

"Hey, love." She called everyone that, but somehow it still made you feel important. "Where's Ace? He was meant to be here an hour ago. He's supposed to be bartending this pub crawl."

"He's right here." I turned to point, but he was nowhere to be found in the crowded lobby. "Ummm, I don't know. He was with me a minute ago. We were out getting food. I didn't know he was working tonight. I'm sor—"

"It's ok, love. It's not your fault. It's typical Ace. I think he actually enjoys showing up late so he can act like he saved me from some type of catastrophe, but in reality, he's just late."

Then, from the corner of the room, a voice exploded. Ace jumped into the middle of the lobby and yelled, "Who is ready for the world-famous The Sun Always Drinks Pub crawl?!"

An enthusiastic "YEAAAAH" moved through the crowd, and Ace looked at Maggie and me and winked. He had the look of a showman who was ready to perform.

Maggie shook her head and rolled her eyes as Ace finished herding everyone into the bar next door.

The bar was named the Zinc Bar, but most people called it Z Bar, or sometimes just Z's. Z's was like the lobby of the hostel and had walls covered with paintings of Vietnam street scenes. On one wall, a woman was wearing a *nón lá* hat and carrying heavy bagged parcels on each end of a large stick that sat balanced upon both her shoulders. On another wall, a young boy was speeding on a motorbike with his feet flung into the air and the wind blowing his hair wildly behind him. Behind the bar, several bottles of liquor hovered in the glow of fluorescent lights. Above the bar, a poem was beautifully written in cursive with dark black ink:

> *If one day it happens,*
> *You find yourself with someone you love,*
> *In a café at one end,*
> *Of the pont Mirabeau at the Zinc Bar,*
> *Where white wine stands in upward opening glasses,*
> *And if you commit to then, as we did, the error of think-*
> *ing,*
> *One day all this will only be a memory . . .*

I read that poem over and over again, trying to think of what it meant, but all I knew was that it was beautiful, and, at that time, that's all I needed it to be.

Ace brought me out of my trance as he jumped up onto the bar and began with what seemed like a rehearsed speech. He used the type of crowd-exciting platitudes that politicians often employ to elicit a large applause while on the campaign trail. To no surprise, it worked here too. He continued with a simple call and response routine, and people gathered closely around the bar, staring up at Ace as if it was he they had come to see, and they erupted with enthusiasm and excitement every time he asked a question.

To keep his fans engaged, Ace began his next trick. He grabbed several bottles of liquor from the bar behind him and began flipping and catching them while intermittently pouring from them into a large mixing class. With each flip, the crowd's reaction grew more intense as people began filming the performance with their phones and watching in awe. Ace, ever the performer, waved his arms around dramatically as each bottle floated gracefully in the air. Each time, he snatched the bottles out of the air just as you thought they were going to smash to the ground. He seemed to revel in the attention and cameras shoved in his face, and as the noise from the other backpackers grew, he seemed to increase the difficulty of his tricks. He suddenly stopped and put his fingers over his mouth. Like trained animals, the crowd went immediately silent. With a quick shake of the large glass, he poured out a colorful rainbow concoction into several rows of shots and yelled, "Who wants some shots?!" He cupped his ear with his hand and stuck his head out toward the crowd, and the call and response continued as everyone on cue shouted back with an enthusiastic "YES!!"

Maggie grabbed the large tray that held the rainbow-colored shots and began walking around, handing them out to eager tasters. They made a great team.

I stood there, just outside the fray of the madness. In front of me everyone clamored for shots or to talk to Ace. Somehow, just like every party I had ever attended, it felt as if I was on the outside looking in, blocked by some invisible glass. Everyone at the bar seemed to know everyone and chatted freely among themselves. I, on the other hand, stood there silently and stared around the room at people taking photos and videos that were soon to be posted on their own social media pages. I quietly continued with my retreat and edged backwards, avoiding the chaos. I found a chair and a small table in the back of the bar. The shy awkward feeling was all too familiar. I might as well have been at one of the few college parties I had attended, the ones where I would leave early, without talking to anyone, and soon enough be making my way back to my dorm room, alone.

Here, thousands of miles away, I contemplated doing the same thing. Maybe it was best if I went to sleep early. I told myself, the same lie I told myself then, I would be more social tomorrow. While I stood silent and hidden in the back, the bar continued to roar, and I sat alone holding my beer with an anxious grip. As my grip tightened, I began to nervously peel off the Tiger label one piece at a time. After having peeled have the label off the beer, I'd done quite well, and I had compiled a small pile of torn papers. Quickly I moved on to the next step of party anxiety and began to shape my piles of trash; the only thing that would take me away from my ever-growing artwork was when I would glance up and see Maggie swaying through the chaos.

She was wearing her Sun Always Drinks Pub Crawl shirt, with the bottom cut out, revealing her tan, pierced belly button, and her face consistently reflected that shining smile as she weaved through the crowd. She had a magnetic quality to her that everyone seemed attracted to. After she handed out shots to eager backpackers, their eyes would linger on her as she walked away to serve someone else. She would then disappear back into the crowd, and I would return to my cumulating piles of trash.

"I hope you bought her dinner?" a soft voice asked.

I awoke from my daze and embarrassedly looked up and managed only a "What?" Maggie was right next to me, looking at me slightly perplexed.

"That bottle you've been manhandling for the past 20 minutes. I hope you bought her dinner."

"Oh, a bit of a bad habit," I replied looking down, feeling a bit too inadequate to talk to her.

"Well, if you are not too busy, how about you help me?" she asked politely. Her job was to sell pub crawl bracelets to the willing particlimands. "I know you don't start work until tomorrow, but I'm shit at math, and collecting money is terribly stressful for me. How about you handle the money, and I'll do the selling? Together, we will help the local economy."

And without waiting for a response, she handed me a new cold beer and a small zipper bag filled with money.

"And this time... treat her like a lady," she said with that gorgeous smile.

11

If Ace was a born performer, Maggie was a born salesman. Everyone Maggie talked to bought a bracelet and most bought a pub crawl T-shirt too. With the bracelet, you were entitled to one free shot at Z's, but Ace kept making drinks without any regard to any rules, and everyone was happy to take advantage of the free alcohol. Every girl who bought a T-shirt would ask Maggie about her custom-made shirt and how she had cut hers so perfectly. While every guy ogled her beauty.

The bar was now almost erupting, and I could barely hear Maggie ask for change. The copious amounts of alcohol being consumed now streamed through the bodies of all the backpackers in the bar, and their voices amplified with each drink. Shots. Beers. Shots. Beers. Repeat. Repeat. Repeat.

While everyone was getting drunk off the generosity of Ace and I was scrambling trying to count the thousands of Vietnamese dong that I was being handed, I worked myself up, trying desperately to do mental math and give back proper change as Maggie breezed through the room selling more and more bar crawl bracelets. It was like walking on the streets with Ace—I was always one step behind, but finally we sold the last of our bracelets.

"Your first shift at Z's is over!" Maggie screamed in my ear.

I was sweating from the heat of the bar and the pressure of the sale. "Thank God," I said, truly relieved.

"Now, let's party!" Maggie yelled as she seemed to leap headfirst into the party.

Drinking games were being organized in every corner of the bar. At one end there was a beer pong tournament. Everyone was shouting out different rules as every player, depending on their native country, seemed to play by a different set of rules and regulations. One or two reracks? Can girls blow? Two cups for bouncing? By the time the game actually started, every shot felt like it was life or death as people screamed across the long tables, trying every form of distraction technique possible.

At the other end the bar, near the exit, a large game of flip cup was taking place. A long table was being transformed into a sports arena. Red plastic cups were placed 10 in a row on each side. Ace had stopped bartending and was playing MC as he marched on the table, shouting out directions.

Without Maggie to follow, and with Ace busy being Ace, I retreated back to my corner of the bar to watch the madness unfolding in front of me. There I returned to my own exciting drinking game: tearing off beer labels. I wasn't sure about the rules of the game I was playing, but I knew there was no winner.

"I hope you at least bought her dinner?" Ace yelled as he shook me side to side.

"Maggie just told me the same joke." I looked up at Ace.

"Well, I never said I was original. How are you getting on? Meeting anyone?"

"I helped Maggie sell T-shirts and bar crawl bracelets," I said, hoping Ace would count that as meeting people. He didn't.

"You aren't here to sell T-shirts. Well, you do work here, so I guess you technically are, but fuck that! You are here to make memories." Ace was obviously still in MC mode, throwing out more cliché lines, but I knew that what he was saying was true.

"I have a hard time starting a conversation," I confided.

"Bad excuse. No one here knows anyone. Look around—these aren't the high school assholes you knew or the stuck-up college rich kids or whatever. No one here knows anyone! Everyone just wants to have fun and meet people. I'm going to give you a little tip. You only need to know three questions, and then you can talk to anyone."

Once again, he lifted his hand and began counting on his fingers. "First question: Where are you from? Second question: How long have you been traveling? Third question: Where are you going next? Those are the three simple questions that all backpackers ask. I sometimes want to pass out cards with my information on them so I don't have to answer those stupid damn questions. But for a newbie, it will be easy for you to chat anyone up. Now, you see those two girls over there? I want you go up to them and ask those questions and invite them to play flip cup with us."

"Now?" I asked.

"No, after we take these?" Ace put two shots of some liquor on the table that smelled like jet fuel.

"I don't do shots. I'm not really a big drinker, and I think I'm feeling a bit jet-lagged." I rattled off multiple excuses in a row, hoping one of them would get me out of taking the jet fuel that was disguised as a drink. They didn't.

"Then we are both in luck because I don't do shots either, so cheers to that!" Reluctantly, I picked up the shot he had poured for me, and we clinked our glasses together.

The taste was awful, and I almost gagged as I hunched over, trying to keep the terrible liquid down.

"Breathe, my man. Breathe. Deep breaths." Ace patted me on my back as he looked around, hoping I wouldn't puke in the middle of the bar.

"Ugh... that was terrible," I said, taking a large swig of beer to wash the taste away.

"It's supposed to be terrible, but now you got some liquid courage. I think it's time you talk to those girls." He pointed to two girls talking, slightly away from the epicenter of the party.

"Now?" Still trying to avoid his request.

"Yes, now!" Ace nudged me with his large arms.

I turned to look at the two girls and turned back to try to protest once more, but Ace had already left and was now standing near a flip cup table, arranging sides and pointing back to me.

I had no choice. I walked toward the girls with my head down, already anticipating rejection and failure. I stumbled awkwardly into their conversation and rattled off the three questions Ace had prepared me with as fast as I could. It lacked any smoothness that I assumed girls responded to, and I fully expected them to walk away. But they didn't walk away, and they didn't seem upset that I was talking to them. To my complete shock, they smiled and began to answer the questions I had asked.

Their names were Emma and Natalie, and they were from Hamburg, Germany. They had most recently come from Australia, where they worked as au pairs, and were now traveling in Asia for three months before heading back to Germany to start university. Then they repeated the questions back to me, and I answered, still amazed at how easy it was. We quickly transitioned into talking about how we had all arrived today and how crazy this party was. Then I heard Ace's booming voice as he waved us over frantically.

"Would you like to play flip cup with my friend over there?" I asked, as Ace continued to wave.

"It looks like we have no choice," Emma said, smiling, and the three of us walked over. It seemed most people caught on pretty quickly that Ace was a hard person to say no to.

"Ladies, I'm glad you could join us," Ace boomed.

"This is Emma and Natalie. It's their first day here too," I yelled over the thumping music.

"Hello, ladies. I'm Ace, the tour guide for tonight's pub crawl, and you've already met Charlie, the official hostel photographer. If you need that perfect Instagram shot, you must find him. He works magic on the gram," he said as he winked at me.

I blushed and shook my head and was going to correct Ace, but he was already getting the game set up and explaining the rules.

Soon the relay race was on, and both teams were chugging beers and flipping cups. Most of the beer ended up on people's shirts rather than in their mouths, but no one cared—except for Ace, who was complaining about the amount of beer on the floor. "Rookies," he kept whispering to me. But he didn't seem to mind my rookie tendencies as I struggled mightily with the flip technique. After a few rounds and a few pointers from Ace, though, I improved, and our team began to win. After each win, we made up a silly dance to celebrate in front of our dejected counterparts across the beer-soaked table. Without noticing, I had sprouted a large smile on my face, and I continued using the three questions to easily talk to everyone playing with us.

"Still jet-lagged?" Ace leaned over and smiled.

12

"Finish up your drinks!" Ace yelled. It signaled the end of Z's and the start of the bar crawl. The pre-party felt more like the party leaving most participates sloppily drunk. Most people now had a drunkenly sway to their gait as we marched out of Z's. Our walk was short, and Ace led us up to a small bar a few blocks away. The bar was empty when we arrived, but soon we filled it up, and more complimentary shots were immediately dispersed.

As soon as I entered the dark and run-down bar, I spotted Rhys and Henry. Rhys, who was drunk and struggling to stand, swayed on his feet and talked closely to two pretty but uninterested girls standing next to him. Henry stood there, slightly away from the group, and looked annoyed.

"Hey, Henry," I shouted over the music.

"Hey, party planner. Crazy night. Almost a bit too much for Rhys."

"CHARLIE!" Rhys shouted as his head came close to my ear. "Mate, these are the two birds I was telling you about. The ones from Sweden. Stockholm—right, ladies?"

"No!" they shouted in unison. "We are from Umea!" They both seemed ready to leave the conversation.

Not perceiving any of the obvious cues, Rhys introduced me. "Ladies, this is Charlie!" he said as he elbowed me hard in the chest.

They were both pretty and had gorgeous blonde hair that contrasted well with their tanned skin. Rhys then nudged me aside and blocked me from interacting any more with them. It didn't bother me, and I talked to Henry, taking occasional glances over at Rhys, who looked as if at any moment he might fall flat on the ground.

"I think we might have to go home soon. Rhys got a little carried away at Z's tonight," Henry shouted.

"Looks like everyone did." I looked around and saw that everyone was now dancing in a large mass of bodies and singing some pop song that I didn't know. "I may join you, as I'm feeling a bit tired myself."

Then someone grabbed me underneath my arms, and I screamed, only to find Ace giggling away at my reaction.

"What up C-Note!" Ace handed me a new cold Tiger beer, his eyes clear and focused as he dived into a story about his past escapades.

Spotting a drunk backpacker during a pub crawl was easy, but I could never quite tell if Ace was drunk. He never slurred his words, never looked out of control. And he was just as loud and boisterous sober. Nothing gave away that he was drunk. Only later, after weeks of long nights with him, did I start picking up cues when Ace had had a few too many drinks. Never did he present himself as obviously drunk like Rhys did, but if you were around him long enough, you would be able to notice something—something of a sadness in his voice when the night was late and he'd had a few drinks too many. He still told his stories and tried to put on a smile, but sometimes you would catch him alone outside a bar rolling cigarettes and looking with foggy eyes out into the distance. And if you were there, late at night, when he was alone and the crowd was gone, he would often mention how he wanted to write a book about his stories and his travels.

"I want it to be like a new version of On the Road and The Sun Also Rises," he would say with a soft voice and sad eyes. "Something for the modern traveler. The true version of hostel life. I just need a sober morning, mate. You watch." He would then take a long drag from his cigarette and watch the smoke rise and disappear into the dark sky.

However, the next day you would never see him write or talk about the book, and if you ever brought it up, he would quickly change the subject, and you wouldn't hear about it again until later in the night, after he had had too many drinks once again.

"It's a bit, ummm, wild!" I screamed in his ear. "I'm a bit tired, too, and I may go back to the hostel with Rhys and Henry."

"Sleep? On your first night out? Bullshit! I'll be right back."

Ace ran off and disappeared into the sea of bodies and beers. The two beautiful Swedish girls quickly used the distraction of Ace's arrival and followed him to the bar.

"Bloody hell. Ace stole our girls," Rhys stammered, looking angrily toward Ace. The two girls were now laughing at Ace as he was probably telling some type of story. He moved his arms around wildly and was making funny faces as he laughed with amusement.

"I think you helped them make that decision," Henry said snarkily, but Rhys was too drunk to follow.

Rhys seemed both jealous and envious of Ace as he watched him talk with the girls from Umea as he swayed drunkenly, staring at them with his eyes half closed.

"Every night all the fittest birds try to angle up to him when he's already got Maggie. Selfish... I tell ya. Around him, I got no chance. Then he stopped talking and a light green color flushed across his face and his hands rushed to his mouth but nothing could stop what was coming next. "uggghhhhh." Chunks of vomit emptied out of his mouth and onto the floor.

"Alright, mate, come on," Henry said in a tone that was angry but also sympathetic and dragged him to the bathroom. Rhys wiped his mouth with his shirt as he spit out remaining bits of vomit onto the now cleared-out floor where we had just been talking.

"I'm going to take this drunk arsehole back to the hostel. If you want to come with, please do, but I don't want to ruin your night," Henry said as he passed me.

"I'll catch up in a second; I just want to say good-bye to Ace and Maggie."

"Yeah, ok. Goodnight, mate!" Henry said as he held Rhys up.

Ace reappeared with the two Swedish girls. He looked down at the floor that was being cleaned up by a young Vietnamese man.

"Bloody savages. That Rhys gives us backpackers a bad name. Anyways, this is Elsa and Julia from Umea," Ace said, reintroducing us. "This is Charlie, who I was telling you about. He is the hostel's new walking tour guide. If you have any questions about Ho Chi Minh, ask this man. Today, he took me to an amazing little spot for pho in District 6. A good locals-only vibe."

After that introduction, Elsa immediately began quizzing me on the pho dinner Ace had taken me to just hours before. I somehow managed to fake my way through surface-level knowledge about District 6, trying to pull out any information I could remember and had learned from Ace. I even managed a joke about tour companies setting up there, which got a surprise laugh.

"You have to take me there before we leave!" Elsa said as she grabbed my arm, looking excited.

Before I could reply Ace stepped in. "Ok, you two. Less talking and more drinking. How about a shot and a beer?"

"Just a beer for me," I said, already feeling a bit drunk. "I wasn't joking before; I really don't drink shots!" My attempts at saying no were once again thwarted as Ace disregarded my objections and moved forward with his plan and began handing out shots to the girls. I reluctantly took one as well.

"Again, we are in luck; I don't do shots either. Tonight is, truly, our lucky night," Ace said with a smile. The smell alone made me nauseous, and I closed my eyes and looked away.

"You ok, Charlie?" Ace looked down at me, looking confused about my lack of enthusiasm over the drink in my hand. Elsa and Julia, on the other hand, were ready and eager to consume whatever awfulness was in this small, one-ounce plastic cup. Elsa smiled at me, held her cup up and looked me in the eyes.

"Cheers to new friendships?" she said as her blue eyes stared at me.

"Fuck it. Cheers to new friendship!" I shouted. I didn't often swear. But I also didn't often drink to excess and spend evenings talking to beautiful girls. I took a deep breath and prepared myself.

"HAHA yes! That's the spirit. FUCK IT!" Ace yelled, smiling ear to ear and thrilled that I was taking part in his debauchery. All four of us clinked our cups together and finished the shot.

Before I could catch my breath from the shot, Ace had all four of us on the small, makeshift dance floor. The alcohol now coursed through my veins, giving me newfound energy, and I tried my best to keep up on the dance floor. Some American pop song played over the PA system. I didn't recognize it, but everyone else seemed to know it, and they were all dancing and singing to the generic tune.

Ace bent down and gave me a knowing wink. "Better then peeling the labels off bottles?" I nodded. Then Ace yelled in my ear, "But, remember, Charlie—the night is young. You got to pace yourself. You don't want to have your guts spilled out onto the floor like our friend Rhys."

I should pace myself? That was ironic. He was the one forcing me to drink shots that I didn't want, but I felt indebted to him for rescuing me from the self-made bottle-label trash piles, so I stayed quiet.

While I was on the dance floor, something odd began to happen, and not just my dance moves. Several people from our hostel approached me and asked me several curious questions. *Can I add you on Instagram? Can you follow me? Where should I go for pho? Where is the best district for banh mi?* Unbeknownst to me, Ace had been busy spreading fabricated stories about my life. Now I wasn't just the hostel tour guide or the party planner; I was also either a professional travel photographer or a person who had traveled to 50-plus countries or an all-knowing expert on the local food scene. Every time someone new approached me, I shot Ace a look. He just smirked and spun his fingers in a circle, encouraging me to play along. *He* would repeat to me throughout the night, *"Here you can be anybody you want. In a few days everyone here will be gone. Why not have a little fun?"*

In my drunken state, I went along with the lies and even surprised myself about how well I played up the stories, or maybe everyone was too drunk to notice that I had no idea what I was talking about. But it was fun to play a part in Ace's ridiculous stories. As much as I liked playing the role of a travel nomad, however, I really just wanted to talk to Elsa. I escaped the sea of colliding bodies on the dance floor and found her talking with Julia and Ace. Alcohol confidence now seemed to have imbedded itself in me, and I initiated a conversation with Elsa with my now-memorized questions.

"How long are you traveling for?" I yelled over the music.

"Only one more month! Ugghhh—I don't want to go back to a Swedish winter! How about you? You seem to know everyone. You must have been traveling forever?"

"Not that long," I said. If only if she knew.

Then Ace came up behind us and put his large arms around both of us.

"One more shot for the road?" he said, flashing that big smile.

"No more for me. I think I'm heading back to the hostel soon. Had a long day at the Củ Chi Tunnels. I'm exhausted," Elsa replied quickly.

"Boooo! You got to come to the last bar. Charlie has been challenging me to a dance battle all night."

"Sounds enticing—let me talk to Julia about it." Was anyone ever able to say no to Ace? Happy with another victory, he smiled and turned to me.

"Hey, Charlie. Go find Mags! See if she needs any help." He was then quickly off into the crowd only to appear a moment later on top of the bar. The local bartender swatted at his leg to get him off, but he paid no attention as he yelled, "Last call!" and instructed the drunk herd that it was time to move on to the next bar.

I was gathering myself and ready to continue my night when Elsa tapped me on the shoulder.

"Hey! Don't tell Ace, but I think we are leaving. That guy is impossible to say no to! We are going to escape in the chaos. Shhhhh." She held her fingers up to her lips.

We both stared at each other for a second. I wasn't sure what to do. She was silent, and because of the silence I grew nervous and anxious. We just stood there as bodies furiously drifted around us and out of the bar. I glanced at the depleting bar and saw that the only people still staggering behind were paired up and wildly kissing without regard to anyone else around. I looked back at her, and still only silence hung between us. I had survived the night with a steady combination of beers and shots and a mixture of lies and fabrications. Now, I stood dumbfounded and drunk and looking for the right words to say. But the one true sentence I desperately searched for never came. So I swayed in my drunkenness and stayed silent.

"Let's go!" Julia yelled from behind. She was waving her hands frantically as the bar was emptying out.

"I guess I should get going. Don't want to get stuck doing another shot with Ace. Are you staying?" she asked, pausing and ignoring Julia's waving, waiting for my response. I could only manage a weak nod of my head. The alcohol that had earlier caused my confidence to soar now sent it plummeting back down to earth.

"Ummm... ok then. Maybe I'll see you tomorrow at breakfast. Really nice talking to you." Elsa turned and rushed down the stairs with Julia.

I slowly made my way down the stairs of the dingy pub, my eyesight a bit fuzzy, my balance a bit off-center and my mind full of regret and the missed opportunity with Elsa. I carefully navigated down the dark, ill-lit stairwell, concentrating on each step as my head hung low in the shadows, only to have it forced up as I emerged out of the darkness and into the brightness of the street outside. The street was now swelling with people, and the once-organized herd of sheep in our pub crawl were now disoriented and distracted by the lights and sounds and smells of Bui Vien Street. Closed off to cars, the street was full of bars and nightclubs. Backpackers had free reign of the area.

They were everywhere. Backpackers and only backpackers. Nowhere did you find locals drinking. Everywhere you looked, all you saw were Western travelers roaming the streets loud and drunk. One big homogenous group. Same style. Same wide eyed look. Same endless pockets for spending. I limped alone, trying to find my way through the sea of similarities.

Every bar had a group of pretty Vietnamese women sitting up front trying to convince drunken travelers that their bar was the best. Each offered a different drink special. Food carts had also taken up their regular nightly residence on the streets. Smoke was rising from every cart, and the air smelled delicious. It was all one big show, and like Ace had said earlier... the city was now fully alive.

The crowd moved at a snail's pace. The street's distractions were almost too much for our drunken group and soon one by one people began migrating away. Ace continued to walk quickly through the busy streets unaware of people drifting off. Maggie, on the other hand, was doing her best to corral them together, and in my drunken state, I thought I could somehow help.

"Need any help, Maggie?" I asked. She looked beautiful, and not at all drunk like the rest of us.

"Hey there! I've heard you made quite a name for yourself, Mr. Back-packer," she responded as she interlocked her arms with mine.

I blushed. "It seems Ace has enjoyed building me a reputation."

"He seems to like you. He doesn't normally like new travelers unless they are girls, but it seems he is fond of you. Just be careful." I nodded. I didn't know what "be careful" meant, but at this stage of the night, I couldn't be counted on for any thoughts.

"Where is Elsa? She was a stunner. Looked like you two were getting on quite nicely?"

"She left," I said solemnly.

"Oh, that's a shame. Well, I'm glad you can help me now." She pulled me in tighter against her. "But be warned—at this time of night it's like wrangling wildcats. Ace gets everyone so drunk before we leave Z's that most people can barely walk straight... Hey! Hey! Let's go!" she yelled at three drunk boys stumbling and laughing as they tried on goofy sun-glasses from a Vietnamese man who was telling them about the quality of glasses by hitting the lenses with a metal coin. The three boys listened to Maggie and soon got on their way with the rest of the group.

"You boys did look good in those glasses. It's a shame you didn't buy them," she said casually. Immediately the three drunk boys ran back to the sunglass seller and exchanged cash with him before hurrying back to her to show them off.

She turned to me and nudged me, winking. "Just helping the local economy."

While Ace was leading the pack up ahead, Maggie and I stayed in the back and made sure food and other bars didn't distract our participants. Maggie did a much better job, as I had a hard time convincing anyone to keep moving or to buy sunglasses.

When we finally arrived at the last destination, the lights of the nightclub flashed in various sequences of colors. I sat on the barstool and watched the dance floor sway with the motion of the music. Hands were in the air as people jumped up and down to the hard-thumping bass. Several hostel bar crawls seemed to have converged here as differ-ent pub T-shirts were sprinkled among the sea of dancers.

"Charlie boy! Why aren't you on the dance floor? My job is now done; it's time for me to have some fun!"

He wasn't having fun before? Ace seemed to live in an alternate world, with a carefree nomadic lifestyle that seemed to consist of telling stories and drinking.

I replied, "My leg is a bit sore, and I'm a terrible dancer." I didn't want to tell him that I was upset that Elsa had left and that I had let her go without even saying a word to her.

"Not a good dancer? Look at those drunkards on the dance floor. Not one of those drunk assholes have an ounce of rhythm between them. Now, me and Magaroni here were born to dance." He bent down and kissed her softly on the forehead as she closed her eyes, but just as quickly she pushed him away.

"You! A good dancer? I think that drink has stung you a bit too hard tonight." She leaned over to me and whispered, "He's an okay dancer, but we can't let him get a big head."

"And I don't want to hear any excuses about a limp or clubfoot," Ace said.

"Drop foot," I corrected him sharply, feeling a bit annoyed.

"I know, drop foot. Usually caused by a peroneal nerve lesion." He smiled a cocky smile as if he should be awarded for listening and remembering. "But I did just witness you walk across Phạm Ngũ Lão Street today without looking! And now you are telling me you can't dance to this shit music and have fun with me and Magaroni because of some little limp?" Again, saying no to Ace proved harder than expected.

"I guess I—" Before I could finish answering, Maggie took me by the hand, and we rushed to the middle of the dance floor.

It was sweaty and hot. It had to be 10 degrees warmer inside the inferno of people. We carved out a little spot for us, in the middle of the crowded floor. Maggie was beaming as she moved effortlessly to the music. She was a great dancer. She swayed her hips and closed her eyes and let the music control her. Her shoulders rolled rhythmically with the thumping beat. Ace was a pretty good dancer, too, and he moved fluidly around the two of us. I, on the other hand, swayed chaotically side to side with very little timing or attention to beat. Maggie at times would hold my hands, and then we would move together as I tried to keep up.

Ace kept us hydrated with beers, but as we danced, most of it spilled onto the already-sticky dance floor. Periodically, Maggie went off and chatted with some people from the hostel. Everyone loved her. Ace would take breaks to go outside and roll cigarettes. Each time, some girls would try to talk to him, but he would always return to Maggie and me. I just kept dancing. I felt as if I left the dance floor, I would fall asleep standing up.

Soon the night turned to morning, and my first pub crawl was finally ending. I hadn't noticed the dance floor was almost empty. Only a few pairs of couples remained. The rest of the party had migrated back to the hostel or onto the street to eat from the local food vendors.

Maggie, Ace and I walked out of the now-quiet club. Drunk backpackers moved sluggishly through the streets in search of food to fill their drunk appetite. The food carts were still serving to the last remaining souls who had not made it back to the hostel. Off the dance floor I was struggling, and couldn't wait to sleep. Maggie, also looked ready for bed as she interlocked her arms with mine as Ace skipped gleefully in front of us, turning around occasionally, walking backwards to talk to us.

"Charlie boy, you are great! You are a machine. Jet-lagged and yet you made it a full night with Magaroni and me."

"Don't include me in this!" Maggie shouted. "I'm exhausted, my feet hurt and I would have gone home hours ago. You are lucky Charlie was here to keep me entertained," she added as she squeezed my arm.

"Watch out, Charlie. Don't fall in love with this one. Remember rule number two of backpacking. Never fall in love!"

"That's awful advice," snapped Maggie in a tone less flirty and more serious than her previous exchanges. "And it's just because you only love yourself."

Maybe picking up on her tone or maybe just because he was drunk, Ace started skipping and yelling.

"I loooooove Magaroni!" he shouted as he grabbed a street pole and swung around it as if he were in some old-time Broadway play.

"You are so obnoxious," she hollered and rolled her eyes, but she also had a big smile on her face.

He might not have been in love with her, but she was in love with him. Despite her ability to attract everyone and how she made everyone feel important, she smiled a certain way only toward Ace, and he knew it.

Ace, still ahead of us, yelled back, "Hey, Charlie! What's our plan for tomorrow?"

"SLEEP!" Maggie yelled back.

"I was talking to Charlie!" Ace responded quickly.

Maggie looked down sadly.

"I got it," Ace said, not waiting for my response. "How about we go to my favorite place in the city? You like books, right?" Again not waiting for my answer, he went on, "Meet me in the lobby around three p.m.?"

I nodded. I was too tired to talk or argue, knowing there was no point trying to change his mind, and I needed all my energy to walk.

"Hey! Didn't you promise to take me there last week?" Maggie said, still looking slightly sad for being left out.

Ignoring her, Ace stopped and yelled out, "Woo hoo! We did it!"

"Did what?" I asked, confused.

"The Sun Always Rises!" He pointed down the long Phạm Ngũ Lão Street as the tip of the sun was beginning to peek over the dark streets. With Ace now satisfied I finally got to go to sleep.

13

The outside of the café looked like a Maurice Utrillo painting. It was pink, and the green ivy was just starting to send its vines up the sides of the building. Inside, Café Lavender was dark, and only dim lights were on. The brightest light in the café peeked through the windows at the entrance. It almost felt like the café was closed, but the door swung open and Ace took up a spot near the window where the rays of the weak winter sun were warming a wooden chair. Despite the darkness of the café, the room felt warm and inviting. Above Ace hung several plants that draped over their pots.

In the front of the café, a glass case presented a collection of pastries and chocolates and a few cakes. Next to that, a small bar made of dark wood sat still with two empty barstools. Above the bar, a small menu was written beautifully in colored chalk with a listing of an assortment of teas and coffees as well as a few wines and beers. Along the walls behind the plants hung black-and-white photographs. Ace turned his body and peeked above him where one had been placed. It was a beautiful image of a man and a woman sipping on coffee and holding hands inside a café that looked similar to this one. The couple looked very much in love and happy. After staring at the photographs for several moments, Ace realized that he felt both hungry and thirsty, and he thought a croissant and some tea would be a good combination on this cold winter day.

He walked up to where a woman was perched on a stool behind the bar, her back turned to him. She seemed to be fussing with a camera and paying little attention to see if anyone had entered the café. Ace didn't even realize she was there until he had walked right up to her, and even then she barely moved and expressed absolutely no interest in his presence.

"Bonjour!" Ace said, trying to get her attention.

"Bonjour," she replied without turning around, still fixated on her camera.

"Can I have a croissant and a tea?" he asked.

She took a deep breath and looked up but did not turn in Ace's direction. Instead, she stared straight at the blank wall in front of her and replied sternly, "S'il vous plaît?"

Ace didn't have the slightest idea what she had said, and in previous countries when he hadn't understood the language, he had often gotten by with a yes, so he said, "Oui," hoping it would suffice.

She sighed and answered in a long sentence again in French. Ace stood there unsure of any of the words she had spoken, but this time he didn't think a "oui" would suffice. She finally turned around and pointed to the chairs where Ace had just come from. She wore thick, black-rimmed glasses that covered her big, dark-black eyes. Her hair was equally dark, but her skin was a fair, milky tone. The two shades contrasted beautifully together, and he couldn't stop staring. She was stunning, and he was stuck in a trance as he stared at her.

"Asseyez-vous, je vous en prie," she pointed again at the chairs behind him, but Ace didn't respond. Half unsure of what she was saying and half paralyzed by her beauty.

"Asseyez-vous, je vous en prie!... Ugh. Can you please have a seat? I'll bring you your croissant and tea," she said in perfect English.

"Oh yes, I'll sit. Ummm, thank you, ummm... merci," Ace mumbled.

He hurried back to his chair in the sun and waited for his tea and croissant. She floated around behind the counter as she made his tea. She wore a white V-neck T-shirt that clung to her slim body, with black jeans that she wore slightly baggy and a dark black scarf wrapped tightly around her neck.

"Tea and croissant, monsieur," she said, dropping the items down loudly on the table.

"Merci," he somehow was able to get out.

She smiled slightly, and her eyes softened as she turned away and returned to the back of the bar. For the next hour, he ate and drank as slowly as he could, hoping to catch another glimpse of her face, but she rarely turned around. Her only interest was the camera that sat in her lap.

He picked at crumbs on his plate until he knew that he had stalled long enough. This was his chance, he thought. Finally, a real-life Parisian girl had appeared in front of him. Never lacking confidence, he stood up tall and walked calmly over to her. He had it all planned out. With a line rehearsed and ready, he opened his mouth, his heart racing, but nothing came out; instead, he simply lowered his head and dropped a five-euro bill down on the counter and walked out into the cold winter afternoon.

The rest of the afternoon, he walked through the hills of Montmartre and thought about the girl in the café as he made his way back to Le Village. He beat himself up for not talking to her and having no idea of what she was saying when she spoke French. That afternoon he told himself he would finally open up the *Lonely Planet* book that had spent much of the trip tucked away at the bottom of his bag and learn some French phrases.

He rustled up a small empty notebook that was meant to be a travel journal but looked as empty and pristine as the day he bought it all those months ago. He walked into the On the Road Pub and began copying French words and phrases into his book. It was early in the evening, and most of the hostel occupants had not yet returned from their day's adventures. The only other person in the bar was the Australian bartender, who was sat there reading a cookbook.

"Cookbook?" Ace asked.

The Australian put down the book. "Yeah, mate. Bit of a hobby. What did you get into today?"

"Have you been to Café Lavender?"

"Nope."

"Dude, I think I just met my French girl."

"Oh yeah? Good on ya! When is the date?"

"No date yet."

"Oh, the mighty Ace. Unsuccessful, eh?"

"Something like that." Ace had no interest in sharing his failure with the bartender.

"I'm just taking the piss. You need to be taken down a notch or two, mate. Like a pint?"

Ace nodded, looking down at his translated words in his notebook.

"Happy hour 'til seven p.m. On the Kronenbourgs?" the bartender asked.

"Yeah, that's fine," Ace said, still studying his new words in this new language he was desperate to learn.

"What you got there, mate?"

"Oh nothing. Just some notes for the diary." Ace also didn't want to give the bartender the satisfaction of being right about learning French.

"Ahh, don't be shy with me, mate. You look like a schoolboy studying for a test."

"Really, it's nothing," Ace said.

"This beer is on the house if you share. There is no one here, and I'm keen for a laugh."

Ace was never one to turn down a free beer, so he indulged the bartender.

"I'm trying to learn a little French so I can go back to the café and talk to that girl. This little notebook is going to be my mini dictionary. Hopefully I'll learn enough to win a proper date," Ace shared.

"HA! I was right. She must have been a real beauty if you are trying to learn French. HAHA!" The bartender was bent over at the hips, laughing. Ace immediately regretted telling him. "But it's not going to work that way, mate," the bartender continued.

"No?"

"You can never learn a language that way, reading from a book."

"I'm not trying to be fluent. Just enough. And where is my free beer?"

"Just enough? Enough for what? And what happens if you get lucky and she says yes? Are you just going to repeat *Je m'appelle Ace'* a hundred times?"

"I guess I'll figure it out if I get that far, plus she speaks English, too, I think." He actually wasn't sure if she did. Maybe she just knew a few words for stupid tourists like himself.

"You better hope so, but I'll tell you another gem while I'm at it. The only true way to learn a language, especially French, is in bed with a woman," the bartender claimed.

"And how would you know that? I haven't heard you speak a lick of French."

"I'm still looking for my French *amour*. That means love. Is that in your little book? You can keep plugging away in your book, but I'm telling you, mate. You will only learn French in the arms of a beautiful Parisian woman who talks to you in that silky-smooth language while you lie in bed and think of nothing else but those words she is whispering to you. You will be so desperate to learn what she is saying that you will then, and only then, learn French."

"Thanks for the free advice. Now can I have my beer, please?" Ace drank it quickly, left the bar and went upstairs to his room. For the first time since he started traveling, he was the first one to go to his bed. There with his book out and his pen racing to fill empty pages he sat and practiced his French until he fell asleep.

The next morning, and the days that followed, the streets became his classroom. He wandered around in the mornings until he got lost and then attempted to read the signs on the cafés and in the markets. He kept his little notebook with him and wrote down all the words from his daily adventures. Soon the notebook was several pages full of French words and English translations.

> *Pomme. Apple.*
> *Banane. Banana.*
> *Rouge Café. Red Café.*
> *Chat. Cat.*
> *Chien. Dog.*
> *Sourire. Smile.*

He wrote down all different kinds of words on his long walks and practiced them slowly as he tried to master the pronunciation. He sat at the bar and practiced each word over and over again, but he did not dare use them because he was still unable to piece any words together to complete any form of intelligent thought. He just sat there alone and read and reread the words.

Most days he returned to Café Lavender. Some days she was there, and some days she wasn't. He had not yet talked to her more than ordering his tea and croissant, but one day when she was there and he approached the counter, she asked, without looking at him, "Tea and croissant, monsieur?"

Without hesitation, Ace replied, "Merci, je vais m'asseoir maintenant." He stood there in a bit of shock, surprising himself, as the simple phrase rolled off his tongue. He had not planned it—it had happened naturally, as naturally as someone would say "please" after ordering. The way the words eased out of his mouth felt good, and maybe they even sounded like passable French. He stood there, waiting for her response.

Those four simple words must have caught her off guard, as she turned away from the camera and looked him in the eyes for the first time—those dark and beautiful black eyes—and she smiled. Ace took a bit of pride in himself, but like the other days, he didn't say another word, and after he had finished with his food and drink, he placed a five-euro note on the counter and walked off.

That evening, still feeling the satisfaction from his French accomplishment, he went back to his classroom and roamed the streets of Montmartre. Late at night, the area around the Sacré-Coeur basilica was quiet, as most of the tourists had left and gone back to their hotels in the Latin Quarter or in Saint Germain. It was a good time to walk around and hike up and down the hilly neighborhood. Ace was often surprised how much more he was starting to enjoy those walks instead of drinking in a busy bar.

This area was no longer the magical and vibrant scene crawling with painters and writers that his mother had talked about, but Ace enjoyed the rolling hills and views of Paris that were offered at the top of the small peaks in the otherwise flat city.

It was a wonderful cold night, and a light white snow fell on his head. He was now comfortable reading most of the signs he passed, and as he walked, he read the French words that scattered across the shops like they were a living dictionary. Most nights he was the only person out, and he often talked aloud, repeating small sentences to himself. His tongue still moved awkwardly around most of the words as they fought their way out of his mouth.

"Bière et vin à vendre."

He read the words that embroidered a window outside of a closed wine shop.

"Mange vino," he said out loud, the few combinations of words he now knew fluently.

"Very good pronunciation. What's your favorite? I hope it's French wine and not those overly fruity Napa wines," a voice behind him said in a recognizable accent.

Startled and embarrassed, he quickly turned around, and he found that he was not wrong about the voice that he had guessed he heard. There she stood below the lit streetlight, which brightened the small white snowflakes that fell on her dark black hair. The familiar scarf clinging tightly to her neck led up to the face that took his breath away. At that moment, neither English nor French would come out of his mouth. It was she, the woman from Café Lavender.

"Bonsoir, monsieur," she now spoke in French, obviously noticing that he was having trouble finding words.

"Bonsoir," he was able to meekly get out.

"Quel genre de vin aimez-vous?" she asked.

Rattled, his mind went blank. Nervousness hit him like a truck, and he stood there wide-eyed and dumbfounded. Her words were spoken so beautifully when they rolled off her tongue, he wanted to swallow them and keep them with him.

"I suppose you haven't learned that yet?" She smiled in a way that comforted him in his embarrassment. "Well, my traveling French student. Learn what I just asked you, and meet me here tomorrow at five." She pointed to a café that was closed called Café Chat. "Au revoir," she smiled and walked away, fading back past the light and down the dark street.

"Comment t'appelle tu?" he yelled as she walked out of the light and into the darkness of the street.

She turned and smiled, responding, "Caroline," and then quickly turned back to him once more to yell again, "Quel est votre vin préféré?"

She disappeared down the hill, and he was left standing alone in the light. Immediately he pulled out his book from his belt loop and feverishly scribbled out the phrases she had repeated.

He raced back to the hostel. The Australian bartender was there. Ace put down 10 euros. "I'm buying you a drink," he said, and began to translate the new words in his book.

14

They met the next day at the café. The day after that at the park. The day after that at a museum. Every day they would meet and talk in a mixture of English and French. In the beginning, it was more English, but Ace was picking up new words each day, and these short meetings motivated him to learn more. Back at the hostel, he would write down his new words and phrases and practice them tirelessly on the balcony. He rarely noticed other travelers now and was consumed with Caroline. As their meetings became more frequent, Ace's vocabulary grew, and their conversation soon transitioned to mostly French. The conversations were easy and flowed with only short pauses for Caroline to correct his pronunciation or to help him with a word that he didn't know. She was patient with him, and he was not afraid to make a mistake around her.

Caroline was a student at the University of Paris and was studying photography. Her mother was French, and her father was from Sweden. Her mother had died when she was young, and she had spent her childhood in Sweden but would spend as much time as she could visiting her grandparents in Paris. When her grandparents passed away, Caroline took over their apartment in Montmartre and Café Lavender that they had owned.

Most days Caroline and Ace would meet late in the afternoon after she had finished her classes. Often they met at the hostel pub or at Café Lavender. Ace would usually be there studying his new words, and Caroline would walk in, always with her camera slung across her body. She always wore some combination of black and white clothing, and her dark hair was always pulled up into a messy bun. She would often explain that having hair just interfered with her photography, and she would joke that if she were a true photographer, she would shave it off.

She spoke with confidence and never filled up the conversation with fluff. No American small talk. She would just come out and say what was on her mind. When she was in the On the Road Pub, she would smile with happiness as she looked around. She loved the enthusiasm of new travelers as they came to her city. She cheered on the new arrivals as they drank the welcome shot that was the Australian bartender's special, and she would laugh as they made a face full of cringe after they had finished.

"These hostels are so fun. I would like one day to travel like this."

"We should! We would have the best adventures together. We can run away and travel together forever," Ace said enthusiastically.

"I don't know about forever, but maybe for a time, yes. Forever seems like you are just running away from life. Mr. Ace, what are you running away from? Why you aren't home living the American dream?"

Always a bit cynical about his home, Ace replied, "The American dream is dead if it ever existed. Every day people work too much and have too little to show for it, yet they blame everyone else except for the greedy people who have everything. I saw life from both sides and didn't want to be a part of the rat race. So I thought maybe I would travel and figure something out, but mostly I just drank my way through Europe."

He was more honest with her than he had been with anyone else but still not completely honest, as some things remained too deeply buried to be dug up.

"Ah, yes. So go travel and find your way. Lost youth and coming of age in Europe. Yet all you have done is party and meet girls?" She smiled. "Sounds a bit cliché. Like an American movie, no?"

He hated things that were cliché, but maybe that's what it was.

She was eloquent and harsh. Smooth and abrasive. Patient and honest. She would tell you how she felt. There were no games, and she never held anything back as she was probing. She didn't hide her feelings in order to avoid an argument or worry about your feelings. She told you her truth. It was refreshing. She was refreshing.

"Since we are asking the tough questions, why did you ask me out on a date?" Ace asked.

"I asked you out on a date?" She tilted her head and smiled, confused.

Ace explained, "Well, in America if a girl wants to get a drink, it's a date. Hmmm, ok, let me rephrase it then. Why did you want to get a drink with me?"

"You looked so lost that first day in the café. I thought, maybe too lost and that you would float away back to the hostel and vanish like the thousand other tourists. But you surprised me that day, that day you first spoke French. I could see that you were trying to learn despite your French being no good."

"Hey now! I wasn't that bad, was I?"

"It's much better now. You have a good teacher," she smiled. "But let me finish. You were lost yet still trying to learn your way. Those are my favorite qualities in people. If you are not lost, then you are too comfortable, and if you are not learning, then you are not changing, and if you are not doing those two things, then you are truly lost. I was also thirsty, and you have a pretty face," she chuckled to herself.

They continued talking and ordered another cocktail. The conversation was quick and riddled with wit and humor, unlike any he had ever shared with anyone before. The empty drinks scattered around the table and were the only measure of time. The rest of the bar seemed to disappear as they laughed and talked until she asked him to walk her home.

That night they went back to her apartment. The next morning as they awoke, she whispered something in his ear, and he smiled, and they made love again.

15

My neck and chest were clinging to the thin sheets with sweat. Every inch of movement rattled my brain. I attempted to stay as still as I could because even tiny movements seemed to cause my head to explode. My stomach turned over and over as if I were on a ride at an amusement park. My lips and mouth were dry, and my tongue searched desperately for moisture. I tried to retreat back into sleep, but sleep teased me and punished me for drinking. I stayed there half-awake, lying curled up in a ball on my tiny bed. My first morning in Vietnam was spent feeling the heat rise in the small room.

I watched the slow-moving fan rotate in the room and then checked my watch. It was just past one in the afternoon, and I still hadn't left the bed. My only thought was trying to lie still enough to quiet my pounding head. Only after the heat became unbearable did I gather the courage to go for a shower.

The slow drip of the shower seemed to help ease my head. When I returned to bed, I stopped paying attention to the time and had completely forgotten about the bookstore. Unfortunately, Ace hadn't.

"Charlie!" He burst into the room and took one look at me. "Oh, man, you look like death."

"I feel like death. This is why I don't drink!" I exclaimed. "How do you feel?" I asked, mentally noting that he had bounded into the room as if he had had a full night of restful sleep.

"Not bad, my friend. Not bad. Here—try this." A big bottle of coconut water landed on my bed.

"You'll need some hydration. I drink one of these before I fall asleep after a big night.

"I don't think I'm ever drinking again," I said, believing that I really meant it.

"Tell me that tonight," he said with a sly smile.

I grabbed the coconut water, put the bottle to my dry lips and drank as if I hadn't had water for days.

"Damn, mate! I didn't mean for you to finish it. I guess you needed it more than me. Now that you have the good liquid goodness in ya, let's move."

After the coconut water, my head calmed down as my body began to rehydrate and my brain turned on.

"Oh no!" I yelled.

"What?" Ace asked, trying to get any remains of coconut water out of the plastic bottle.

"I wanted to meet Elsa downstairs for breakfast. I wanted to see if she wanted to get pho! Maybe she is still there." Hoping I could redeem myself from the previous night's failure. I pulled on my jeans as quickly as I could.

"Once again, do you only react with girls around?" Ace said, laughing to himself. "But sorry to burst your bubble, but I just talked to her and—what was her friend's name?"

"Julia!" I said quickly, still trying to get dressed quickly.

"Oh yeah, Jules. Elsa and Jules. They just left on a bus and are heading up north."

My head dropped. I had only met her for one night, and I didn't want to sound disappointed, but I think my face said otherwise.

"Charlie, did you get your first travel crush? Elsa was good-looking, can't blame ya. But, listen, that is hostel life. Here today and gone to-morrow. Either got to strike while the iron is hot, or the moment vanish-es in an instant. But don't think too much about it. Plenty of new girls will be checking in today. Just gotta be quicker with those moves next time," Ace said.

I nodded, trying not to show that I cared. Secretly I wished I could have stayed in this room and the sleep the day away, but soon Ace soon dragged me out and we were back on the busy streets.

I wasn't paying attention to where we were going. I was only thinking about Elsa and trying not to get sick, but the bustling streets of Saigon somehow made me feel better. The images I had gawked at less than 24 hours ago had become somewhat normal sights and sounds by now. As we walked, Ace continued on with the tour and telling me about the his-tory of Vietnam. We passed through the Bến Thành Market. We walked through the large hangar-like structure, and it seemed to be an endless grid of vendors. They sold everything, from knock-off Nike shoes to an endless assortment of tropical fruits and fresh fish.

"Don't buy nothing! Wait till you leave. You don't want to carry around things until your last few days. Don't worry about all this shit. It will be here every day," Ace said as we hurried through and I barely had time to look around.

Then we walked past the Independence Palace, where the tanks that had effectively ended the Vietnam War—or the American War, depend-ing who you talked to—still stood. Now, looking around this city, you would never guess that a civil war was in full blaze here less than 50 years ago. Even having been here myself for such a short time, I was amazed at the spirit and hospitality and fortitude of the people in this flourishing city. I was quickly falling in love with Saigon.

"What district are we in now?" I asked, trying to somewhat get my bearings.

"We are now in District 3. It's full of hotels and upscale bars and rooftop restaurants. It's quite posh, but in this little area lies my favorite place in the whole city."

After walking for several minutes, Ace stopped at an ordinary gray building. There were no signs or evidence that an actual business be-longed there; it was just a quiet gray building at a busy roundabout in-tersection. It was a place you could pass by a thousand times and never notice. Even as Ace stepped through a small entryway that led up a flight of stairs, I wasn't sure where we were going. Could Ace's favorite place in the city really be a bookstore? Maybe this was some type of traveler initiation or a practical joke and we would soon end up in one of the dingy prostitution bars that I had heard were common in Asia. Even with my reservations I didn't question him and followed him up the stairs.

The door we stepped through bore a small sign with the letters BOA written out by hand on a simple white piece of paper. To my relief, it was indeed a bookstore: a small one-room bookstore attended by a small Vietnamese woman. She had a shaved head and wore a baggy T-shirt and light blue jeans that just covered her dark black boots. She greeted Ace with a friendly smile and whispered, "Chao Ahn," and Ace responded with a hello.

"It really is a bookstore," I said, still surprised, and secretly relieved.

"Where did you think I was taking you? A blow job bar?"

"Umm, no."

"Yeah, those don't open until later, so we will need to eat first." I wasn't sure if he was joking or not. "Isn't this place great?" He smiled and waved his arms around in obvious pride of the small store.

"Yes, it's very nice," I replied.

"And the best part about it is that no one knows about it. You should feel lucky. I never take anyone here. Not even Maggie," Ace said.

The small woman walked back behind a counter in the back of the room and sat underneath a sign with a small menu containing a list of coffees and teas. Ace went over and quickly came back with two warm cups of tea.

"You can't be in a bookstore and not drink tea." He handed me a cup. I sipped slowly as I walked around the small room. "It's chai tea. I got hooked on it while in India, and here they make the best version I've had in Asia." I took a big sip, and it was good. Soon I didn't even notice my head or stomach bothering me anymore.

Ace continued talking, "In here I feel like it's my own little Shakespeare and Co. I can come here and read or just sit with the books. My mom used to read books to me when I was young, and it reminds me of her. She was a big reason I started traveling, and she… ," he trailed off.

It was the first time he had shared anything about his past that was not an elaborate, maybe fabricated, travel story.

"Do you see your mom when you go home?"

"No. I don't go home much," he responded softly and walked away.

I thought I had said something wrong, so I tried to redeem myself. "You should come here and write!" I said enthusiastically, remembering his telling me about his ambitions to be a writer during the bar crawl the previous night. I looked at his face and waited for a smile and a whimsical story about the story he was writing. Instead, he only nodded with an embarrassed look on his face and turned away again. After that, I gave small talk a break.

The room's perimeter was stacked floor to ceiling with books, and in the middle of the room, a smaller bookshelf separated the room into two sides. Throughout the room, small pieces of paper stuck out, separating the books into sections. Each paper was handwritten with a different style of font and color. Sci-fi. Horror. Romance. Poetry. Travel.

The two of us wandered around, sipping our teas and fingering the spines of the books. I found some of the books I had brought with me and pointed to the section of Hemingway books that occupied one large row. I stared at the titles; every room in the hostel was there.

Seeing me in that section, Ace started talking again. Staying quiet was not one of his skills.

"You know that the hostel wasn't always called The Sun Always Rises Hostel. A few years ago, I changed the name of the hostel and the rooms and started the bar crawl. The owner didn't know shit about anything, so I helped make that hostel come to life. In return, I stay for free and get paid tips from the bar crawl. Just enough to keep me on the road."

"You've done a good job. Maybe you should open up your own hostel?" I said gingerly, hoping that was an okay question.

"Have you read this one?" Ace ignored my question and pointed to *Hemingway: A Complete Collection of Short Stories*. This is a good book to read while on the road."

"I'm looking for something different. I would like to learn how to meditate while I'm here. Do you meditate, Ace?"

"Meditate?! No! Did I misread you, Charlie? Are you an *Eat Pray Love* guy? Just when I thought I was starting to like you," Ace snapped in a snarky tone.

My face turned bright red. "No. Just curious. Have you ever heard of Thích Quảng Đức?"

"Yes, of course, the monk who killed himself in protest of the Vietnam War," Ace said confidently. It was actually in protest of the Vietnamese government's persecution of Buddhists, but I didn't correct him.

"Yes. He is one of the reasons I became fascinated in Vietnam and Buddhism and meditation. That photograph of him was shown at least once in almost every photographer class I ever took, and it was on the cover of my favorite records. That image is so haunting and beautiful, and meditation seems like a superpower. I don't think I'm an *Eat Pray Love* guy, just curious."

"I didn't think so." Ace nodded in approval. "Ask Mhi up there. She might help. I'm going to read a bit of Hemingway."

Mhi was sitting behind a counter that separated the bookstore from the café. On the stereo that played lightly overhead was Jawbreaker, one of my favorite bands, singing a song that I would play endlessly in my room at home while I looked through new photos my father had just brought home.

You're not punk and I'm telling everyone
Save your breath, I never was one
You don't know what I'm all about
Like killing cops and reading Kerouac

"You like Jawbreaker?" I asked her.

She nodded and smiled.

From the beanbag where he was now lounging, Ace yelled, "They were good before they sold out!"

I shot him a look and was ready to stand up for my childhood heroes, but Ace was already nodding off on the beanbag with the book lying unopened on his chest. I shook my head and went back to Mhi.

"Ummm, do you have any books on meditation?"

She smiled and nodded. She bent down underneath the wood counter and walked to the corner of the bookstore. Ace was now fully engulfed in the beanbag and was quietly napping.

Her fingers moved up and down the spines of books and reached in to grab the smallest book on the shelf and pulled it out: *Thich Nhat Hanh: Everyday Mindfulness.*

She handed it to me.

"This man is a Vietnamese hero. You will like very much."

"Thank you," I said.

She smiled and walked back to her spot behind the wood counter. I thumbed through the pages of the small book. It seemed like a good start. Ace was deeply sleeping now. I tapped him on his shoulder, and he snapped awake.

"I think I'm ready," I whispered to him. We walked out of the bookstore as the song faded into Blake Schwarzenbach singing:

You're on your own
You're all alone
You're on your own
You're all alone

16

Work at the hostel was slow and easy. Be at the front desk at eleven in the morning. Check people in and answer any questions about the hostel. Usually, they only had one question:

"What's the Wi-Fi password?"

My only real responsibility was to sign people up for the daily excursions to the Cu Chi Tunnels and the Mekong Delta and, most importantly, for the bar crawl that happened every other night. Most of the time I would spend my morning trying to drink enough coconut water to take away my daily headaches.

After the first week, I had exhausted the cliché tourist activities. I had done the tours, visited the museums. What I had not yet done was take a single photograph. I had an anxiousness, an almost paralyzing fear, that I wouldn't be able to be the photographer my father thought I could be, and my camera stayed safely tucked away in my bag.

I slowly began to fall into a routine, but not the routine I had expected. I hadn't touched my *Everyday Mindfulness* book, and I had barely lifted my camera. Every morning I repeated to myself, *Tomorrow I will start*, but every night I would spend my evenings with Ace drinking at Z's, and then I would be too hungover to be functional in the hot Vietnam heat the next day, and I'd make up another excuse not to unzip my camera bag. Up to that point, my daily accomplishment would be getting out of bed to make my eleven o'clock work shift. I would spend the morning at work half asleep, and then around five in the afternoon, Ace and I would get dinner and continue our daily tour of the city that I was slowly beginning to learn.

During those walks, Ace would continue to discuss the different rules and regulations for what it meant to be a real backpacker. He defined terms: backpacker versus a flashpacker. A backpacker was an actual traveler, those people on the road for an unspecific time and a flashpacker was someone who traveled less than a month, a person usually on an extended work holiday. According to Ace, you never wanted to be one. Also, he described in detail how backpacking in Southeast Asia was dead, and everyone here was just a rich westerner trying to get that perfect Instagram shot to show off to friends and strangers with cliché poses and cliché hashtags boasting about their perfectly manicured lives. He would repeat to me that they were not here for the right reasons.

I never learned from Ace what the right reasons were, and Ace's disdain for people at our hostel typically dissipated after he had had a few drinks, usually around the time when he would begin telling stories of his past exploits. Then he loved having backpackers and flashpackers alike hanging onto his every word.

But he was right, well... half right.

Everyone I met at the hostel seemed to have a perfect future lined up. Either they were here on a gap year and soon to be starting university or they had just graduated from university and were awaiting a cushy job back home. Everyone seemed to have life figured out. Being out here was just a brief break from reality. Travel the world for a few months and then head right back home where they could once again resume their comfortable lives.

The only two people who didn't seem as if they had a plan for the future were Ace and I. Everyone at this point knew about my photography because of Ace's fabricated stories, but at this point I had done more talking about photography than actual photography. And for Ace, if talk of university or jobs or future goals would spring up, he would find an excuse to leave. Usually to get a new beer or to roll cigarettes.

Even though I knew nothing about Ace except what he told me in long-winded stories about his past adventures that he repeated to everyone, people assumed that we had been longtime friends because we were always together. They all seemed envious of his lifestyle and kept asking me about his personal life or how long he was staying on the road. From their perspective, he seemed to be living the dream. Traveling. Partying. Hooking up with the prettiest girls. Everyone wanted his lifestyle because for them it was temporary, but for him it seemed permanent.

But his life was a mystery. I would get snippets of those writing ambitions during drunken nights, but even those were gleaned from tempered conversations, and never did he tell me too much. Every so often I would see those sad eyes that told me that maybe he wasn't living the dream that everyone thought he was.

But those eyes were not apparent to most of the backpackers that drifted in and out of Z's. Those backpackers that came and went so quickly saw only one side of Ace: the bar crawl showman, and there he was always the star. On those bar crawl nights, the many travelers who came to The Sun Always Rises for Ace would rarely be let down. He would run through his normal routine, and everyone would be drunk and happy. It was something to watch. I would laugh to myself at his one-liners as I circled the bar collecting money with Maggie. It was all a show. But like every show, even the best ones, eventually come to an end. The lights turn off and the curtain closes. But so far, Ace was fighting the inevitable, and to this point he was not ready to be anyone but that showman.

When there was no bar crawl scheduled, Z's was still a gathering place for most people. On those nights, instead of making endless shots, Ace would usually set up card games. Primarily we played Shithead. Most backpackers seemed to know the game, and if they didn't, Ace had no problem explaining it to them. During those quieter evenings, I tried to go to bed early, despite significant protests from Ace. He always wanted to stay out, and he never left the party early.

If I was able to escape at evening at Z's getting to bed early was still no guarantee of sleep. There was nothing natural about sleeping with a room full of people. You either got drunk enough to pass out, or you would be tortured by the loud party at Z's down below. The noise would rattle the walls, and you would be constantly woken up with the flickering of lights and the whisking of people coming in and out of the room. You would only really get to sleep once the pub crawl left for the first bar, but inevitably a few hours later, you would be woken up by the crashing sounds of drunk people trying to make their way into the room.

On the nights I left early, Ace would drunkenly preach that the best part of traveling is not waking up early and going to see museums or having to endure the five o'clock wake-up to go see the sunrise at some overcrowded temple. He always ignored the part that I was here to work and that I was finally trying to start my photography project.

He would continue on his soapbox. "You know, Charlie, the best part of being a backpacker is meeting people." He'd get close to me and look at me earnestly. "You won't remember what you felt like standing around thousands of people at Borobudur, but you will remember the friends and memories you made from the crazy times on bar crawls." He was a walking contradiction. Sober he lashed out at the new backpackers, and drunk he loved their embrace.

I always nodded and agreed; it made life easier to agree with him. "Friends," however, was a loose term, as people rarely stayed anywhere long enough to actually make real friends. No one shared any deep personal information because they were here to party for a day or two and then off to the next city. Here today, gone tomorrow. A rapid turnstile of people and situations. Best friends for two days and then an acquaintance for entirety on social media just waiting to be forgotten. That was the hostel life.

A life that, somehow, I was becoming more familiar and comfortable with. The longer I stayed, the more it grew on me like weeds in a garden. At first sight they are an eyesore and all you can see are their imperfections, but with time, even weeds can blossom into flowers. The Pilar Room was always in a shambles, as the revolving door of roommates never ended. You would have the roommates that spread out their belongings as soon as they checked in, with dirty clothes seeping from their beds and onto the floor; the roommates that would sleep at all hours of the day; or the roommates who would ramble on about every place and thing they had done since they'd been on the road. The bathroom floor would always be brown with dirt and soaking wet from multiple daily uses.

I rarely woke up rested, and the room was always dirty and had the smell of a locker room, but I always woke up smiling, because during my time at the hostel I realized I didn't require much. What I had thought were essentials became a luxury. I didn't need privacy because there was none. I no longer required air-conditioned rooms because there were none. Clean clothes were rare because laundry was more expensive than beer. And like all things that aren't easy to like because they are rough around the edges or flawed, if you stay with it long enough, you develop an appreciation for them, and of all things, you end up loving them the most. It was all so simple and uncomplicated. Maybe I was also a bit naive, but that's how the first few weeks went. I was a new traveler on the road in an uncomplicated life. That would soon change.

17

Procrastination is rarely a form of laziness but, rather, a form of insecurity. I was scared to start something I wasn't sure I could finish. Or finish something I was not proud of. Drinking made the project float off into the distance as I laughed and danced my evenings away. Then in the mornings, those doubts about my photography would find a way back into my head as I lay in my bed fighting off my daily headaches. Luckily for me, Ace and Maggie had just left for a weeklong trip to the Phu Quoc Islands.

Without Ace's presence and consistent pressure to keep drinking to the wee hours, it was much easier to motivate myself. Feeling rested and trying to push away any doubts that I had simmering just below the surface, I would rise early, before the heat. I would hurry down to the free breakfast, and I would feast on toasted white bread and Nutella and would amass an assortment of fruit that overflowed my plate. From there I would spend long days away from the hostel with my camera, exploring the city.

The city itself seemed to be made for photographs. Every square inch could be framed in a unique way.

I would return frequently and often to District 6, where there would be endless images to shoot. I would watch the old ladies cooking. I'd observe them hovering over their pots on the sidewalk restaurants. I'd watch the details of their movement and their facial expressions. Steam from their boiling pots would rise to their faces, and they would dip their noses toward the aroma that flooded the streets. Then they would assess and adjust their creation by adding a little of this and a pinch of that until they were satisfied. I moved my camera and focused. *CLICK*. Then my lens would move to the patrons eating on the small chairs, shoveling perfectly cooked noodles into their mouths as they laughed among friends. *CLICK*.

Then other subjects caught my attention, such as the young boys and girls speeding down the road on their bikes, smiling ear to ear as the wind rushed through their hair. *CLICK*. The people of this city provided such a beautiful canvas for my camera. Sometimes I would spend hours on the same small block or sitting on a bench in an unnamed park just photographing the people that moved around me. There was never any shortage of inspiration or eager models. Then I would disappear in the thick traffic and be off to the next location.

At the end of my day, I would wander over to District 3. I rarely took the taxis despite the slowness in my walk because I never wanted to miss a photo opportunity. On these long walks, my muscles and endurance began to improve. I sometimes surprised myself with the amount of walking I was able to accomplish in order to not miss that old woman sitting outside her small store selling old communist propaganda posters and smoking an endless cigarette. *CLICK*. Or the young boys in the park playing a game that I had never seen before, a cross between badminton and hacky sack; Ace would tell me it was called Da Cau. They would display beautifully coordinated kicks and maneuvers that looked graceful and effortless as they kept the birdie floating high into the air. *CLICK*.

Eventually, I would end up in the now-familiar comforts of BOA Books. I would chat with Mhi about music. She liked hard rock music. Mostly 80s punk and hardcore, just like I did. We would discuss Black

Flag and the Misfits, and she would make me the most delicious tea. There, after hours of walking, I would give my achy legs a break and read on the beanbags. I liked being there, surrounded by books and the soft buzz of punk rock that drifted around the room.

I would read my Thich Nhat Hanh book. The book was simple in its words but complex in meaning and even more difficult in its execution. I would read the simple passages about mindfulness—being present with everyday thoughts and actions—and I would then try to meditate. I would sit awkwardly on the ground and hold my fingers in an ok sign, but immediately my mind would wander.

Deep inhale one, deep exhale out; deep inhale two... *Is this "Teenage Kicks" by the Undertones?... deep exhale out; deep inhale one... my ankle hurts... deep exhale out; deep inhale two, deep exhale out; deep inhale three... deep exhale out... What time is it? Should I go back to the hostel?... Are my photographs even good?* I would then open my eyes feeling more anxious than before and realize my meditating practice needed a lot more practice.

18

My favorite part of the day was watching the city awaken just as the sun rose and the markets opened, when the sidewalks were still empty and before the city was buzzing with motorbikes. That was a good time to start walking.

I floated around several ideas of what I wanted my project to be. Who did I want to be the focus? What story did I want to tell with my photographs? After days of being immersed in the streets of Saigon and finishing several rolls of film, I knew the story I wanted to tell.

Something about an everyday worker in a massive metropolitan city resonated with me. They were the cogs in the machine that cranked and powered the engine. They were everything that made the chaos organized. An anonymous taxi driver. The sidewalk chefs. The boys and girls who played in the parks. I was excited to highlight everyday citizens of the city, maybe as an ode to my father and his silent walks throughout Philadelphia.

Now I set out to find my models.

The motorbike mechanics were happy to accommodate me. They laughed among themselves as I jumped with fright when they revved their bikes loudly. The nail salon ladies invited me into their shops and didn't mind me taking photos of them as they bent over their western tourist patrons, performing pedicures and manicures. The construction workers who moved with quickness and efficiency to build the elaborate skyline and rooftop restaurants they themselves would never be able to afford to eat in but still hammered away as they took their place on my rolls of film. And of course my favorite subjects, the amazing chefs in District 6, whom I returned to over and over again. They smiled and laughed as I took photo after photo of them as they worked over their steaming pots and pans.

After long days of working and sweating my way through Saigon, I would return to the hostel in the late afternoon. There I would see backpackers glued to their phones, editing and posting photos. Immediately after, those photos would appear on their social media pages for the world to see. They spent more time thinking up witty hashtags and captions, and cared more about how many likes and comments each photograph would get, than they did about having actually experienced whatever they were posting about. Everyone was so dependent on the gratitude of the follower. The follower was the new critic of the art world.

In contrast, I was left questioning the rolls of undeveloped images that juggled around in my bag. Had I captured life in Saigon? Were my photographs a cliché of thousands of other photographs? Had I done my subjects justice? So many thoughts weighed on my mind. Did anyone really care about print photos that you could feel and touch? Or was everyone just sucked into bad-quality compressed digital images that were made for mass consumption to share electronically?

All of my photography teachers had told me that print was either dying or dead. I had been warned, but I didn't listen. While all professional photographers I knew had left the creative world and become wedding photographers or were in photography purgatory doing photo shoots for perfect families performing perfect poses, I, on the other hand, held on to a father's opinion. My dad had thought I was different, and for a fleeting moment, so did I. I was going to prove there was still a market for what I could do with a camera. I clung to my romantic image of people still wanting to see photographs in big, bright, bold and colorful print that resonated across large, glossy pages. I was going to inspire that young boy or girl who sought out adventure so that they'd find it in a magazine or books just as I had. I had fed on that dream for a long time; now I was drowning in its reality.

In a moment of melancholy and self-doubt, I grabbed my Thich Nhat Hanh book. *Meditation might help*, I thought. *That's what it's for, right?* But as soon as I was about to walk out of the hostel, Ace suddenly walked in.

"Hey, Buddha. Are you enlightened now?" he shouted, his big grin stretching from ear to ear.

"Back so soon? Where's Maggie?" I was confused. They weren't meant to be back for at least a few more days.

"Not sure. She got a bit sick, so we pulled the plug." Ace was wearing his large backpack as he walked around the desk and grabbed the key to one of the rooms.

I was still confused. "Sick? Does she need any help? Any medicine?"

"Naw, she's a strong girl; she will be fine in a few days."

I was going to continue my line of questions, but Ace was too quick and took over the reins of the conversation.

"How's it been here? Any big nights?"

"I actually haven't gone out since you left. Trying to do some work and take a break from partying, but I've taken a lot of—"

Ace cut me off. "I leave you alone for a few days, and you turn back into a hermit?" he said, seeming slightly disappointed.

"Not really a hermit, but I got a lot of wor—" Again he interrupted me.

"Well, let me ask you something."

"Yes?" I replied, unsure of where this was going.

"Since I'm back early, I didn't get my proper leave. Let's say you and I head up to Hoi An?"

"When?"

"Now!"

Hoi An was a town far north of Ho Chi Minh. Most backpackers I'd met the last few weeks had all raved about its splendor and the local cuisine. But I wasn't done with my photography project in Saigon, not even close. I still had several locations I wanted to scout out, with only two more weeks left in Vietnam before my visa expired.

"I think I want to stay a few more days here, as my one-month visa is almost over," I said, for the first time trying to disagree with Ace.

"Mate, you've been here for weeks and haven't even started back-packing. I'm beginning to doubt your authenticity."

"Who's keeping score? You told me you don't like all the travelers who talk about how many countries they've been to and how many flag patches they have on their bags. That you'd rather be in one city and see it right than visit 10 cities and only skim the surface. Isn't that what you said?"

"Well, I wanted it to be a surprise, but it looks like I'll need to convince you somehow. I have an old mate up there who develops film, and I thought you might want to see what you've already shot."

I had been quite curious about the several rolls of film I had stored away, especially after my lapse into self-doubt earlier in the day. I wasn't sure if I had really captured my subjects the way they deserved. This would give me a chance to see my work.

"I'm not sure... I... ," I hesitated.

"I promise we will return quickly, and you will have more than a few days to finish up your photography tour of Saigon." Ace should have been a lawyer. "Plus, Hoi An is a stunner! Great place for photography and the best place to buy a custom suit."

He was either a damn good salesman or I just had difficulty saying no to him—or both. It was a bad combination. Soon my bags were packed, and we caught the next bus to Hoi An.

19

The large bus rumbled north from Ho Chi Minh. We passed endless miles of rice paddy fields and countryside towns. I had been expecting the bus to resemble the buses I had seen in my *National Geographic*, that classic-looking bus often pictured in developing nations: packed to the brim with overflowing cargo and locals, with live animals scattered about. This bus, however, was filled only with backpackers and their gear. Equipped with fully flat beds and Wi-Fi that kept all the backpackers connected to their phones, it would have been an upgrade to any Greyhound bus in the United States. As the night fell and the outside world grew darker, the faces of the travelers were perfectly illuminated by the light of their bright phones. Even Ace, who rarely used his phone, was busy messaging someone. I assumed it was Maggie.

I sat there in disappointment—disappointment in high-tech buses that I was spending the better half of two days traveling on when I could have been working. But I was working on being mindful and not letting things from past decisions, or things I couldn't control, bother me. I had read through the *Everyday Mindfulness* book twice now and started a daily routine of personal mindfulness. Brush my teeth mindfully. Shower mindfully. Eat mindfully. I wasn't sure if I felt any more at peace, but I liked that the pace was slow and calming.

The journey was long, and when Ace wasn't on his phone, he slept awakening only when we stopped at a roadside restaurant, where we would get out and eat fried rice or noodles. When we got back on the bus, he'd roll right back to sleep.

When we arrived in Hoi An, it was late in the evening and the hostel was quiet. The bar contained a few people drinking beers, but the party atmosphere that had permeated Z's every night was nowhere to be found. I couldn't have been happier, while Ace didn't seem to share my feelings.

"Man, this place is a bit tame, eh?"

"Probably just an off night," I said, trying to sound surprised. I had booked the hostel myself and had purposely chosen a hostel that was not as lively as ours in Ho Chi Minh. I only got away with it because Ace was too lazy to help book the accommodation.

My plan for the next day was to see the city and get my rolls of film developed. If we were going to be here, I didn't want to spend my days hungover in a hostel room.

Ace seemed to have other plans.

"Well, tomorrow we will liven this place up," he pronounced as he fidgeted in the bunk below.

I didn't say anything, soon dozing off as Ace continued talking.

20

Everyone who had talked up Hoi An was not wrong, as the city was a marvel. As we walked along the streets, my camera was rarely away from my face. The well-preserved historical town that had once been a booming trading port had my lens spinning in every direction. If Saigon was Vietnam's future, Hoi An was its past.

Bicycles weaved in and out of the small streets, and colorful lanterns hung and streamed from the French-influenced buildings crossing the bustling streets that were filled with tourists and locals. Ace pointed and talked about the city as I clicked away on my camera.

We entered several small tailor shops, as apparently Hoi An was the place to get a tailored suit or a custom dress. I didn't have any extra money, but Ace was determined to get a sports coat. He haggled over the prices and the type of fabrics, each time saying that he had just been offered a lower price from a shop a few stores down. The women working in the shops didn't put up with his bargaining technique, and rarely did they lower the price to his demands. Unable to persuade them, Ace gave up and finally got fitted for a burgundy-colored sports coat at a price just slightly lower than the shopkeeper had first demanded. He looked great and older, in a good way, out of the backpacker's clothes he usually donned.

We continued our tour, crossing over the most famous landmark in Hoi An—the Japanese Bridge—and soaked up the 17th-century architectural marvel. Then we made our way to the waterfront, where a river flowed gently downstream and away from the town. On the quiet river, large wooden tour boats moved slowly as wide-eyed tourists took photographs of the beautiful landscape. Sprinkled in between the tour boats were several fishing boats operated by locals testing their luck and hoping for a hefty catch.

"Look at those fishermen there." Ace pointed toward the open water.

I scanned the water and saw there were several.

"Get your camera ready! Right there, Charlie—six o'clock!"

Out on the water, on a narrow wooden boat, floated two men both wearing Non la, the traditional pointing hats that were also a favorite purchase of backpackers. One of the men manned the back of the boat and gently held a large wooden paddle that guided the vessel as the man up front was gathering up a large net.

I tossed my camera around my shoulder and brought it up to my face. I peered through the eye slot and found the boat that rested on the calm water. I focused my lens on the man up front as he completed the gathering of his net. Beautiful gray clouds hovered overhead and emitted just enough light for me to use an aperture of f/18. I then shifted to a high shutter speed to catch the speed of the upcoming action.

I had the boat completely in focus as the fisherman in front of the boat began to balance himself and spread his feet as wide as he could in the narrow craft. He made a few rocking motions with his arms as he gently swayed the boat back and forth, never once looking off balance, and then with a burst of energy, his arms swung violently down and then upwards across his body as he released the gathered netting into the air. The loose netting unraveled as it left the man's weathered hands and, for a split second, floated weightlessly in the air. It expanded in the air below the gray clouds, and just as it reached its apex, it hung in the air just long enough for me to drop my finger on the button of my camera.

CLICK. The net then fell softly onto the still water. The men watched the net sink into the water, hoping to find a catch when they would once again reel it in. Whether they did or didn't snare a catch, they would roll up the net and repeat the dance on the water.

"Whoa!" I exclaimed, still looking at the men through my camera.

"Those are really fishermen too. Not like the ones in Inle Lake that charge you money for a photo. Beautiful, ain't it?"

"Yes. Very." I pulled my camera slowly away from my face. "I can't wait till I get this developed. Thanks, Ace, for helping me out with that."

Ace nodded and smiled and turned away quickly, telling me he needed a nap and was returning to the hostel.

"Mind if I stay out and walk around? I want to finish off this roll of film," I told him.

"Sure, I'm just feeling a bit knackered."

The town was definitely worth the trip. The feeling of resentment I had briefly felt at having been pressured to leave Saigon had now vanished, and I was happy that Ace had brought me here. I was also excited about seeing my pictures developed.

"Thanks for bringing me here," I yelled.

But Ace was already walking away.

21

"**Charlie boy! Come over!** I need one more player," Ace screamed. Beers and people had accumulated around him.

I entered the hostel and barely recognized it. Yesterday, the hostel bar had been dead. Now, less than 24 hours later, it was piping with energy and very much alive. What kind of magic did Ace possess?

"How was the city?" he asked. I looked around, puzzled by the transformation of the hostel from the night before.

"It was, ummm... it was good." Everyone seemed to be centered around Ace. "The lanterns on the streets are great for some night photography. Oh, and did you get a chance to contact your friend? I'm really looking forward to getting my films developed."

"Oh, that's great! I told you this town was great, but what I really need now is a fourth player in this game." Ace was teaching two young females the traveler's Shithead game.

"Did you message your friend?" I asked again nervously, thinking he had spent his whole time trying to start a party at the hostel.

"Of course. Don't worry, Charlie. I'm on it. Now go get four beers for us." He handed me some crumpled-up dong.

"When are we meeting him?" I asked as I counted the dong.

"He hasn't got back to me yet. But he will," Ace said as I left to get beers for the game.

We played several rounds of Shithead, and everyone had gotten sufficiently drunk when a beautiful blonde girl whom I thought I recognized walked into the bar.

Ace looked over and yelled, "FINALLY!"

She smiled and hugged Ace tightly around his neck.

"Sorry the bus down from Hue took forever," she said.

"You remember Charlie, right?" Ace grabbed me over.

"Yes! The food guide. I was disappointed that I never got that tour," she said, still smiling at Ace.

I couldn't believe it. It was Elsa, the Swedish girl from Umea whom I had met on my first night in Saigon.

"He will make it up to you!" Ace shook me gently. "Now, how about you get another round and Elsa can join the game." Ace again stuffed my hand with crumpled-up Vietnamese dong, and off I went in a haze of confusion.

What was she doing here? Was that who he had been messaging on the way up here?

The next few hours ticked by with the usual activities: cards and drinking games at the hostel and then marching as a group through the small town, finding bars to infiltrate. Ace and I weren't talking. He had evaded all my questions about whether his friend had gotten back to him and had spent most of the night chatting with Elsa. I tried to avoid looking at them. I still couldn't believe she had come to see him or, better yet, that he had encouraged her to meet him here.

I didn't drink much that night. I was feeling a bit out of sorts as I tried to piece together Ace's motivation for having Elsa, the only girl he knew I had a crush on, meet him here, with me to observe it all. On the other hand, Ace seemed intent on drinking, even more aggressively than normal. Every time I looked over, he and Elsa were finishing up another shot. As the shots multiplied, so did his stories, and once he was drunk enough, as I could have predicted, I heard him talking to Elsa about the book he was writing, repeating the same lines he had told me. She stared at him with eyes of admiration, and it filled my heart with jealousy. I had had enough.

"I think I'm taking off," I told them as they talked closely.

Ace limply waved good-bye and barely even acknowledged me as he continued to talk to Elsa.

"Goodnight, Charlie. Great seeing you," Elsa interrupted Ace and hugged me good-bye. I turned and walked away when I heard Ace tell Elsa, "My writing attempts to find beauty in the ordinary."

No longer did I feel jealousy, but now anger burned through me, as Ace had fulfilled his earlier promise in stealing my dad's favorite line. I wasn't familiar with this feeling but it overcame me, and I felt my vision blur. Then, without warning, my fist flew through the air, landing squarely on Ace's jaw. His head swung back and then recoiled just as quickly, like those inflatable punching bags that always bounce back. He just looked at me. His eyes didn't look angry or sad but oddly satisfied with my actions.

That's how I thought it would have gone if I had actually done it, if I had actually punched him. But I didn't, I just stared at him and walked away. I still looked up to Ace; I was still feeling indebted to him for helping me acclimate to this hostel life. Tears began to well up in my eyes, and the anger still bubbled up inside of me as I stormed out the bar.

I was asleep when they loudly stumbled in. Ace could barely stand, and I could hear both of them giggle and laugh as he lost his balance a few times. They drifted together, using each other as crutches to stand up. You could hear them kiss sloppily because they made no attempt to be quiet. Ace then turned on his phone light, and I could sense everyone in the room roll over in disgust because they knew what was about to come next. Ace rummaged through his backpack, and then he and Elsa made their way into the tiny bathroom. I tried to roll over and sleep, but the sounds of them in the bathroom a few feet away kept me up.

22

The next morning, I climbed down from the top bunk. Ace and Elsa were sleeping peacefully in the small bed together. I couldn't have left the room more quickly as I walked downstairs to get breakfast. After breakfast, I stayed away a few hours, and when I walked back to the room, Ace was still snoring away. The morning hours soon vanished, and the afternoon was ticking by. I was starting to get an uneasy feeling in my stomach. I was still in the lobby with my film ready to be developed when I spotted Elsa walk by me.

"Hey! Hey! Where's Ace?" I yelled as she briskly strode past, holding her head, which was half hidden under a hat and dark sunglasses, and looking embarrassed to see me.

"Oh, hey. Ummmm, still sleeping, I think. I don't think he is feeling well." She didn't look too good, either, and she quickly left the hostel. As the afternoon kept dwindling away, I had finally had enough. Maybe I couldn't punch him, but I sure could wake him up. I walked back into the room and found Ace still in the same position.

"Ace! Ace!" I was tired of waiting.

"Mate, I'm sorry. I feel like shit." He tried to roll over.

"We were supposed to get my film developed. Did your friend get back to you? We leave tomorrow and I wa—"

Just then, Ace bolted to the bathroom. Several minutes and sounds of sickness later, he slunk out of the bathroom and lay back down on his bed, wiping his mouth and looking pale.

With his eyes shut, he whispered, "Mate, bad news. My friend moved back to Germany. Bad luck."

BAD LUCK! My heart plunged, along with the high expectations I had been holding onto. "You mean you weren't sure if he was here or not? Bad luck? Ace, you know I came up here specifically to get my photographs developed!" I yelled.

"Well, you weren't going to get them developed in Ho Chi Minh, and now you got to photograph a new area. Not a complete loss, mate. I don't owe you an apology; now get outta here, and let me sleep this off," he said as he turned back around in bed.

"If you owe anyone an apology, it's Maggie." It just steamrolled out of my mouth, without a single thought. I couldn't see his face from my bunk, but I knew he was now sitting up. I was sitting up myself, almost in shock that I had brought her up.

"What the hell is that supposed to mean?" Ace said.

"Ummm, you and Elsa last night," I said shyly.

"Listen, Charlie. This is traveling. Maggie and I are not married. We are not anything."

"I know that, but . . ."

"You don't know anything. You think she is an angel? Did she ever tell you she had a boyfriend back home? That's right, she has a boyfriend, and you know what? She calls him when we are together in bed. So do you think I have to explain something to her about anything? Leave me alone, and go take photos or whatever you want to do." Ace rolled over and fell back to sleep.

I sat there, stunned. After our argument, I felt like I had done something wrong. Like I was the one to apologize. I hadn't even brought up why he had had to bring Elsa here or that I was upset that he had used my dad's line to cheaply impress her.

We didn't talk the rest of the day, and the bus ride a few days later was the same as on the way up: Ace slept, and I read my book, but now I was unable to stay calm as we headed back to Ho Chi Minh.

23

After being misled by Ace and losing a few working days I felt extra pressure to continue my work in Saigon. As busy as the lobby was on bar crawl nights, the mornings were equally quiet. The Sun Always Rises hostel's lobby was a ghost town this early in the morning as most didn't rise till the early afternoon. To my surprise, Maggie was up and in front of a computer. She was rarely up this early, and I was surprised but happy to see her.

"Good morning, Maggie," I whispered.

She jumped slightly, as I must have scared her. "Oh, good morning, love. Wasn't expecting anyone this early."

"I've got to do some work today." I held my camera up.

"Where are you going?"

"Not sure. But I have three rolls of film I need to finish before I leave. Only got a few more days."

"I know, I'm quite sad about that. Mind if I join?" Normally I liked to work alone, but I welcomed her along, and we headed out for the day.

This early in the day the heat had not yet taken over the city. Today there was also an unusual cool breeze that brushed against my face, and the sky was full of thick, black clouds. It looked like at any moment there would be a heavy rain. I had almost trained my eyes to watch for the rain because of Ace's hatred of it. He was always watching the skies and if there was any chance of rain he would disappear quickly to Z's and start drinking. But I didn't mind the chance of rain and was actually hoping to get some dramatic rain photographs as Maggie and I walked the busy streets.

It was the first time we had had a sober conversation together since the day I had checked in, but we felt comfortable around each other, and talk came easily as we walked. She talked freely and openly about her life, particularly about her childhood in Mexico, and I listened with great interest.

She had been born into a privileged family and had lived in a tight social circle of friends and families who were all connected by their family business. The children had been pushed to be competitive and were pitted against one another. Children and their accomplishments had been paraded around like trophies. Soon, competitive rifts had formed between the young children, and, hating the pettiness of it, she had rebelled.

"You don't strike me as the rebellious type," I said as she strolled slightly ahead of me.

"Don't let this smile confuse you, Charlie. I'm a fiery Mexicana full of power and rebellion!" She quickly looked at me with a stern face.

I nodded in agreement, as I was now too intimidated to argue with her.

Despite her family's wealth, they never did anything she deemed exciting. They would take vacations only to the beach towns in Mexico, like Tulum or Puerto Vallarta, and stay in large resorts with unoriginal names like Dreams Resort or Paradise Village. She called them "do nothing" vacations, places where other rich Mexican families would vacation—or fat, sloppy Americans with bad tans and bad tattoos, those Americans who would vote in a heartbeat to keep her family out of the United States but down here, in her family's land, would try to get a tan like a Mexican. They would sit out all day baking in the hot Mexican sun, but they would never get brown and would have to settle for turning red, which made their bad tattoos worse. She hated those trips to those resorts. Do nothing. See nothing.

As she went into high school, she began to get into trouble and make friends with the poets and artists from her hometown. Usually they were the poor men and women who liked to drink and smoke too much. Everyone from her life looked down at them, as they lived in small homes and never vacationed on the famous beaches of Mexico. But she envied the freedom of their lives and creativity they all shared. Her favorites were the photographers. She would sneak out of her home when it was dark and watch them take photographs. During that time, they would tell her stories. They had the best stories. Stories of travel and adventure in Central and South America. Also the sad stories that most of them carried around with them. Something about a sad story felt more real to her. More truthful. They enjoyed having her around as well. They could feel her attitude was similar to their own, and the men and women embraced her and began to teach her how to use a camera.

Her parents eventually began to catch her sneaking out of the house. Upset with her newfound hobby and friends, they banned her from going out with them. After one chaotic fight with her parents, she spent an entire night in anger and wrote a 30-page manifesto about her life and what she wanted out of it.

The next few months, she stayed away from her artist friends, and her parents assumed they had won the argument and were pleased with themselves. Then, on the last day of school, she handed her parents the manifesto she had written months before, and she left with a backpack. She joined a group that was heading south toward South America. She never even attended her own graduation ceremony, where she was honored for finishing top of her class.

"I worked at a café for one year in Chile, and I saved all my money. I still want to go to school and maybe become a doctor, who knows? I'm not like you, Charlie. I don't have a plan. But right now, I'm just trying to figure things out." She paused and took a deep breath. "Enough about me and my sad past. Let's take some pictures!"

I was going to tell her that I didn't have a plan either, that I didn't even know if my photographs were any good, but the moment had passed, and I chose not to bring it up again.

She handled the camera beautifully, and we traded off taking time behind the lens. We stopped at several parks and markets and cafés. Maggie being Maggie, she jumped into some of the Da Cau games at the parks with the young, shirtless boys. They openly welcomed her, and she was a natural. She was fit and athletic and moved effortlessly as she kicked the birdie high in the dark morning sky. I took photos of her while she played. Never actually posing for the camera, her smile always turned out perfectly formed and natural, never forced. After the game, the rains that had been threatening all morning came to life, and large drops began falling furiously to the ground. After several rain photographs are clothes were soaked and we sought out dryer conditions. I knew exactly where to go to wait out the rain.

"How do you know about this place?" she asked as we were being greeted by several nail salon women.

"Just supporting the local economy!" I proclaimed.

"Stealing my lines now, are you?"

Before today I had only took photographs of the women but today Maggie made me sit in the chair where I received my first pedicure. She said it was punishment for a stealing her line.

I giggled every time the salon lady's fingers hovered around my feet. She paid no attention and instead worked furiously on my newly formed calluses. Maggie took my camera and, despite my protests, began taking photos of me in my vulnerable state in between tears and laughter. Maggie and the nail salon ladies became coconspirators as they made me laugh and Maggie clicked away. Soon my nails were freshly painted, and the whole salon was laughing. We left with hugs and smiles. And, as with all Asian rainstorms, the clouds soon parted, and the streets dried up.

With our nails done and our faces sore from laughing so hard, we strolled through the streets talking about photography and taking as many pictures as we could. Maggie wanted to take shots of the motorbikes zipping through the city and portraits of the children playing together in the parks. People responded to her with ease and comfort. As we walked, I told her about BOA Books and how Ace had taken me there on my second day in Saigon and how much I loved spending quiet afternoons there reading and talking to Mhi. I must have sounded too excited because she immediately demanded that we go there. Soon we were in a taxi heading to District 3.

Inside the taxi, we sat quietly until I asked her the question that I had had on my mind for the past week.

"May I ask what happened with you and Ace on Islands?" I felt so comfortable with her that I thought I could ask her anything.

"Whatever do you mean, my dear?" she said in a sarcastic tone.

"You don't have to answer if you don't want to."

"Yeah, I figured you'd ask. I know you and Ace are such great friends, but we both probably know Ace won't say a thing."

I had never thought of Ace and me as great friends. I assumed he had great friends everywhere and that he just considered me a person that he was friendly with while I was in Saigon. I didn't even know if we were still friends now, as we hadn't spoken since Hoi An.

"Well, I try not to show it, but I'm absolutely in love with that man, and when I was drunk and alone with him, I told him so." Maggie was the most upfront and honest person I had ever known. Things that most people would hide away she openly and freely shared.

"We had just arrived on the beach, and the sun was setting. I looked at him and told him I loved him, and guess what he did? He stood there like I had just given him a weather report. He shrugged and told me without a hint of emotion that I was 'too young' for him and that he didn't think I 'truly' loved him. I cried, and he got upset and told me that I was probably just missing my boyfriend. The next day we were back at Z-Bar, and we haven't talked since."

"Yeah. When we were in Hoi An, he said you have a boyfriend?"

"Yes, I have a boyfriend, and we still talk, but he doesn't make me feel the way Ace does. I would feel bad about breaking up with him over the phone, though. I know that when I go back to Mexico, it's over. It wasn't like I was trying to fall in love. I met Ace at—this sounds so cliché—a pub crawl, in KL. I was a perfect target for him. Here is a girl with a boyfriend; she won't get attached. I think that's why he likes backpackers, because none of them are here long enough to actually call him out on his bullshit. But I couldn't help myself. He was the most interesting person I had ever met. He was so well traveled and had been everywhere. I was in awe of him and his experiences and the life he led. He was so carefree but also mysterious, and he had those sad eyes when he got too drunk, and he would talk about this book he was writing. It all sounded so romantic. A handsome backpacker who was writing a book. How could I have not fallen in love, right?"

"HA! Yes, I think we have all fallen for it. Have you actually seen him write or read any of his writing?"

"No. You?" Maggie asked.

"I haven't. But I do believe him. If you took half the stories he told and actually put them on paper, he would have plenty of material. At least, I hope he does and that those stories don't get wasted on drunk travelers." As we talked more about Ace, I began to miss him and our friendship.

"But he can't stay still long enough to write. Too busy trying to party all night meeting new backpacker girls. Like me!" She tried to fake a smile, but I knew she was sad.

"I think he does think more of you as than that... He looks at you differently than other girls."

Maggie nodded silently. A small tear fell from her face, and she quickly wiped it away as we arrived at that inconspicuous gray building.

We got out of the cab and paid the driver. Maggie must have felt the way I felt the first time Ace took me here: confused at standing in front of a random collection of buildings with no sign of a bookstore. We walked through the small gate, up the unassuming stairs and through the door with the small sign that displayed the name BOA Books.

Mhi was in her usual place; I nodded to her politely, and she waved. The Clash was playing through the speakers.

I wasn't born
So much as I fell out
Nobody seemed to notice me

I ordered two chai teas and went over to Maggie, who was scanning the spines of the books.

"Mhi told me that we just missed Ace," I said, with a surprised look on my face.

"What was he doing here?" Maggie said in a disappointed tone, and I could tell she wanted to see him.

"Not sure." I was truly shocked that he had made it here before noon. "I wonder if he went out last night?"

"Let's not let that boy control our day. What is the book I see you reading all the time?"

I pointed to the *Everyday Mindfulness* book that had replaced the one I had bought on the shelf. She picked it up and scanned the pages.

"I can let you borrow mine. I've read in twice already." I handed her a copy of *The Sun Also Rises*. "You could read about our hostel's inspiration. Did you know Ace changed the name of the hostel and all the rooms?" For some reason, we couldn't stop talking about him.

"Haha! Yes, Ace told me that before we came here. He said he would lend me his copy, but you know Ace—he never did. Maybe I'll buy this one and borrow the meditation one from you."

Mhi walked over and handed us our chai.

"My favorite book," she said in her soft voice. "You buy and tea's free."

"I guess I must. You know, Charlie, supporting the local economy."

24

"Where are we going today?" Maggie shouted at me as I walked out of the elevator.

For the next few days, Maggie and I stayed away from Z's. We spent the mornings in the parks reading *Everyday Mindfulness* and trying to meditate, but mostly we just laughed because neither of us could stay silent for more than a few seconds. Having Maggie around also made me more productive. I liked having a second pair of eyes, and she pushed me to find new angles and challenged me to find unique lighting. She pressed me to find a story for every photo I took. *Discover the why for each photo*, she would always tell me. I spent less time taking photographs and more time watching my subjects, trying to take just one photograph when I felt their true self was being represented.

Having someone encouraging me reminded me of when my dad had taken me out and we would wander around South Philly. I missed him, and I knew he would be proud of me and of my work no matter how it turned out. But secretly I was feeling confident and more sure of myself. Maybe there was something in this project.

Whatever this project would become, I was almost finished with it. I had only two days left in Saigon. I had to start thinking about what I was going to do next.

After a month of everyone telling me different places to go, I was left feeling confused and unsure of my next destination. Cambodia to see Angkor Wat, or up north to see Halong Bay or Laos or Indonesia or island hop in the Philippines or maybe check out Thailand, despite Ace's telling me several times to avoid it at all cost?

Before I left home, two months had seemed like an entirety, but now the time felt short and rushed. I needed some guidance, so I went to find the one person who had been everywhere. I also wanted us to patch whatever rift we had between us.

"Two more days, eh? That went by quickly," Ace said as he lay on his bed. "I told you, rule number... ." He talked to me like we hadn't had a fight in Hoi An.

"Yes, I know. I shouldn't have booked a flight home."

"You are learning! You can cancel it, ya know."

I nodded. My flight was non-refundable, and I had told him that several times, but of course he always seemed to forget. Ignoring him, I pressed on.

"Any thoughts on where I should go?" I asked.

"Where do you want to go?" he replied. He never answered anything. A poor man's Socrates method.

"Not sure yet."

"Now that's the traveling spirit!" he yelled. He seemed to be in good spirits and never mentioned that we hadn't spoken in a few days. Maybe we weren't that good of friends after all. "Just wait until something sparks you, and then set off. That's the magic of traveling."

"Hmm. Thanks, Ace." This discussion was about as helpful as I had thought it would be. Ace never planned anything, and he seemed better at telling you where not to go than where to go. Frustrated with him once again, I turned around and was about to walk out.

"Wait, I got an idea." He jumped off his bed and stood tall in front of me.

"On where I should go?"

"Maybe," he said as he stroked his chin a few times. "How about we go to Myanmar?!"

"Together?" Ace never traveled with other people. Did he really want me to go? "Are you sure?" I asked.

"I didn't tell you yet, but I think I'm leaving Southeast Asia for good and finally heading toward Central Asia. I'm tired of this place and the new influx of Instagram travelers."

Ace's worst enemies were the Instagram travelers, as he called them. They were even worse than flashpackers. The Instagram travelers were only there to show off. The ones who would go somewhere just for the photo and then would spend hours in hostels editing their shots. The people with Instagram names like wanderlustgirl, travelcouplesgoals, et cetera. All day he would complain about how they had ruined traveling and that because of them there were no more secrets, no more mystery to travel. No longer were backpackers the outcasts of society, the rare few who left home to seek adventure down an unknown road. Now everyone was here to get the "money shot": the same sunrise photo of Angkor Wat with thousands of people. He missed the backpackers with the sad stories, those who were running away from something. Now everyone traveling was a carbon copy of everyone else. He would have gone on, but I didn't want to hear it again, so I changed the subject.

"Why Central Asia again?"

"The Silk Road, of course! Kyrgyzstan, Uzbekistan and Turkmenistan," he said proudly. For Ace, the more obscure the country, the better.

"I may be naïve, but anything that ends with *stan* sounds dangerous to me," I responded.

"You've been in the U.S. too long. Live there long enough, and everything will scare you. Let me tell you about dangerous... Forty years ago, there was a war right here. In this very country. Twenty years ago, just a short bus ride away, there was a genocide in Cambodia. Killed 25 percent of their population in six years. Ten years ago, you weren't even allowed into Myanmar. Now these places are being flooded with tourists, and I think Central Asia is next. I want to get there before all these Instagram-seeking backpackers ruin it."

"Oh, I see. I'm not sure about Myanmar. I don't know too much about it."

"Maybe we can discuss it tonight over dinner?"

"Dinner?"

"Yeah, mate. You think I was going to send you off without a good-bye dinner?"

"District 6?" I asked, expecting us to go eat pho again.

"You only have a few more days here. Tonight, I'm taking you... out. Out! No pub crawl or pho in District 6, but a proper restaurant."

"That would be great!" I was curious and excited.

"Listen, Charlie. I know I fucked up with Hoi An and not getting your films developed. I want to make it up to you." That was as close to an apology as I thought I was going to get, and I didn't want to leave on bad terms, so I happily agreed.

"Seven p.m. sharp, Charlie, and wear something smart!"

25

Saigon was spectacularly malleable, even in its name. I was never even sure what to call it: Saigon or Ho Chi Minh City. Ace talked about how the city was always evolving and how it could mold into any form or shape you desired. If you wanted a local-only vibe, go here. If you wanted a backpacker bar, go there. If you wanted a fancy rooftop restaurant, go to District 3.

The taxi inched its way across town. It was seven p.m., and the sun was just about done with its daily assault on the city. Ace sat in the front seat. He was trying to chat up the taxi driver and was asking him something about what area he lived in as he floated his hand just outside the open window. I was seated behind him, feeling the nice breeze blow through my now-long hair, cooling my face. Maggie had also agreed to dinner. She sat next to me in the back seat. I guess he thought he could fix two friendships with one night out. She was quiet, and it made me feel uneasy.

"How's my hair look?" I said to her. I knew it was blowing crazily in the wind.

She turned slowly to me, as she had been silently gazing out her window.

"Stunning, my love. Absolutely stunning." She pushed my long, black hair back and tucked the bits that were floating away behind my ear.

The area was familiar to me now, but I had never thought about stepping into the hotel bars or restaurants that littered it. They catered to a wealthier traveler.

The taxi pulled up to a large building that had its own valet out front. It could have been any upscale restaurant from back home. We were greeted by a young man in a black suit with equally black hair that was cut in the popular undercut style that was now trending among the young professionals in Vietnam.

In English, he said, "Welcome to Pali."

We all nodded politely and followed him through the front door and into a beautiful lobby that was well lit with a large chandelier. The young man pushed the elevator button, and we waited to go up.

I shuffled about in my one collared shirt that I had brought with me on my travels. Ace stood there in black jeans and boots, wearing his new burgundy sport coat with his Hawaiian t-shirt underneath. Maggie was still quiet and stood a bit away from us, looking at the old black-and-white photographs of Saigon that hung on the walls next to the elevators. She was wearing a sundress that exaggerated her curves and looked beautiful, and I knew Ace felt the same, as I kept catching him staring at her as she walked by. When the elevator arrived, the young man ushered us in and pushed the button labeled Pali Rooftop.

I could feel the tension between the two as the softly playing piano music hovered around us and taunted the silence. Maggie hadn't forgiven Ace as easily as I had. Ace, however, was grinningly oblivious to any problems, and I could tell he was excited as he bounced like a child as the elevator sped upwards. He liked playing host and showing people new experiences and anxiously waited for our reactions of approval.

The elevator doors opened, and a flood of noise entered the silent elevator. The restaurant was buzzing. It was loud and crowded, and a thunderous beat played overhead. The place was part nightclub and part restaurant. Ace could barely contain his excitement by now and was pacing about as the young man in the suit held the elevator door and motioned with his hands for us to enter the restaurant. Ace sprinted out.

"Whaddya think, Charlie?" Ace said.

Inside, servers zoomed around the patrons who were eating and drinking at large tables. The restaurant was filled with families of western travelers and businessmen and couples on dates. The decor was simple and wide open, and small, colorful umbrellas hung from the high ceilings. The outdoor patio, crawling out past the full tables and into the darkening night, featured a vast view of the emerging lights of the skyline that would soon be on full display.

We were then greeted by a hostess who was dressed in a beautiful tight black dress. Her dark hair was pulled tightly up into a bun, and she had a beautiful smile.

"Do you have a reservation?" she asked softly in English.

"Nope, but is William here?" demanded Ace.

"Mr. William. Yes, he is. Do you have an appointment?" she asked quizzically.

"An appointment?! Man, this guy is important these days. NO, I do not have an appointment. Just tell Mr. William his good friend Ace and company are here," Ace said confidently.

She nodded and left.

"Isn't this place great?" he said again. His face shone with a childish wonderment. To Ace, everything always seemed new and shiny.

"It's very nice, Ace," Maggie chimed in.

"Nice?! Ok. I guess we aren't up to Queen Maggie's standards," Ace said sarcastically.

She looked sharply at him and then quickly away.

"I would have at least known to make a reservation," she said as she walked away.

This was the first time I had witnessed hostility between them. She was not joking, and even Ace felt it this time. Gone were the flirtatious jabs; that comment was a left hook that landed square on Ace's jaw. A line from a Rocky movie, featuring my dad's favorite Philadelphian hero, popped into my head: *It's about how hard you can get hit and keep moving.* Ace was stunned and looked wide-eyed and unsure how to react. He seemed caught off guard by her obvious anger. I could read Ace. He stood there, thinking, *How can she still be mad at me?* His face flushed and his breathing quickened, and I waited for a comeback, but he simply hung his head and did his normal routine when he was told something he didn't like: he ignored the comment and sauntered off. Probably not the type of move Rocky would have coached, but that was Ace.

"There he is!" Ace barked. His smile returned as a man came forward to greet us.

His head was shaved, and the top of it shone from the bright lights. He wore thick red glasses and was dressed immaculately in a three-piece suit. He was good-looking and seemed serious and important as he stood confidently in front of us.

"William! My old friend. How are you?" Ace shouted, all signs of distress vanishing from his face.

They embraced with a big hug.

"I told you last time, Ace, you need to make a reservation. It's Saturday night, and we are slammed. I can get you all a table, but it will not be on the roof." He sounded frustrated as he continued to observe the room, hardly looking at us.

"Come on, Willy! You know I hate reservations."

"It looks like you hate irons also. Looks like you are going to a bloody hostel pub luau," he said with his laid-back Australian accent. Ace looked down and tried to smooth out his wrinkled shirt.

"You know how shirts get in backpacks." Ace half smiled.

"Mate, I haven't traveled with a backpack in years. My wife would kill me if I booked her into a hostel." Then a server came up to us and whispered something into William's ear, and without pause, William answered loudly back in Vietnamese.

"Willy, you sound like a local!" Ace proclaimed.

"My wife is a good teacher. And sorry—where are my manners? I'm William, and I'm the owner of Pali. Thank you for coming in tonight."

"Let me introduce you to my new crew. This is the lovely Maggie, and this is Charlie, a great up-and-coming photographer."

"You still don't know how to dress, Ace, but you sure know how to pick the ladies. I hope you don't fuck this one up, mate." He lifted Maggie's hand and kissed it.

"He doesn't know how to do that either. Hello, I'm Maggie." One more body shot to Ace. Then he turned to me.

"Hello, Charlie. Pleasure to meet you, and please, before you leave, tell me where I can see your photographs." He shook my hand with a hardy grip and smiled warmly.

He walked us through the restaurant and stopped a few times to check on tables and told a few jokes to people enjoying their meals. Several times he barked orders as several servers zoomed by us like they were at a track meet.

"Here is your table. Next time make a reservation so I can seat you at one of our outdoor tables."

"Won't you have a drink with us, Willy?" Ace pleaded.

"I'm working now," he answered, not looking at Ace as he scanned the room with a sharp gaze. "Maybe in an hour or two when things calm down a bit."

"Lovely. I have several new stories to catch you up on—" Before Ace could finish his sentence, William had already hurried off.

"This is really nice, Ace. Your friend is great," I said.

"He is ok." Ace turned quickly to the menu.

"I thought he was lovely," responded Maggie. "Handsome—and he dressed so nicely. Looks like he is doing well for himself."

She was unrelenting tonight and landed a few more body blows. Ace darted up from behind his menu, but once again he didn't say a word. Responding to critiques and challenges was not his strong suit, so he turned to what was: drinking. Lots and lots of drinking.

26

The cocktails seemed to dull the fight in Maggie, and by the time the food had arrived, we already had a nice drunk on. Ace was able to recapture the conversation, as Maggie was now too drunk to punch straight, and we retold stories from my month in Saigon. The presentation of our food was like a work of art, with every sauce specifically measured and poured over the food that was so meticulously cooked and thoughtfully placed onto the plate that you were unsure if it smelled or looked better. You almost felt bad about eating it, until you did, and then you no longer felt bad because it tasted wonderful and you were smiling and laughing and happy in the company of good friends while eating good food.

Ignoring any manners, we reached across each other's bodies to share our plates. Soon we were finished, with full bellies. Ace seemed pleased with himself as we gushed over the food and the cocktails. The cocktails we ordered were each off a special drinks menu that was fashioned into a book. The book and drinks were curated and illustrated by William.

The book included several pen sketches of the Saigon city skyline and landscape and the people who occupied it.

Occasionally, we saw William rush by our table, but he never stopped by to chat. He was too busy schmoozing with other guests. He poured wine and brought out drinks and always stayed long enough to tell a story or two. He stood over the tables of businessmen and posh tourists and was the king of the court. Laughter and drinks followed him as he circled through the busy restaurant.

After several hours of dining, the once-crowded restaurant slowly began to empty. I was hoping to leave, but Ace had other plans as he kept ordering us drinks despite the fact that we were already plenty drunk. With the emptying of the restaurant, we decided to take our drinks outside to enjoy the view.

"God, how this city has changed. Look at that skyline!" Ace shouted loudly.

The sky was now dark, and lights of the high-rise buildings were the only lights illuminating the city. An impressive skyline was growing in all directions, assisted by the large cranes that were mounted in every corner of the city.

"Things like this didn't exist a few years ago. Now every roof in District 3 has a rooftop bar. Hell, a few decades ago there was a bloody war here, and now look. It's becoming just like any other city. Hip and modern. Stupid posh restaurants with overpriced drinks and rich assholes coming here opening their bottomless wallets and consuming everything with their unwavering appetites." Ace was more drunk than usual as he ranted on about things I'd heard him say a million times.

"Sorry to take you away from your carefree and anti-establishment backpacker lifestyle, Ace." William appeared behind Ace and smiled, holding a small glass filled halfway up with whiskey. "You know he is full of shit," he whispered to us. "You can sit here now." He pointed to an empty table at the edge of the roof.

"You know what I mean, Willy. When we came here years ago, we fell in love with Saigon. We fell in love with the streets. Now, from up here, we can't even see the streets."

"Spoken like a true traveler, my old friend, a romantic to the bone. But from the looks of things, it seems like you enjoyed yourselves despite dining in an overpriced posh restaurant full of rich assholes. And don't worry about the bill. It's on me. I always pay for backpackers. I know how hard it is to travel with a budget, and I think every now and then it's good to have a nice meal."

Without thanking him, Ace went into a story. "Old Willy and I traveled through South America together. When was that... eight...ten years ago?"

"Feels like a lifetime ago," William said and took a long sip of his whiskey.

Ace went on, "We were both lost. Neither of us spoke a lick of Spanish, and we were the only backpackers in this isolated part of southern Argentina. We ended up spending a month together hiking around Patagonia and drinking Argentinian wine and eating the best steaks our mouths had ever tasted. Now look at him. A big shot in the culinary explosion of Saigon."

"I don't think I'm a big shot yet. But this city is amazing and has treated me well. Have you seen the drink menu yet? Ha! Of course you have. You almost ordered everything on it," William laughed.

"The book is a bit preten—" Ace started to say just as Maggie cut him off.

"They were delicious! Did you design the drinks yourself?" Maggie chimed in, to avoid a drunken comment from Ace.

"Yes, I did. The menu was my inspiration for this restaurant. I wanted to bring in a new flavor of dining into this emerging city. As you can see, the restaurant aesthetic is new and modern and hip and something you would find in any major city, but I also wanted to look back at the history of the city and its people and pay homage to them. Like Ace said, we fell in love with this city because of the streets. My goal was to mix those two together in a harmonious way. The book itself contains 40 drinks. Forty drinks associated with 40 years of peace. Forty years of no war. I tried to use classic Vietnamese flavors and design a menu that paid tribute to the city. I drew everything you see in the book because I'm an artist at heart and love exploring the different districts and discovering new tastes. You will still find me most days in the streets trying new food, as I continue to try to blend the old school with the new school."

"Then sell them here where no one from the streets can afford them?" Ace said abruptly as he finished his drink and grabbed a waiter to order another one.

Ignoring the comment, Maggie gushed, "These drawings are incredible!"

"Thank you. I appreciate that." He gazed sharply at Ace.

"Yeah, not bad, Willy. Not bad at all. I remember those shit drawings you used to do while we were hiking. Glad you got a bit better."

"Haha, thanks for bringing that up, Ace. Yeah, I didn't have a natural talent like you, so I practiced, a lot. Now it's something I'm proud of."

"Maggie and Charlie, please take one each." He handed us each two books. "These copies we have used for the past month, and they have a bit of damage, but it's my little gift to you."

"Thank you," we both said in unison.

"Not one for your dear old friend?" Ace remarked.

"I'm sure you have some of my old drawings stacked away in those notebooks of yours. Who would have thought I would have a book published before you!" Ace turned red as the waiter placed another drink in front of him. "By the way, how's the writing coming along?" William asked.

Ace took a big swig from his fresh cocktail, almost finishing it.

"You are still writing, right?" William pressed.

"I don't really write anymore," Ace mumbled into his drink.

Maggie and I exchanged glances.

"Shit, man. Ace had these stacks of notebooks filled with his writings. It was also the only time he stopped talking, so I always encouraged him to go off and write." Everyone laughed; even Ace couldn't help himself. "But he hid them like a pot of gold. I felt lucky when he was drunk enough to show me any of it. When we parted ways, I always kept an eye out for a book written by our gorgeous Ace. Of all the people I traveled with, he had the most potential to do whatever he wanted. I truly thought he was going to stop traveling and dedicate time to actually becoming a serious writer."

"I guess I wasted my potential, then," Ace said, as he took another large sip and called for a waiter. William shot the waiter a signal that Ace didn't see, and the server quickly turned around, away from Ace.

"Hey, what the hell?" Ace protested.

"Sorry, mate. Kitchen is closed."

Ace's head bobbed up and down, and he was too drunk to argue. I could see Maggie looking at Ace. She had taken off her boxing gloves and was looking at him now with caring eyes as Ace's drunk, sad eyes stared down into his empty drink.

"I think his muse was this drop-dead Parisian girlfriend. Why you went with me to South American and left her, I will never know. You still in contact with her, Ace?"

Out of the hundreds of stories I had heard Ace tell, never had I heard anything about Paris, or of any past love.

Ace lifted up his empty glass and studied it, hoping to find any brown whiskey that he might have missed. He poured the ice into this mouth and ignored William's question.

Even William was picking up the cues that Ace didn't want to discuss that part of his life, and he turned to Maggie and me. "Enough about the past. What's next for you two? Where are you guys going after Saigon? God, I sound like a backpacker again. Haha."

Maggie answered first. "Thailand! I want to go to all the beautiful beaches!"

"Can't go wrong there. I will give you my contacts there. But I'm sure Ace will be able to recommend the hostels, as I no longer know too much about them," William said, trying to coax Ace back into the conversation.

"Uggh. Fuck Thailand. You couldn't pay me to go!" Ace snarled.

Sensing Ace's hostility, and before Maggie could respond, I butted in. "I'm not sure where to go next. I feel a bit overwhelmed."

"I'm trying to convince young Charlie to join me in Myanmar, the last oasis in Southeast Asia," Ace said.

"Yeah, I'm thinking about that, Ace, but I also wanted to learn how to meditate. I've been practicing on my own and just feel like I need some proper guidance." I was still unsure about traveling with Ace to Myanmar.

"That's great, Charlie. I love meditation, and it's something you'll definitely want to explore while you're out here. I'm sure The Sun Always Rises is a hard place to develop that skill—ya know, in between the bar crawls and hangovers," William laughed.

"Hmmm," he went on. "You know where is a good place to go? For both of you? I know of a great meditation retreat in Pai. You and Maggie can go meditate, and, Maggie, you will be close enough to then head down to southern Thailand and explore the beaches."

"Where?" I asked. I hadn't heard of Pai.

"Pai. It's in Northern Thailand. It's a chilled-out little backpacker city, surrounded by beautiful nature with caves, hot springs and waterfalls. There is a meditation retreat there, and the person that runs it is great! A must-go-to if you are interested in meditation," William said.

"Oh, Willy, don't send Charlie boy to Thailand. Thailand is the worst, and I hate fucking Pai. It's full of the worst backpackers," Ace blurted. "You remember what we used to say when we went there."

Ace was now finished with whatever was left in his drink. Unable to fill his mouth with liquor, words occupied the space instead. "Northern Thailand was great five years ago. There were only a few backpackers there, and it was great. Now it's all 7-11s and assholes."

"Well, 20 years ago it was all farmers and locals, and real adventurers would probably say the same thing about you, Ace, God of Backpacking! Let me tell you a little secret. You will never be the first person anywhere, and things change. Sometimes good and sometimes bad. Let them make up their own mind. This is what they want to do, not what you want them to do," William said firmly.

The two of them bounced back and forth like a tennis match. Old friends maybe; rivals for sure.

"They can do whatever they want. I'm just saying going to bloody Pai for a meditation retreat is as cliché as reading Eat, Pray go fuck yourself, or whatever that stupid book is called."

"Write a better one then, my old friend," William smiled and looked around. We were the last people left in the restaurant. Probably trying to avoid a blowout fight, William stood and calmly said, "I think it's time we call it a night; I need to get home to my wife and child."

We left with our books in our hands, riding back down the elevator with the same silence as when we arrived.

27

Bang! Crash!

After spending time in the hostel, I was rarely bothered anymore by evening noises, let alone woken up by them. I was beginning to sleep through everything, but these noises were different.

Bang! Crash! There it was again.

Bang! Crash!... and again.

I sat up in my bottom bunk. I looked at my watch. It had only been a few hours since I had gone to bed; Z's must still be buzzing. Maybe a new drinking game?

Bang! Crash!

There it was once more.

What was going on downstairs? I made my way downstairs as quickly as I could. A crowd of people had gathered. Phones were out and filming what was going on. In the middle of it all, Ace stood center stage, but this time he was not playing his usual part as king of the court. This time he was in the role of the lowly jester.

He had a bottle in his hand, and he was attempting to spin it around as he moved it behind his back. The routine he had once perfected now looked ghastly amateurish. His usual smooth and rhythmic movements now appeared crude and disjointed; his actions were slowed and his vision blurred from drinking all night at Pali. He no longer possessed his normal sure-fire reactions necessary to catch free-falling bottles. His hands swung through the air either a millisecond late or a millimeter in the wrong direction.

Bang! Crash! Bottle after bottle crashed to the ground. Shards of glass floated in spilled liquor.

Ace swayed side to side as if someone were playing an invisible game of tug-of-war with his waist as he walked to the bar to get another bottle. I couldn't watch anymore. I pushed passed the gawkers, brushed down their phones and walked toward Ace.

"Hey, Ace. How about we put down the bottle and go to bed," I said.

"Charlie!" Ace shouted. "You know I can do this," he whispered in my ear way too close and way too loud, the way drunk people talk when they want to tell you something important. "And fuck all these people. They're not artists like us, Charlie. These people...these people have not suffered like we have, and that's why they can't be artists like us. Now let me finish the show with my grand finale!"

I didn't know what he meant but I tried to back him off the ledge before he leaped into his finale performance. "I know you can, but tonight may not be your night."

"Every night is my night! This . . ."—he spun the bottle around his hand, almost dropping it several times—"This is what I'm good at. This... is the only thing I'm good at." He pushed me back, threw the bottle high into the air and made a quick 360-degree turn. But, once again, he mistimed the bottle's trajectory.

Bang! Crash!

"Ace, stop!" I looked around at the sea of cell phones once again hovering in front of faceless people, then back at Ace, whose eyes widened as he stared at my ankle. I hadn't put my brace on in the rush to get downstairs and hadn't felt it when it happened, but a piece of broken glass had splintered from the last bottle and plunged firmly into my shin. I pulled it out; half of it was covered in blood. My leg was dripping red with blood, and it ran down my ankle, into my shoes. He quickly grabbed a few clean towels from the bar and placed them on my shin.

"It's only a small cut," I repeated. It was only a small cut but it bled as if I were hemorrhaging.

Ace turned to fully face me, in drunken regret and red-faced embarrassment. "Mate, I'm so sorry."

"It's ok. I'll be fine."

He turned his eyes toward the crowds that were usually adoring fans but who were now laughing and pointing, taking photos and filming the debacle that was taking place in front of them.

Sobering up may be an overestimate, but he seemed to have a moment of clarity. He looked at the shards of glass that peppered the ground, the blood that streamed from my shin and the smiling and laughing faces behind the cell phones. His face changed to a look I had yet to see in him.

"Film away! All you do is film film film. You would film everything. Just to make yourself feel better and anything for likes. Is anything off-limits for you assholes? You would probably film my mom hanging if you had the chance!" I jerked up with a glance of pure shock and stopped attending to my bleeding ankle. Had I really heard what I thought I had? Had Ace's mom committed suicide? He didn't talk much about his past, but he did talk about his mom periodically, and I could tell they were close. The crowd holding their phones resembled that of a firing squad, and most began to lay down their weapons as they took in the shocking news of Ace's mom's suicide, but some stayed fixated on their target and kept filming away.

"You want something to film? Film this!" Ace picked up another bottle and threw it over the head of the gathered crowd. They ducked as the bottle smashed against the wall behind them. Brown rum dripped from the walls as everyone covered their heads.

"I'm sorry, Charlie." He pushed past me and left.

I looked back at the shocked crowd, and this time all of their weapons were now laid down.

28

Our bags were packed; we had begun saying our goodbyes around the hostel. It felt bittersweet because I felt very much a part of the hostel family I had made here in Saigon, and I was going to miss all my new friends, but I was also excited and ready to begin a new adventure. It was time to move on. Maggie and I had both registered for the introductory weekend meditation retreat in Pai. All we needed to do was get there. Fly to Bangkok, overnight train to Chiang Mai and bus to Pai.

There was only one friend left to say good-bye to, but Ace had vanished. The last time I had seen him had been the morning after Pali. He had been sitting at the bar drinking an early-morning beer. Z's was clean, the shards of glass removed, the stains on the walls wiped clean. Ace must have used his magic again to remove any signs of the previous night. Nothing looked different. But there he was, sitting alone and blankly staring into his beer. Everything looked the same but felt different. The aura around him of a carefree and confident traveler he portrayed from the outside seemed shattered. The lifelong backpacker living the dream, was gone. He now just looked sad, lost, and lonely.

I took a seat next to him, and he barely acknowledged me. I told him about my plan while he sat there silently, never once bringing up the previous night. I told him Maggie and I were heading to Thailand, that we were going to the retreat that William had recommended. I assumed he would berate me. Tell me how we were no longer real travelers, that I was breaking any number of rules. He simply nodded into his beer. The next two days he was a ghost.

I was worried, but no one else seemed to notice. Hostels were like that. You would meet someone for a night or two and be their best friend, and then they'd disappear onto a train or bus or flight and into the next city, where they would just as quickly meet a new group of people. The cycle would continue and repeat itself. Hostels were fluid, and people whisked in and out so quickly it was hard to keep track of who was coming and who was going. Most assumed Ace had been kicked out of the hostel and had left to go traveling again.

But I knew he wouldn't leave without saying good-bye, and if he was still in Saigon I knew where to find him.

When I reached BOA Books, it was just before noon. I walked up the familiar stairs and pushed the door open. In front of me, perched on a bean bag, sat Ace with piles of crumpled-up paper all around him.

He looked up and nodded. His beard had grown longer and his hair disheveled. "How's the ankle?" he asked in almost a whisper. I guess he remembered something from that night.

"Ahh, it's fine. Maggie helped bandage it up." I lifted up my jeans and showed him the perfectly wrapped cloth. "If you still want to race, I'd suggest now is your best opportunity," I added, trying to make a joke.

He smiled briefly. "She is an absolute sweetheart. She will make a great doctor. And no racing for me. I'm too busy doing nothing."

"What are you doing here?" I asked.

"Writing the next great novel, of course," he said with a forced grin and a shrug. At that same moment, he violently ripped another page out of his notebook and crumpled it up.

Then without warning Ace starting talking, not of his past exploits but how he was feeling. A vulnerability that he never showed. "Seeing William the other night shook me up. What he has accomplished. Who he is now. He and I were one and the same, both traveling assholes, looking to get drunk and get laid every night. But now he's this successful grownup with a restaurant, and I'm still an asshole. And then I had this idea. I had this stupid idea that I should write again. I thought I would come here and I would be able to put pen to paper and words would just flow like they used to. But... nothing. Absolutely nothing." He swiped all the papers to the floor with a quick stroke and dropped his forehead into his hands. "In my head, I have a million swirling ideas, but as soon as I touch pen to paper, the words vanish out of my head and I'm left with nothing. I haven't been able write one sentence I can be proud of. Maybe I've dulled my abilities. Maybe I never had them. All I know is, I used to love to sit down at a café and write. I haven't written a meaningful word since I left Paris."

"What about South America? William said you wrote there," I said, trying to raise his spirits.

"I wrote there like I'm writing now. Nothing but absolute dog shit," Ace said angrily.

"But he read your writing and said it was great!"

"I only showed him my old writing from my time in Paris."

"Well, maybe you should go back to Paris."

"I can't!" Ace yelled.

"Why not? Commit a crime there?" I said jokingly.

"Because I just can't, ok!" Ace screamed.

I looked over at Mhi, hoping she hadn't heard that. She obviously had, though, because she had a concerned look on her face, and I think Ace noticed it too.

"Sorry for yelling, Mhi!" He looked at me with a calmer face. "Sorry—I'm all messed up right now," he whispered to me.

"I understand how you feel." I shifted uncomfortably in the bean bag. I hadn't talked about this with anyone, but I felt Ace needed to hear it. "My dad died before I left on this trip. My mom and dad never told me he was sick, until it was too late. Too late for me to tell him how much he meant to me. And after he died, I was angry. At him. At my mom. My leg. At his camera that hung in my room and taunted me, reminding me that he was no longer there."

Ace looked at me and, for once, did not interject with his own story but instead sat there silently. Listening intently.

"Then I realized. My anger wasn't going to bring him back. It wasn't going to cure the disease that killed him. The anger was only stopping me from doing the thing I loved. The thing my father and I had spent the happiest years of my youth doing. That day, I made a choice that his camera wasn't going to remind me that he wasn't here but would instead remind me that he will always be here. I feel him and smile every time I take a picture." Maybe Ace needed to hear it, but after I finished, I realized I needed to hear it too.

Ace pursed his lips, and I could tell he wanted to say something, but he just looked away at the books behind him, as if something there would give him the words he couldn't say.

"Well, I'll let you get back to writing. But I wanted to tell you we are having a big leaving bash tonight as Z's for Maggie and me. Wouldn't be the same without you," I said.

Ace continued staring at the books, so I got up to leave. "Hey wait, Charlie." I turned around. Ace was now looking at me and softly said, "Thank you."

"For what?" I asked.

"Sharing that story about your dad."

"You are welcome, Ace. And will I see you tonight?" I asked, hopeful.

"Yeah, wouldn't miss it for the world."

"Okay, I need to get back and go to the Bến Thành Market. You know it's my last day. I gotta buy all my touristy things now."

"Haha! Now you're talking like a seasoned backpacker," Ace said.

"I learned from the best." He gave me a full smile, and then I got up to leave and said, "And, Ace, if you ever want to talk about anything, I'm always here."

"I know you are, Charlie. Thank you."

I went over to Mhi and said good-bye. I promised I'd send her the photographs I had taken of her and of the bookstore. She smiled, we shared a nice embrace and I walked out. A Lawrence Arms song snarled in the background.

There's a park in the city where I used to go
But now it's covered with fences and cops and light posts
And I'd never go back even if it was the same
But it kills me to know that it's changed

29

That night, Z's was like it always was: drunk and loud. I circled the bar, collecting money. Ace was making drinks behind the bar, and Maggie was walking around passing out the complimentary shots. Everything was the same, but yet so different.

I yelled for everyone to finish up their drinks—it was time to start my last Sun Always Rises bar crawl—when I felt someone grab me.

"You are a good friend, Charlie." When I first arrived, I used to think Ace was never drunk. But now as he stood next to me, I could see that his eyes were clearer and more full of life than I was used to seeing them.

"You are my friend too," I said earnestly.

"I haven't had many real friends in a long time, the ones that actually call me on my shit," Ace shared. "After you left today, I thought a lot about what you said. About you and your dad and your photography. You made me think about my mom. Sometimes I forget why I find peace at BOA. Why that place, of all the places, is my favorite place in the city. You helped me remember why. That bookstore is where my mom is still with me, surrounded by her favorite books. It reminds me of the library at our house where she would go and hide when the world was too much for her. Where she introduced me to stories of adventure and travel. There I don't feel sadness about her death, but happiness that we both share the love of the words in those pages. Thank you, Charlie. You are a good friend."

"Thanks for sharing that Ace. I replied, and we both smiled."

"Can I ask you something? Would you mind if I join you on your trip?" I looked at him, thinking he was joking.

"Are you sure? I know you hate Thailand."

"I know a great hostel in Chiang Mai, and I couldn't let you travel there without a great recommendation. And I want... well, to be honest, I think it would be good for me. I'm not really doing anything here," Ace said.

"Of course, Ace. I would love to have you join."

"Thanks," Ace said as backpackers drunkenly rushed past us. He put his hand out and shook my hand. Then he walked out of Z's and back into the hostel. I looked around, and everyone was drunk and laughing, and I glanced up over at the now-unmanned bar and read:

And if you commit then, as we did, the error of thinking,
One day all this will only be a memory.

I think I finally had a better idea of what those words meant.

30

The apartment Caroline lived in sat on Rue Lamarck, a stone's throw away from the Cemetery Saint Vincent. On all accounts, it was an ideal house for a young woman at university. The house had belonged to her grandparents. They had also owned Café Lavender, which sat a short five minutes away down the street.

Both buildings had been inherited by Caroline when her grandparents had died. Caroline had adored her grandparents. Caroline's mother had tragically passed away when she was young, too young for Caroline to remember, so she looked to her grandparents to fill in the blanks and tell her vivid stories of her mother. Her father had moved back to Sweden after his wife's passing, as Paris was too sad a reminder of his life with his wife. Caroline had been raised in Stockholm but wanted to maintain the family home and café, so she moved to Paris to attend university.

The house was spacious and contained three bedrooms. There were two identical bedrooms that were simple and old-fashioned in their decor. Ace assumed that most things had been left untouched when her grandparents died. Then there was a smaller, third bedroom. That bedroom was really Caroline's room and had now been converted into a darkroom. It was her workspace and her sanctuary. When she and Ace weren't together, she spent most of her time working in that room. In that room, there was an endless production line of negatives and small prints that were sorted in stacks across the apartment. All of them were black and white, and at the bottom right-hand corner, they all read C.S., for Caroline Struddenberg.

Everything was in stacks since there was hardly any shelving in the house. Stacks of books. Stacks of records. Stacks of her photography. The abundance of stacked items resembled miniature mountain ranges, yet they were somehow organized enough that Caroline always knew where to find any particular item. Caroline referred to it as organized chaos.

The simplicity of the bedrooms contrasted with the dining and living rooms, which were filled with life and energy. Plants hung from the ceiling and took up almost all the empty space on the floor next to the windows. Natural light engulfed the apartment from early morning to mid-afternoon, and the plants thrived in that environment as they grew and shot upward, spilling over the sides of the pots. Caroline was meticulous with watering her plants and spent time each morning investigating them and attending to them accordingly. She was very motherly to the plants and took great pride in their growth. Sometimes she told Ace that if you looked close enough, you could see them leaning toward the sun. Ace never saw it. But she did. She had an eye for things that no one else could see.

A record player and two large speakers were placed where other people might have had a television. She had a large collection of jazz records and American rock and roll, from Miles Davis and Chet Baker to Tom Petty and Bruce Springsteen. It was a wonderful apartment, and Ace quickly found it more welcoming than any home he had ever been in.

During those first few months, they couldn't get enough of each other and made love frequently with an unbridled passion that he had never felt with any other woman. They never rushed while they made love, and it would be hours before they both fell asleep, exhausted and satisfied.

In the mornings, when the light arrived early and warmed their naked bodies, they would talk for hours, making up adventures they would go on. In the summer, they would go to Spain and eat tapas and drink sangria and dance the salsa until sunrise. In the fall, they would stay in Tuscany, where they would eat pasta and drink red wine. Winters would be spent in the mountains of Switzerland, where they would ski in the shadows of the Alps and read books near an open fire. In the spring, they would ride bikes in the warming Dutch countryside and watch the flowers bloom and then make love in the colorful fields under the large windmills.

But now they were in Paris, and it was August, and it was hot and sticky, and the city felt like it belonged to them. Most of the locals were away on holiday, and they could sleep late into the morning and then walk the empty streets in the afternoon. They would drink chilled white wine in the parks where there was shade from the sun, and they would kiss each other with lips that still tasted of the silky-smooth sauvignon blanc. It was a wonderful summer they enjoyed together, and they knew they needed to be nowhere else but here, in Paris.

During the long Paris days, Caroline's camera was never too far away. Ace adored her creativity and how her mind worked, the way she saw a photograph before it happened. Her ability to visualize a photograph before she took it was artform in itself. At one moment, she might fall to her knees; the next, she might climb up on a tree or lie prone in the grass to get just the right angle, with just the right lighting. She was completely absorbed when she was behind the lens, and Ace often thought she may have even forgotten he was there when she was in the middle of a shot.

Ace never knew exactly what she was photographing. He would follow the line of sight of her camera lens, usually to some mundane subject they had encountered: a man on a park bench, children playing on the street, or a young couple sneaking away into a shadow of a secluded alleyway, but never could he fully grasp the exact image her camera was capturing. Ace would usually press her about the photographs after each shot.

"Is that going to be a good one?"

She would shrug and say, "Let's keep walking."

And like that, she would hop out of whatever pose she was in, and they would continue with their tour of the city. Rarely did she take more than one photograph of any particular subject, and after she finished a roll of film, she would throw her camera behind her and grab Ace's hand and they would walk together, fingers intertwined in the warmth of the summer night.

When they arrived home, she would tuck herself away in the seclusion of her darkroom to work. Eventually, feeling fascinated and curious, Ace would pour himself a whiskey and peek into the room being careful not to emit any light in and quickly he would slide in and take a seat on a stool that sat against the door.

He sat at the edge of the darkness in silence, his eyes fixed on her as they adjusted to the red light that illuminated the room. Caroline stared at the drying photographs with an intensity that he had never possessed, a passion that he had never known and a talent that he had never felt. He loved that silence.

He watched her glide from side to side in the room with grace and purpose. She never seemed to notice his presence as the small red light in the room illuminated her face. It highlighted the contours on her cheeks that led to the shadows of her neck, and it projected a perfect silhouette of her face over her drying photographs that hung on the opposite wall.

He took small sips of whiskey, and she made small gestures with her face as her mind worked. If she was really focused, a slight scowl would appear on her face and her eyebrows would furrow ever so slightly. At those moments, he couldn't help but think how lucky he was. She was the most beautiful creature he had ever seen. He would finish his whiskey, and the same way he had come in, he would leave, quickly and in silence.

When Caroline was finished, she would lay the prints down in a stack of previous prints. Always in black and white and always with her tiny signature on the bottom right corner: C.S. They would remain there in an unnamed stack with several other hundreds of photos, and Ace didn't think she would care if she ever saw them again or notice if one went missing.

Ace loved it when she finished new prints. He would flip to each one, carefully studying the details and trying to figure out what she was trying to capture and what story she was trying to tell. She would tell him to stop.

"You are making too much fuss over my photographs!"

He would argue back, "They are great. There is a story in each one. You should have an exhibit at your café! I can bartend and make drinks, and everyone can come in to see your work." She would shake her head and say no. The photographs were special; Ace knew that. What she captured never seemed flat like most photographs but rounded with emotion. As he looked through the newly finished stack of photographs—an old man on a park bench remembering what it was like to be young and in love; little girls splashing in the summer rain puddles as their expensive toys lay untouched; lovers intertwined in a dark alleyway engaged in a kiss that would never end—he would often retrace their walks and remember where they had been for each shot. Despite Ace's overwhelmingly positive appraisal of her work, she would always wave him off.

"These photographs are not mine. I have stolen emotion from someone, and I think it would be unfair to present them as my own and share them with strangers without their permission," she would counter. Ace eventually thought he could force her hand but knew if it wasn't truly her idea, she would never go for it, and so her photographs stayed in the unnamed stacks for his eyes only.

That year, like every other year, summer ended too quickly, and the quietness of the city evaporated. The city that, for a moment in time had seemed like it belonged to them, was now returned to the locals, who were back from their summer holidays. Gone were their long mornings in bed and long afternoon walks around Paris. Caroline had returned to school, and her side of the bed was empty and cold in the morning; Ace was left to his own devices in an empty apartment with nothing to do.

Their evenings, which used to be occupied by cooking dinner and making love, were now filled with going out to bars with Caroline's art school friends. Ace hated those nights.

He hated her friends, not because they were rude or because he believed most of the men at her school were in love with her, but because he was jealous of them. He always felt inferior to them in talent and in life experiences. They were wealthy kids from wealthy families and had spent their youths traveling the world much like the school kids

Ace loathed from his high school days: the ones who would whisper about his mother and him, and the ones that ostracized him once he and his mother had moved into that shitty house that was smaller than the bedrooms some of his classmates lived in.

Most of the bars were in Belleville and Ménilmontant, where most of Caroline's friends lived. Her friends all seemed hell-bent on being the most unique person in their group. In stark contrast to Caroline, who liked to stay in the shadows of the art world, her friends were always looking for their next big break and had a burning passion to be discovered, to be the next big artist discovered in Paris.

Often the nights revolved around sitting in dark, loud bars drinking tremendous amounts of alcohol and rolling cigarettes while discussing topics that ranged from new music or art they had discovered, or whatever project they were currently working on. Mostly, though, they just complained about everything.

Every established artist was always better years ago or had now sold out. Each of them bashed whatever established artist was now making their way into the Paris art scene, and each of them searched feverishly to find a new underground musician or painter or writer, or whatever they could find, to showcase to the group. The more obscure the better. A great new discovery would fly by with a nod of approval if it was able to pass through the group without being critiqued.

"Oh, I just love this new band called The Displaced," someone shouted. "They have this raw energy, and their lyrics are absolute poetry. Think Jawbreaker before they sold out."

And, of course, no one had heard of The Displaced or really knew even if they existed. Every band name sounded made up to Ace, but everyone nodded and said they had heard of them.

Caroline would whisper over to Ace, "You know they are full of shit, right?"

Maybe they were, but it didn't stop Ace from feeling self-conscious and insecure about being lost in every conversation they had. He had absolutely no idea what any of them were talking about. He only knew writers who had long been dead, and once he was ridiculed by the group for bringing them up. He knew nothing of the current art scene. Despite Caroline's attempts to help him feel comfortable around them, he disregarded her friends and their boorish attitudes, but yet they still fascinated him in a strange way.

He had never met anyone like them before. They talked about art the way his old friends would talk about sports. The group would rattle off names of artists from every corner of the world, and everyone had an opinion about them. The conversations would move fast and bounce back and forth quickly between people, which would eventually lead to shouting and arguments about Artist A or Artist B. They were either great or terrible; rarely was anyone designated anything in between.

During the long, drunken nights, Ace would try to remember the name of a specific artist or band mentioned and would research them when he got home so that if they were ever brought up in conversation again, he would be able to add something to the debate. But the names from past nights were never brought up again, because by the time the group met again, they were always moving on to something new and fresh, and soon Ace gave up and fell into a permanent side player during these meetups.

He was relegated to spending the nights rolling cigarettes and drinking excessively. He had mastered the skill of rolling a perfect cigarette. It was a calming and soothing action, and it kept the conversations out of his ears. He would just sit there and watch his fingers. His fingers would gently roll the loose tobacco into the fine, thin paper, and each time a perfect cylinder would form. Piles of cigarettes would collect next to him as he drank endless amounts of whiskey and beer. After a long night, Caroline would have to help him home, and he would stagger up the stairs to her apartment, where sometimes he would make it to bed and some nights he would not. On those nights, they did not make love.

31

Maggie and I stood huddled in the cold morning air of Chiang Mai. Ace had run off to the row of tuk-tuks that waited outside the train station. I pulled out the sweater that I had stashed away in the bottom of my bag, and it provided me just enough warmth as we waited for Ace to sort out the transportation to a hostel that he assured us was the best in the city.

From a small distance away, I could hear Ace bargaining with one driver and then saw him violently shake his head and move to another driver just a few meters away. It was a game that everyone played, even though most westerners would end up only saving a few pennies. The first driver then walked over to Ace and began to renegotiate prices. Ace looked like an auctioneer pointing and gesturing to the different drivers; finally, he pointed to one driver and yelled us over.

"Ok. Who has Thai currency? I need 50 baht," Ace demanded. Of course, he didn't have Thai baht. Maggie also shook her head. Luckily, I had pulled some money out at the Bangkok airport to get some food. I handed over my 50 baht.

"Get your bags, and let's go. I'm freezing!" Ace shouted.

The three of us stuffed our bags into the tiny little compartment in the back of the tuk-tuk. We huddled close together as the driver started the tiny motor that sounded more like a lawnmower and slowly drove us away from the train station. The tuk-tuk chugged slowly through the quiet and empty streets of Chiang Mai. Here there was no traffic and little noise. As the tuk-tuk moved us slowly toward our hostel, the cold air brushed up against us, and we all shivered and secretly wished for the heat of Vietnam that we had been accustomed to.

Ace acted as our tour guide, again. He said the city contained 250 pagodas, and he pointed out the walls that surrounded the city and the canals that surrounded the walls as we entered through the Tha Phae Gate. It was imposing and almost medieval-looking as we entered into the heart of the city. Ace told us that for years it had been a quiet place that no one visited, as everyone was too busy island-hopping and partying in southern Thailand. But as Thailand became more popular and word of mouth spread about this beautiful town and the surrounding area, it now was a bustling hub of backpackers. As we moved through the town, we kept an eye out for The Dharma Hostel. An old travel friend of Ace's had opened it a few years ago, and we were expecting to stay there for three nights until we continued on to Pai.

Inside The Dharma Hostel, the lobby was lively and full of people going in and out quickly.

"People are up early here," I said, observing the difference between this and the hungover-sloth pace that people moved at during the mornings after a night at Z's.

"This is definitely not a party hostel. More a kind of hippie dippy vibe." Ace put his hands in prayer position and rolled his eyes.

A young woman was working behind the counter with her back to us. Ace instructed us to wait for him as he went to sort out our accommodation. When he approached, the woman turned with a smile. She had light-brown hair, blue eyes and a tanned face. I had assumed this was Ace's friend, but immediately I knew it wasn't, as her smile vanished when she saw him. She didn't warm to Ace's attempts at charming her, but I was just hoping that he had made a reservation. He hadn't, of course, and the hostel was full. The woman behind the desk quickly became annoyed that he didn't understand that they were fully booked and there were no rooms available. Ace was used to getting his way and became easily frustrated if he didn't.

"Are you sure? Every room?" He persisted, thinking he could persuade her to get someone to give us a room.

"Yes! I'm sure! There are plenty of hostels in the area, but we are full!" she said.

"I'm an old friend of Mia's. She always told me that if I was ever in town to come here. This is The Dharma Hostel, right?"

"Yes, of course it is, and, well, I've never heard of you, and my sister isn't in, so you will have to find accommodation elsewhere," she said, sounding annoyed.

"Sister?" Ace said, taken aback as he quickly stopped talking and started studying the young woman's face.

Watching the whole scene unfold, I almost smiled and enjoyed the attitude she was giving Ace even though now it looked like we no longer had a room for the evening.

"I can see the resemblance," he smiled at her. She didn't return the gesture. "And are you sure she never told you about her dear old friend Ace?" Ace still not giving up on trying to charm his way into a room.

"Yup. Positive. Never once have I heard of you," she said sternly.

Ace, knowing that the battle was over, finally submitted and, changing his tone, asked, "Can you tell me when Mia will be in? I at least want to say hi to her."

"She will be here around noon, but she will tell you the same thing I told you."

"Ok! See you at eleven! You mind if we leave our bags in your storage room?"

She reluctantly led us around the corner to a small room that she unlocked. Several other bags of people who had arrived too early for check-in occupied the room. We dropped our bags off beside them and left the hostel.

"We will come back at eleven," Ace said as we walked out of the hostel.

"Didn't she say noon?" Maggie said, sounding frustrated.

"She is always early. And I promise we will get a room. It looks like

Chiang Mai is even more popular than I thought."

"I hope you're right, Ace," Maggie said as she shook her head.

"We will be fine. It's all part of the adventure." Maggie and I looked at each other and smiled, trying to stop each other from getting frustrated.

"I'm starving. You know what I feel like? Pancakes! You can't find good pancakes in Vietnam, but Thailand caters to more of a western cuisine. I'm sure we could find some good pancakes here in tow," Ace said.

Sure enough, there was a breakfast place a short distance from the hostel. It was called Early Riser and had a complete western-style breakfast menu: pancakes, french toast, bacon and sausages. It was all there; it felt like being back home, even down to the décor. It looked like any hipster diner in Philly with graphic designed artwork that decorated the walls and servers with fashionable hairstyles and arms with tattoos that crawled out from underneath their T-shirts.

"Why do you hate Thailand so much? It doesn't seem so bad," I said as I drank a warm and delicious hot chocolate.

"It just got too safe and popular too quickly for me. Backpacking used to be a challenge. I used to have to communicate with people who never understood English. I wasn't able to simply book a hostel online. I would have to show up to a town and find my own way around. That weeded out all these assholes who now come in search of that perfect Instagram photo. We used to be a band of adventurers, and now it's just people who want to post photos of themselves and brag about working with elephants. They all rush to Thailand because it's easy and safe. I wouldn't even call it backpacking. I mean, for Christ's sake, most of these places have hotel-style beds with warm duvet covers."

"Says the guy who wanted pancakes," Maggie blurted out.

Maggie and I both laughed as Ace continued to shovel the warm, buttery pancakes dripping with maple syrup into his mouth.

"Just remember, though," Ace said, talking and chewing with his mouth full, "all jokes aside, we have to follow one rule while we are here."

"What's that, Ace? Never book hostels or make dinner reservations so we look like assholes thinking us westerners deserve some kind of special treatment?" Maggie quickly responded.

"Nooooo! She's punchy today, isn't she? The one rule and the most important rule while in Thailand is... never go full Pai," Ace stated.

"What is full Pai?" I asked.

"Happy to explain," Ace ranted on.

"Of course he is," Maggie said underneath her breath.

"When we get to Pai, you will understand. It's one of those weird suckhole places when you travel. People come to stay for a few days and then boom... a month goes by, and if that happens, you most likely have gone full Pai."

"I don't have a clue what you're talking about," Maggie said.

"Listen, Pai is a town that almost completely revolves around back-packers. No hint of local culture. If you stay too long, you will start with wearing 10 bracelets on each wrist. You know, one for good blood flow, one for body harmony, one to find love, or whatever. On your bag, you will have a stupid dream catcher or something stupid you made in an overpriced class. And, of course, you will trade in shorts for elephant pants and T-shirts for poncho-looking things. If you ever meet one of these people, all they talk about is Pai and how great it is, and how you must go," Ace sighed. "That's full Pai. Never go full Pai. Now where are these pancakes?"

We ate silently the rest of the time and waited for Ace to finish his second order of pancakes.

32

We arrived back at The Dharma hostel just after eleven a.m. We were all full from the pancakes and tired from the long journey and were in need of a bed that we didn't have. Behind the front desk there were now two women. Both had the same light-brown hair. Without looking up, one of the women yelled, "Mr. Ace! I never thought I'd see the day when you would be in Chiang Mai. Thought you'd be in Uzbekistan by now."

"I'm working on it!" Ace said, smiling.

"I hope so. You've been talking about it for years!" She looked up. She had a beautiful face—lightly tanned with blue eyes—and long, brown hair pulled up into a loose topknot. She wore a small tank top and a flowy skirt that moved rhythmically as she walked over and hugged Ace.

"And how'd you know it was me?" he said, smiling, anticipating a compliment.

"My sister told me some asshole was claiming to know me and de-manding rooms like he was more important than the people who had actually booked the rooms. I also heard your loud voice from a block away." Ace stopped smiling. "It's great to see you, my old friend," she said with a disarming smile. "Who are your friends?"

"This is Maggie and Charlie. We're doing a meditation retreat in Pai in a few days, and we wanted to stay here before we head up," Ace replied.

"A meditation retreat... you? I don't know which one of you has magical powers, but Ace going to a meditation retreat is quite the trick. Hello, Maggie. Hello, Charlie. I'm Mia. Welcome to Chiang Mai."

I looked back over Mia's shoulder at her sister, and I could easily see the resemblance now. But while they were both very pretty, Mia was smiling and charming while her sister looked annoyed over the situation and had returned to whatever work she was doing, paying little attention to us.

"Meditation retreat," Mia said softly, repeating it multiple times, as if the more she said it the more she would believe it. "Unfortunately, like my sister said, we are full. I was going to tell you to get lost, but since your friends look nice and you are doing a meditation retreat, I'm graciously going to let you stay at my house. It's a few minutes away, and there is a pullout couch and an air mattress on the floor for you to share. I'll have my sister show it to you. Don't let me regret this, Ace!" Mia said.

"Never!" Ace said as he hugged Mia tightly and easily lifted her off the ground.

"Put me down!" she demanded but smiled happily as she walked away. She went behind the reception counter and talked to her sister, who, from her expression, was not happy with us now crashing at their home. They argued briefly, but I couldn't pick up what they were saying because they were a bit too far away. After several intense moments, Mia smiled and hugged her sister, and her sister gave a half smile, obviously still not happy with the results of the conversation.

Ace greeted Mia's sister again as she walked toward us, and he introduced Maggie and me to her. "I'm Sophia," she offered up, and walked briskly out the front door.

"Beers tonight? Catch up?" Ace shouted back to Mia as we walked out the door.

"Sure. I'll be home around eight tonight," Mia shouted back, not looking up from the computer screen.

They walked down the small streets. There were women hanging wet clothes on laundry lines and tuk-tuks moving slowly and loudly past them. The morning cold was slightly burning away, and the sun was slowly warming up the streets as they walked together down the quiet road, passing several hostels and cafés and finally reaching the sisters' house.

I knew I was happy with our new accommodation when I walked in. On the walls were photographs that were mounted nonuniformly in a way that gave the walls a dramatic feel and made your eyes dance and seek out the next photograph. All of the photographs were in black and white and of quick action shots. The black-and-white photographs contrasted well with the lush green plants that surrounded them. The kitchen was small, with pots and pans hanging from homemade wooden shelves. It felt like a home.

While I was wandering the room, studying the prints that hung on the walls, Maggie and Ace had already taken up residence on the pullout futon and were both fading into a nap.

Sophia was shuffling around the apartment, picking up small things from the floor and gathering up blankets and pillows for us. I could feel her watching me as I stared at each photograph. I should have asked her if she needed any help, but the photographs were too good, and I was sucked in. She placed the blankets and pillows on the floor, looked up at me and asked, "Anything else? I must go back to work soon."

"No. You have been more than generous. But may I ask you who took those photographs on the wall?"

"I did." She smiled briefly, then looked down, and I sensed she was half embarrassed and half proud. Her smile was perfect, and a small dimple emerged on her left cheek.

"They are beautiful. I'm so tired, but I think I could stare at them all day," I said shyly.

"Thank you. That is very kind of you." Sophia said slightly blushing.

After the episode with Elsa, I was determined not to regret not saying anything, and maybe because I was tired and a bit sleep-deprived, I talked to her with more confidence than I should have. "I take photographs too," I told her as I pulled out my large carrying case and started showing her several rolls of finished film that were still waiting to be developed.

"Film?" Sophia asked.

"Yes!" I said, no longer feeling apprehensive about that answer.

"I know someone who can help develop those for you, if you'd like," she offered.

"Oh really? Yes, that would be great!" I looked over at Ace and saw they were fully asleep, and I whispered, "He said he could help me, but that fell through."

"I'm not surprised from what my sister has told me about him," she replied, showing that she did know who he was. Then, just as quickly as we had started talking, she said her good-byes and walked out the front door.

I made my little bed on the small rug next to the pots on the floor. Maggie and Ace were sleeping peacefully above me, and I lay there thinking about Sophia.

33

That afternoon I had a wonderful dream. I was on top of a high mountain looking out over everything. I could see the city below me. It was busy and noisy, but where I was it was quiet and peaceful. Behind me a trail led up along a small stream and into the woods. I floated up that trail, my feet never touching the ground, and there in the woods the trees grew as big as skyscrapers. I continued to float up the mountain to where the large trees could no longer grow.

Car-sized boulders were stacked on top of each other. The larger the boulders became, the higher I went. Soon I was at the top of the mountain on its highest peak. My eyes gazed out to a view with no end. I was somewhere in between space and Earth. From there, I could only make out small lights, which danced and flickered below me. Above me, the space was so vast and decorated with so many millions of stars that there seemed no end. I was alone, and yet I felt connected with all the animals that roamed the forest ground, the people in the busy cities below, the birds that soared between the trees and the stars that hung above me. As I stood there on the highest peak on the tallest mountain, a pleasant stream of water flowed down on either side of me. I followed the path of the water that carved into the mountainside, and down it went through the boulders and past the trees and on down into the cities. The stream fed the green grass and tall trees, and animals bathed in and drank the cool water, and finally I followed it with my eyes to the people on the outskirts of the cities who used it to grow crops and to drink after a hard day's work. I sat there and watched everything from the highest peak on the tallest mountain.

I awoke on the floor, unsure where I was. I was still in between the dream and real life. I rolled up my pillow and sat up as straight as I could. I wrapped my blanket around my shoulders. I placed my fingers together in front of me, just lightly touching the fingertips of each hand to those of the other, and began to breathe. Under my breath, I began to say to myself a little mantra that I had memorized from *Everyday Mindfulness*:

> *Breathing in, I know I'm breathing*
> *Breathing out, I know I'm breathing out*
> *Breathing in, I'm aware of my body*
> *Breathing out, I calm my body*
> *Breathing in, I smile*
> *Breathing out, I release*
> *Breathing in, I live in the present moment*
> *Breathing out, I enjoy the present moment*

For the first time since I had begun my meditation practice, I was able to clear my mind. I was able to reach that mountain peak from my seated position on the floor of the apartment. I heard some outside noises of tuk-tuks passing by, of birds chirping in the early evening, and of people laughing as they walked by. But on the highest peak on the tallest mountain, I could not be disturbed. I heard the sounds and appreciated them and was able to let them float into the stream next to me and watched them disappear down off the mountain. My legs felt light and painless as I seemed to float just above the pillows. I don't know how long I was there, as time seemed to disappear. It was a wonderful feeling.

Worries seemed to tumble away and dissolve into nothingness. I sat on that mountaintop, and a small, carefree smile appeared on my face. I opened my eyes and smiled as I looked at Maggie and Ace still sleeping peacefully on the futon.

34

"You looked mighty peaceful this afternoon," Maggie said. "Maybe they will ask you to teach the meditation class."

"You saw me? I thought you were asleep," I responded.

"I got up once, and you were like a monk sitting there with a blanket." We both laughed, and I told Maggie about my dream.

Soon darkness took over the room as night approached. Sophia and Mia returned from work, and everyone scattered to get ready for the evening. While Mia was chatting with Maggie, Sophia and I talked about photography. She was easy to talk to, and I learned she had recently finished university in Switzerland. After university, she had worked at a job she was unhappy in, so her sister had invited her to live and work in Chiang Mai. Mia was involved in the growing art scene in Chiang Mai, and that's where Sophia learned to take photographs. I could have stayed in the apartment all night to talk to Sophia, but Ace was itching to go out.

Soon the five of us arrived at an open-air courtyard that was surrounded by bars. We were soon seated outside in front of the Yellow Bar. In the bar, there was a colorful dance floor that was reminiscent of a 1970s disco that I was told would soon be crowded with drunk backpackers. Out on the patio, the five us of sat on a large picnic bench.

"I'll get first round. Five changs?" Ace announced as he walked over to the Yellow Bar. No one argued. While we waited, Thai women would approach us with large cardboard displays full of bracelets. Hundreds of colorful bracelets. At first, we just brushed them off, but Mia told us if we wanted a laugh, to look more carefully the next time they came around. Maggie and I called one of the women over to investigate.

"Two for 100 baht," the woman said, already in negotiation mode.

"What are these?!" Maggie read the first one silently in almost disbelief and then read it out loud, and we all started laughing. "It says, 'Pussy Pizza.'"

Then I read one. "This one says, 'Cunt Puncher.'"

"'My Dick Smells,'" Mia said, laughing.

"This is the best one: 'Fuck Cunt 24 hrs'!" I hollered.

We were all laughing hysterically at the absurdity of these bracelets.

"Four for 150 baht," the woman yelled, still on the hard sell.

"Who comes up with these things?" Maggie was able to say in between her laughs.

"It's one of the greatest mysteries of all time," Mia said, wiping tears from her eyes.

"Could you imagine a boardroom with men and women in suits sitting around thinking these up?" Maggie said. She straightened her fake tie and said in her business voice, "I got it! I got it! Our next slogan for this year's bracelets: 'DICK MY BUM, PLEASE,'" as we all bowled over in unison.

"Four for 125 baht!" The woman was now upset at how little we were negotiating and seemed to be at the edge of her price range.

"How about 1 for 50 baht?" Maggie asked. The woman agreed. Maggie pulled off the DICK MY BUM, PLEASE bracelet and paid the women 50 baht. She looked over at me: "Gotta support the local economy. Plus, this will look great around Ace's wrist."

"You know what Ace will say," I said.

"What will I say?" We all bent over again in laughter as Ace returned with five changs, looking confused and upset that he had missed out on something.

"This is for you! Even though it might make you break one of your beloved rules." Maggie handed him the bracelet.

Ace shook his head but was a good sport and wore the bracelet on his wrist, reminding all of us that one bracelet was an acceptable number. We quickly drank one chang after another. We were all in good spirits, and we were having a great time. As predicted, the bars filled up quickly with travelers ready to drink themselves silly. Soon there were empty changs scattered across the table, and Ace kept ordering more. Still, no one protested.

"Let's play a game!" Ace announced. "It's called, Never Go Full Pai!"

"Oh God. Is this one of your snobby backpacker rules?" Mia looked at me and winked.

"What are the backpacker rules?" Sophia asked.

"Ace has invented his own set of rules for backpacking, and if you don't follow them, you are not considered a true backpacker," Mia answered.

"Do you want to play or not?" Ace said.

"Ok ok. How do you play?" Mia asked out of curiosity.

"Hmmm, let me see." Ace scanned the crowded bar. "Ok—right there! Look at that guy over there. Elephant pants, check. Matching elephant tank top, check check. Prayer necklace, check check check. Five bracelets on each wrist. Fucking checkmate! Yup, that dude went full Pai."

"Ugghhh. You are such an asshole, Ace." Mia shook her head with disappointment. The drinks had escalated their voice volume and de-escalated their filters. "I thought you might have changed, but you are just the same old Ace with all your rules and regulations for what a backpacker should be. You know you weren't the first person to travel, and you sure as hell won't be the last. But you may be the oldest." Everyone laughed.

"HA HA. It's just a fun game. No harm in that, is there? Just if you see men or women with elephant pants or shirts, you have to call out Full Pai and tell someone to drink."

"That's a bit mean, Ace! They are comfortable pants. Sorry, we can't all share your unique sense of style," Maggie chimed in.

"Why does everyone pick on my style? I should tell you, cutoff shorts and makeshift tanks are the epitome of backpacker chic," Ace said proudly.

"Well, Mr. Chic, finish that beer because I see five girls all wearing matching elephant pants," yelled Sophia and pointed, "Full Pai! Right, Ace!" The four of us cheered as Ace happily finished his chang.

The night continued that way, and soon we were all yelling Full Pai and making everyone drink. In between the drinking, Ace told old stories of Mia and him in Australia. There were stories of them drinking and partying in Sydney, of them sailing in Whitsunday and of them diving on the Great Barrier Reef. I was enjoying them rehashing old stories as they laughed and teased each other in a flirtatious way, but Maggie was not smiling, and I could see that she felt uncomfortable as the stories continued. Maybe the stories hit a bit too close to home. I think that Mia felt it, too, and she slid a bit away from Ace. When it was getting late and we were all drunk and the backpackers had now fully invaded the bars and it was taking longer and longer to order drinks, Mia looked around and suggested we leave. With no one wanting the night to end just yet, she recommended a bar just down the road, away from the all the backpackers and loud music. We all agreed with one condition: no more beers and no more playing the Full Pai game.

Mia directed us to her favorite bar. It was busy, but we could talk without shouting. Ace went to the bartender to order drinks, and we waited while a young man on stage was playing acoustic covers of old American rock and roll songs. When Ace returned, he placed the five cocktails down at our table, and the young man up front started his next song:

La la la la la la la la la
Now that I lost everything to you
You say you wanna start something new
And it's breaking' my heart you're leavin'
Baby, I'm grievin'
But if you wanna leave, take good care
I hope you have a lot of nice things to wear
But then a lot of nice things turn bad out there

"Ace! I love this song. We must dance!" Maggie shouted.

"No one is dancing!" Ace said.

"When has that ever stopped you? Let's go, old man!" And just like that, Maggie and Ace were on the empty dance floor. They moved perfectly together. At the same time, Sophia got up to use the bathroom, and Mia got up to come sit next to me.

"Still the same old Ace," she whispered in my direction.

"Excuse me?" I asked.

"I was in her shoes a few years ago. I met Ace and fell madly in love with him. It was my first time on the road when I met him in Australia. He tells you all the good things, and most of it is true. He impresses everyone with his stories of adventures and travel. Everyone gathers in awe. And somehow out of all the girls, he talked to me the longest. He encouraged my adventurous side, and he inspired me to travel and take risks. What he leaves out are the bad things, because just as easily as I fell in love with him, he fell out of touch with me. As soon as he could feel my feelings grow for him, he pushed back and grew distant. He then did some really shitty things to me. Some of the things I'm still not over. He crushed me, and I don't think he blinked. Ace will test you. He will make you want to hate him. He will make you want to leave. That's why he has no friends, and he keeps no one around to challenge him. Once he feels anyone get too close, he shuts his door. I was with him for months, and I still don't know anything about him—his family, his life before backpacking. All I know is the 'traveling Ace.' Maybe one of those stupid rules of his is what kept him from feeling anything." She took a sip of her cocktail and watched Ace smiling and laughing on the dance floor.

"Don't get me wrong, though. He has an amazing spirit and soul, and I wouldn't have opened my own hostel and led the life I have if it weren't for Ace. I'm just sad he is still doing the same thing: meeting and traveling with younger and younger girls, and then at some point he finds a flaw and bolts. He talks about rules of not falling in love in hostels, and he is right. Falling in love isn't meeting someone backpacking in Paris or in Thailand. Because love is not three days with someone when everything is perfect. Love happens when you want to stay, when things are not perfect. It's showing someone your scars and flaws and hoping they love those just as much as the rest of you. But our Ace—he doesn't have scars. He still has wounds. Wounds need time and attention to heal. He gives them neither. I hope Maggie is stronger than me," Mia sighed.

"She's one of the strongest people I've met," I said proudly.

"That's good. She seems it. Well, the Ace I know would never go on a meditation retreat, so maybe he has changed and he's ready to heal. Please take care of him for me, okay?" Mia's eyes were tearing up, and she wiped them off with her shirt. "I'm sorry. Alcohol is making me all emotional. I don't drink like this much anymore."

Ace and Maggie were now in full dance mode as the guitar player sang a Cat Stevens song perfectly.

"Now go talk to my sister already. I know you like her, and she thinks you are cute." Mia smiled at me. She was as pretty and as smart and as strong as they come, and she glowed underneath the dim light in the bar.

We both looked over at Ace and Maggie still gliding to the music. Everyone at the bar was transfixed on them, and Ace had gotten everyone to sing along. Maggie looked at Ace. I knew she was still in love with him, too, but I could see she also knew where that road led and she wouldn't let herself go there again. She was truly a fiery Mexicana.

The last chorus came in as the whole bar erupted together—even Mia and I joined in and sang.

> *Oohhhh baby baby it's a wild world*
> *It's hard to get by just upon a smile*
> *Ohhhhh baby baby it's a wild world*
> *I'll always remember you like a child, girl*

35

My portrait lens sat in front of me. My hands were a little shaky from the alcohol. I was holding a small brush as I began cleaning the lens. With full concentration, I made smooth, soft strokes back and forth, removing any dust. Then I dripped a small amount of liquid cleaner onto the lens, and then once again, with full concentration, trying to steady my hand, I wiped the dry cloth across the lens and wiped it until it shone and reflected like new. I reattached the lens to the body of the camera and heard the satisfying click the lens made as it locked into place.

Wielding the camera, I began to observe the room. It was still early, and after the late night everyone was still sleeping.

Ace and Maggie slept quietly together on the futon. *Click.* The morning light was just beginning to peek through the blinds, providing just enough light against the hanging plants. *Click.* I spun around with my eyes pushed against the camera, and Sophia appeared in front of me. I panicked and clicked again.

"Ohhhh, no photo, no photo," she said, shaking her hands and hiding her face as she stared at the ground.

"I'm sorry!" I screamed.

"Shhhhhhhh." She pointed to Ace and Maggie and put her finger against her lips. I made a face of regret and rushed over to the kitchen. "Would you like some water?" she asked.

"Yes, please." I felt oddly calm and relaxed when I was talking to her. I must have been still drunk.

"We had too many drinks last night and too much of that stupid game your friend made up." She shook her head but stopped as she winced and put her hands over her head.

"Why are you up so early?" I asked.

"I can't sleep when I'm hungover. It's early. You should go back to sleep."

"I want to see Chiang Mai before I leave and maybe take some photos."

"Hopefully you will get some photos of something other than zombies today." She lurched rather than walked, with her hands out in front of her, but she managed to pour a large glass of water and bring it over to me.

"Thank you!" I took a long gulp.

"Are you ok? Your hands are shaky," Sophia asked.

Drunk or not, I could now feel myself get nervous. I could feel my face turning red and warm, and I looked at Sophia blankly. She patiently awaited my response. I took one more sip of water and closed my eyes, and as I opened them, the words jumped out.

"Would you like to come with me... to take photos?" I said as rapidly as I have ever pieced together a sentence. I composed myself and added, "I would really like a local's perspective."

"I'm not sure if I'm a local, but I can take you to my favorite places in Chiang Mai. We can also take your film to my friend to get developed."

"Yes, that would be great!" I said, probably too excitedly.

"Can I shower first? Too much smoke from the cigarette smoke from last night. I smell like an ashtray," Sophia said.

"Oh yes. No rush. I'm just cleaning my camera. So, no rush. Take your time. I'll wait here. No rush at all."

"Ok. So just to be clear, no rush?" She smiled and headed back into her room.

I sat down. I felt exhausted and a bit dizzy, but I was delighted that we would get to spend the day together.

"Nice one, mate. I couldn't have done it better myself," Ace said as he peeked out of the covers.

Half an hour later, everyone at the house was up. Mia was making eggs and Sophia was preparing toast with jam while a hot pot of tea was sitting on a small stove. I poured myself a cup and sipped it slowly, letting the warmth soak into my body as we started eating our wonderfully prepared breakfast.

"This sure beats Nutella and white bread," I said. Everyone laughed.

We all noted how much better we felt after the food, and everyone discussed their plans for the day. Ace was the first one to leave; he was going to sort out transportation to Pai. Maggie had been warned by Mia that Pai gets cold and advised to get a sweater. Mia even agreed to take Maggie to her favorite local shop to find one, and soon they were off. That left Sophia and me. I had finished cleaning my camera and packed away the films I wanted developed into my small day bag when Sophia came out of her room.

"I'm ready!" she announced.

She was wearing jean shorts and a loose-fitting white T-shirt, and her hair was pulled back into a ponytail. We walked out of the apartment and down the street. The camera store did not open for a few hours, so she decided to give me a small tour in the meantime. She did most of the talking as I happily listened. She talked about Switzerland and how she missed her small village, and the snow on the mountains, but she was enjoying the year-round summer that Asia provided and was happy to be with her sister.

As we walked, I expected us to enter one of the many beautiful temples or take photos of the monks that passed us. They were all dressed in traditional orange robes and had shaved heads. But we didn't stop. I tried to ask her about monks and meditation. "Have you ever tried to meditate?"

"Several times, but I'm no good with meditation. I have a hard time sitting still," Sophia said.

"I've tried many times too. I hope in Pai I can learn how to be better." I was picturing our instructor with a bright orange robe calmly instructing us on how to meditate as we sat with our legs crossed in a big Buddhist temple.

"You must tell me how you get on, but now let me show you my favorite place in Chiang Mai."

What I was expecting and where we showed up could not have been more different. From the outside, I heard shouting and screaming and a noise that sounded like hammers hitting concrete. I wasn't sure what was happening within those walls, but I was getting nervous. We walked into a large open warehouse building. Inside the room it smelled like a gym bag full of dirty clothes. Several fit young boys and girls moved frantically around the large room. What we entered was no temple, at least not for religious purposes.

"What is this place?" I asked.

"It's not a Buddhist temple, but for me it's how I can relieve any problems in my life. Great way to relieve stress. It's a Muay Thai gym."

A boxing ring sat in the center of the room. On the far side of the gym hung a large banner that read Chiang Mai Muay Thai and was decorated with images of fighters kicking and punching. Inside the ring, a young boy was kicking and shouting as his feet sprung up from the floor and straight into the body of an older man who wore protective padding around his waist. The movement was repeated, and a flurry of kicks were unleashed in seconds, each kick with the same velocity and force as the last. An echoing thud rang loudly in the gym each time the young boy's feet smashed into the protective padding of the older man. With each thundering blow, the older man shouted at the young fighter. The power of the boy's legs was unbelievable. I watched in amazement and looked down at my own tiny legs, especially at my right one, where the brace ballooned out of my shoe. It would be an impossible feat for me to produce such power. I hadn't thought about my legs in a while, but that display of athleticism powerfully reminded me of my own limitations.

I stood a bit hesitant as Sophia walked toward the ring. After several more rapid-fire kicks, the boy stopped and looked exhausted as he bent forward, putting his hands on his knees. The older man, who had been shouting seconds earlier, now stood calmly over the boy and tossed his wet hair around and playfully hit him on his ribs.

"Always beating up people when they are tired!" Sophia shouted into the ring.

"Soffiyaa!" he shouted back.

"Hello, Anurak!"

"Training today?" he asked.

"No, not today, but I brought my friend here to take a few photos, if you don't mind? He is really talented."

"Of course. As you know, my young fighters love their photos being taken," Anurak replied.

"Do you fight?" I whispered to Sophia, feeling extremely intimidated by the whole scene.

"I don't fight, but I work out with Anurak," she smiled as she got in her fighting stance. To counter, I raised my camera, but she quickly moved out of the frame and gently pushed my camera away with a sweeping hand motion.

"You gotta be quick with us Muay Thai fighters," she smiled and laughed.

Anurak joined us as we walked around the gym and watched all the young fighters working on kicks and punches, all the while screaming and yelling. As we walked, Anurak talked about the gym. He had opened it a few years ago after having been a successful fighter. His main priority was to train young Thai boys and girls not only to fight, but to acquire an appreciation for hard work and discipline. He pointed to a sign that had those words displayed in large bold type.

Sophia had been training there since she arrived in Chiang Mai and was now friends with most of the people in the gym. Many of the young boys and girls eagerly came up to her with a smile and a hug. She had done several photo shoots with the young fighters, so she told me they were now almost as good as professional models.

She discussed her work and what she attempted to capture in her photographs of the young fighters. She particularly liked the action shots; her goal was to express the speed and power of Muay Thai while still showing the skill and finesse needed to perfect the movement. It was that combination of power and finesse that drew her into the sport. She told me about the many kicks and punches of Muay Thai and said, "If you only have power, you will miss your target and be off-balance and susceptible to a counterstrike. If you only have finesse, you will not strike your opponent with enough force to do any damage. The key is finding that balance. This is what makes a great Muay Thai fighter."

Not only were our preferred activities different, but our photography styles were in stark contrast to one another. While Sophia looked for action shots, I preferred more subtle shots of the fighters. In the peak of training, these young boys and girls looked invincible. Superhero strength seemed to exude from them as they punched and kicked. I attempted to humanize them by finding them in the stillness of recovery, underneath their outward strength. In this exhausted state, I found a beautiful sense of vulnerability in them.

When it came to having their pictures taken, all the fighters were eager participants. I took close portraits of faces as sweat raced down the contours of their foreheads and cheeks. *Click*. I had the fighters lift their hands up as I zoomed in on their cracked and bruised knuckles. *Click*. I aimed my camera through the ropes that surrounded the ring and found Anurak putting his arms around a young fighter and consoling him after losing a sparring match, bending over and whispering words of encouragement as the fighter's head hung low in disappointment. *Click*.

As I paced about, Sophia talked to the young fighters and began hitting the large, heavy floating bags after encouragement from the young boys and girls who surrounded her. From her resting position, her kicks happened almost instantaneously. Her body went from gathering energy in a squat position to quickly twisting and rotating as her back foot lifted and exploded through the air, slamming hard into the bag. Then, just as quickly, she returned to a balanced position on the ground. She repeated this action several times as the sound of her leg whipped through the air, making contact with the bag. The sound of impact echoed in the large room. Loud cheers from the boys and girls rang out with each kick.

"Remind me not to make you mad," I said as I walked over.

"Ha ha. I'm just learning but would never fight anyone in real life. I only fight this bag." She swiped at small strands of hair that had come loose from her ponytail. "Would you like to give it a go?"

I immediately felt warm and stepped back. My head floated downwards, and all I could see was that ugly brace.

"Oh no. I can't do that." I stared down at my legs and felt embarrassed. She looked at me with a stern face, and I thought she was going to protest my objections, but then she smiled and nodded.

"Well, if you don't want to kick this bag, maybe it's time we leave and let these boys and girls get back to training. That is... if you are done taking photographs."

"Umm, yes. I think I'm done," I said, feeling a bit embarrassed.

We thanked Anurak and all the young fighters, and they sent us away with excited waves. As we walked out, I regretted not at least trying to kick the bag, but I didn't think I could move like that without looking foolish.

"Where are we going now?" I asked, trying to spark up a conversation again.

"Getting you a haircut!" Sophia said enthusiastically.

"What?"

"Your hair is a bit crazy, and I think you spend more time whipping the hair away from your face than actually taking photographs. If you are going to be a photographer, you can't have any restrictions, plus these barbers are the coolest people in Chiang Mai."

I agreed with her. "Maybe it's the pho; I think it's making my hair grow faster than it ever has." We both laughed, and the awkwardness that had hung briefly between us evaporated as we chatted about photography and our varying styles as we entered a barbershop that was only a short walk away from the gym.

The barbershop was new but was trying to go for that retro style that was popular in the hipster-style barbershops in the States. Old-timey photographs hung on the wall, and customers sat in old-fashioned barber chairs. Barbers circulated the room with full-sleeve arm tattoos, wearing blue jean overalls and tight, white T-shirts with side-part hairstyles.

Sophia talked to several of the barbers and hugged them as one of them escorted me to one of the open chairs in the back of the shop. I told him how I wanted my hair cut, but I think he decided in the end to just do what he thought would look best, and he started buzzing and cutting away. Mass amounts of hair cascaded down from my head, and I watched it pile up on the floor as my barber moved quickly around me. He pushed my head down and side to side, studying my hair. He wore a dark denim shirt that was rolled up to his elbows, exposing arms neatly covered with colorful tattoos. His left arm showcased a straight edge knife that trickled with blood, and his right forearm featured a pair of scissors, both of which I photographed when he had finished cutting my hair.

After putting his tools away, the barber whipped his fingers into a jar, pulled out some paste and began to rub his fingers through my hair, carefully teasing out specific strands and shaping it like it was a piece of art, and then he quickly spun me around to face the mirror. I sat there silent, as I was barely able to recognize myself in the mirror. Sophia came up behind me and looked at me in the mirror.

"Very handsome." She quickly blushed when she said it and turned away. That was the first time any girl had ever said I was handsome.

As we walked out of the barbershop, I kept touching the sides of my face and skimming the freshly cut hairs. I felt lighter as I walked and stood a little taller as we made our way to the camera shop.

The outside of the shop was plain and simple, with a small design banner that read Cameras and Camera Equipment. True to form, the inside of the shop was scattered with cameras and camera equipment. Behind the small desk was a shaggy gray-haired man who looked to be in his fifties. The shop was small, with an incredible amount of new and used cameras that took up every inch of open space. The room felt tight as we wiggled down the hallway to the end of the shop where the man stood.

"Hello, Mr. Jake," Sophia said as we approached. Mr. Jake removed his glasses and greeted her with a big smile and a hello that was welcoming and warm.

"This is my friend Charlie. He has some films he wants developed, but he leaves the day after tomorrow. Can we make that work?"

"Of course. Pickup will be at nine a.m.; I will open early that day."

"Oh, thank you, Mr. Jake! You are the best."

Mr. Jake smiled as we dropped off my eight rolls of film. As we left, he shouted, "I'm excited for your exhibit next week, Sophia!"

I didn't know what he was talking about, and she didn't say anything about it as we walked back to her house.

36

Bartending; Make drinks. Tell stories. Smile. Ace thought he could do all of that well enough. He had learned how to make drinks at the On the Road Pub, and the rest he would improvise. He was immediately offered employment due to his good looks and charm. Soon his evenings were spent behind a bar.

The bar he worked at was a cliché replica of a place someone might have found sometime in the 1920s, when Paris roared and Montmartre was filled with poor artists and drunks. Now almost a century later, that scene had been replaced with deep-pocketed tourists and a bar cheaply decorated with cliché photographs from that previous time period and poorly copied prints of Toulouse-Lautrec posters.

He wore a ridiculous outfit that went with the 1920s theme, but it was good money, and drunk Americans would always leave large tips that filled his pockets. Usually customers asked and talked about the same things. Where did Hemingway live? Is the Moulin Rouge! show worth it? To keep himself from complete boredom, he began to fabricate stories about himself, painting himself as a modern-day poet on the road. Gullible tourists ate it up. He soon learned that the longer he talked, the more they drank and the more they would tip. So he talked until his throat ran dry.

He also drank, always more than he should, and by the end of the night he would usually end up as drunk as the people he had been serving. The owner of the bar didn't seem to care because people stayed longer and drank several more cocktails with Ace behind the bar. Caroline would often stop by after school but would leave shortly after if Ace was too drunk or if too many women were surrounding him.

Besides brief encounters at the bar, they actually saw very little of each other. She woke up early and would be away at school while Ace slept off the hangovers, and she would be asleep, or pretend to be, when he came home drunk.

This went on for months. Silence grew between them, and they both grew unhappy. One day, after a full week of not talking, Ace stumbled up the stairs, and to his surprise, Caroline was up and waiting for him.

"Good evening!" he bowed. He was drunk.

"Looks like you had another great night at work."

"Sure did," he said, pulling out crumpled-up euros and messily tossing them on the table.

She looked at him with those eyes, and he knew she was upset.

"Do you think we can keep going like this?" Caroline asked.

"Ugh, Caro. Do we have to do this now?"

"We haven't spoken in a week! How long do you think we can continue like this?"

"Continue what?"

"This. Us. Staying together. Maybe the summer was just a fantasy, and now it's just our time to wake up."

Ace knew she was right, but he would have kept going on like this for another few months. He didn't know how to fix it, so he had ignored it.

"And do you have to drink so much while you work?"

"Hey! I need to do something. And I'm good at bartending."

"If you want to be a bartender, then be a great bartender. But all I see is a person who prefers to drink free alcohol and get paid to flirt with old rich women."

"What the hell does that mean?"

"I see you, Ace. Bartending is not your passion. I see so much potential in you. I want you to do something you love."

"You're one to talk. You have all these amazing photographs here, and you won't share them with anyone. You keep them hidden away because maybe your asshole art school friends won't approve," Ace said bluntly.

"Don't bring this back on me. I don't take photographs to become a famous artist or to share with my classmates or whoever you think I take them for. I do it because I love it. I take them for me."

"That's a cliché cop-out!" Ace said.

"You are one to talk, Mr. Traveler. Going off on the road and becoming... a bartender!"

They had never really fought before. Actually, Ace had never fought with anyone before. If any girl in his past would say something that Ace didn't agree with, he would simply walk away and move on to the next girl. This lack of practice now showed, and he soon learned that Caroline was much more skilled in the art of fighting than he was. While he threw wild haymakers, she calmly and methodically landed jab after jab. Not enough to knock you out, but just enough to toy with you and show how out of your depth you were.

"I needed to do something. I can't just sit here all day."

"I agree, but I see more potential in you than you becoming some drunk tourist bartender."

"Potential! Not you too!" Ace jumped up and stormed out of the room, only to race right back in when he realized Caroline had not left her position in the bedroom. She stayed silent and stared at Ace. Unsure what to do with the silence, Ace started talking. What started out as a counterargument quickly turned into something more, something closer to a confession, and it all poured out as if from a broken faucet. Words spilled out with reckless abandon.

"I've been told my whole life that I have potential. Everyone always looked at me when I was young because of who my father was, and because I could jump high and run fast. 'That boy there has so much potential.' Potential to become a great athlete. Potential to go to a great school. Potential to marry a beautiful woman. Potential to have equally beautifully kids. Potential to fall in line at my dad's job and live some potentially perfect life. But then I got hurt, my dad's company failed and he left, and then... then my mom, my mom... killed herself. And, you know, people only use the word 'potential' when you don't live up to anything. The fuckups that don't succeed. Those are the ones who get labeled for having potential."

Caroline's eyes remand fixed on his as he talked himself into tears.

"And that's me! I fell short of expectations. The one who is lost. The one who didn't succeed. I can hear it now even here; I can hear the whispers of those snobby fuckers back home. 'I knew that kid would never amount to anything' and 'So much wasted potential.' I can see my dad's face, his smug face, thinking I'm just as crazy as my mom. And now you, the woman I love, telling me about how much 'potential' I have, like I can't even live up to being with you," Ace blurted out.

Immediately he realized that he had said he loved her for the first time, but his mouth was a runaway train, and he continued without pause, "Oh Caroline, you should've known me when—"

She got up and without saying a word threw her arms around the shaking man who stood in front of her. His mouth closed, and he finally took a breath.

"Listen, Ace." She stared deeply into his eyes. "I know you now."

The embrace soothed Ace, and he slowly began to calm himself. She pulled away from his chest and looked into his eyes, which now swelled with tears.

"I'm sorry about your mom. But that is not your fault. And those potentials you had in your past were always someone else's potentials. You rejected them and took a risk and came here. I believe in you, just you, not in a silly word. I want you to find something you are passionate about, and if it truly is serving drinks in a bar, then I will be happy for you and I will stare at your face as you make people laugh while you serve me vodka tonics, but I can see in your eyes, and in your heart, there is something more in there, and a passion is waiting for you. You just have to find it," Caroline said.

She placed her head back on his chest. His breaths were now deep and calm. And she whispered, "I love you too."

After that night, Ace never returned to work at the bar.

37

Block after block zoomed by. His legs whipped underneath him. The cold fall air cooled his warm face. It had been years since he had run, but the ground felt good underneath his feet, and his knee felt stable, and his brain cleared as he zipped around Paris. He liked observing how the city moved in the morning and watching the city come to life. When he arrived back home, happy and tired, he would walk around the apartment plucking different photographs from the stacks in the apartment. He would stare at them with fascination and wonderment. At some point, he began to make up little stories about the people in the photographs.

His quiet mornings alone were now spent analyzing Caroline's photographs. He would stare at the subjects' eyes. He stared at their postures. He stared at what was in focus and what was blurred. What was she trying to show, or hide, in her photographs? It felt like a puzzle to Ace, and soon he began to write down these observations, and some of them turned into little stories.

He no longer felt alone as the images on the wall came to life. Every day after his morning run, he would grab a pen and off he'd go. At first, words came slowly. He was clumsy with them. He erased. He crossed out. He rewrote and erased and rewrote some more. He had no idea what he was doing. He struggled, trying to convey the feelings that Caroline's photographs gave him. Each word and each sentence took time, but every time he felt like he got something right, or somehow gave Caroline's photographs life, a euphoric high would carry him through until his next struggle. Soon the stories became more elaborate.

The old man sat and warmed himself in the sun on a park bench in the summer afternoons. Always a fresh baguette in his small bag next him. One bite for him, and one for the birds. He liked feeding the birds. The birds liked his bread, and he liked their company. His wife was sick, and he would leave the hospital while she napped and spend his afternoons here. He would smile as young lovers walked by hand in hand. He would remember how he and his wife had once been young and in love, and now they were old and in love. But she was dying, and soon he would be alone and in love. He would then take out another piece of bread. One for him and one for the birds.

He bought a small notebook. Bought a new pen. He kept his writing a secret, and his stories stayed hidden away in his black notebook.

He left. She stayed. Work took him around Europe, and school kept her in Paris. At first, they would send letters filled with I miss you's and I love you's. As their time apart grew, the letters became less and less frequent and the words more and more detached. They both began to spend time with other people, but both refused to take another lover. They had promised that to each other. He was off in Eastern Europe, where drinks were cheap and bars were lively. On a cold winter night in Budapest, he was with colleagues from work and had been joined by a few locals. They spent money fast and without caution.

They would repeat drunkenly to each other, "You are not wasting money if you are having a good time."

That night was a particularly big night, as they had closed a deal that would make them each a lot of money. First it was the beers, and then the cocktails, and then the cocaine they scored off some teenager in an alleyway. The bar was playing some shitty music, but alcohol forced everyone onto the dance floor. Soon he had his arms wrapped around a young Hungarian girl. She looked up at him with big beautiful eyes, and he could feel her pressing her breasts against his chest. His heart began to race, and he tried to focus on anything other than her hands that were gliding up and down his back. It was useless, and soon they were back at his hotel room making drunk, clumsy love.

The morning came, and the young Hungarian girl was gone, leaving only a huge hole in his heart that he filled with regret. He boarded the next flight to Paris. His passion for his true love had returned, and he no longer cared about work, wanting only, to be with her. First, he went to her house. She wasn't there. Then to her school. She wasn't there. To the cafés where they used to drink coffee and laugh at nothing. She wasn't there. The park where they had kissed and fallen in love. Nothing. He was walking home silently when he spotted a familiar dress run into an alleyway. He gave chase with his heart racing, ready to rekindle his love. There she was. In the arms of another man, giving him a kiss full of the passion that used to be reserved for him. He walked away and never saw her again.

At times, his fingers could barely keep up with the words. His mind began to feel more and more clear as he wrote, and stories and characters sparked rapidly out of his brain, flowed down his arms, and crawled out of his fingertips as he quickly pushed the tip of his pen onto the white paper. He could feel himself improving.

He learned that mornings were the best for his writing. His mind was the freshest in the mornings. He would crawl silently out of bed, where Caroline was still asleep, and he would make a small cup of tea and walk around the apartment to gather up his things, the blue pen and his notebook. He would close the door and walk down the narrow stairway. As he faced Rue Lamarck, the cold autumn air would gently rub his face, and he would take a deep inhale and exhale, watching the smoke from his lungs rise into the darkness of the early morning sky.

Most mornings he would stroll leisurely among the tree-lined boulevards. The streets were quiet, and the cafés and bakeries were not yet open. As he strolled in the darkness, he let his mind run free. He would think of nothing, and his breath was the only sound he could hear. He would never rush his writing. He would allow it to simply come to him. Sometimes he wrote frantically, and sometimes he didn't. During the best mornings, words and sentences would magically appear in his head, and small stories would begin to formulate out of thin air. If those mornings happened, he would find a bench, wrestle his notebook from in between his belt and his pants and begin to write.

At first, he would fatigue quickly and be easily distracted, but soon he built up an endurance for writing. It was as if he was becoming a trained athlete in his mind instead of his body. Soon he was able to sit for hours and write as words flowed effortlessly onto the paper. He liked how he could manipulate the speed of the words coming out of his brain. He liked that he could be the dictator of the story. He could choose a sad ending or a happy ending. Mostly, he chose sad endings.

He would write about things he knew. Places he had traveled. People he had met, and examples taken from his own life. All were fair game for that small notebook.

One short story bled into another, and soon 5 pages became 15, and 15 became 50. He had never felt so powerful and prideful in something. Periodically, he would glance up and watch the sleeping city begin to waken. The young men would gather on the streets to open up their small cafés. Chairs were placed outside on sidewalks, and lights began to illuminate the boulevards. Taxis began to multiply as they started their long shifts of driving around the big, bustling city. He would smile at the small children in their school uniforms as they passed him on their way to school. When he was finished and the words had stopped flowing, he would flip through the completed pages, rarely rereading any of it. He would roll up the notebook and slide it behind him, in between his belt and his jeans.

He would finish his morning routine of walking to the nearest bakery, where he would choose the freshest morning bread. He would walk back along the boulevards, up the hill and back up the narrow steps into the still, quiet apartment, where he would heat up a pan and crack eggs and spread warm butter across the fresh bread. Caroline would rise just as the sun began to enter their apartment, and they would share breakfast and smile at each other.

She never asked where he went on those mornings. She could tell he was happy when he got back, and she knew that if he wanted to tell her, he would. This was how it went for a while, and they were both happy and creative, both of them finding inspiration in the other.

Then came the winter.

38

"Hey Sophia! Who is this handsome stranger? And where is my friend Charlie?" Ace shouted when I walked into the apartment, my hands still feeling the freshness of my new haircut. Everyone was in Mia's kitchen, helping her prepare tonight's dinner.

"Charlie, you look great!" Maggie said.

"Sophia made me get it," I said, feeling a little embarrassed by all the attention my haircut was getting.

"It suits you! Sophia is much cooler than me and knows the best barbers in Chiang Mai. I just hope you both are hungry, because we are about ready to eat," Mia said as she presented a beautiful display of food.

That night it felt like we were a mini family. It was my first home-cooked meal since I had arrived in Asia, and I enjoyed eating at Mia's crowded dining room table with everyone laughing and telling stories. We didn't even drink that night, and we all headed to bed early. Before we did, Sophia pulled me aside.

"Would you like to go on a proper adventure tomorrow?" she asked.

"What kind of adventure?" I said.

"I have the perfect spot, but I want it to be a surprise." After such a great day, I wasn't about to say no.

The next morning, we awoke before anyone else was up. We walked downstairs, where I saw two shiny bike helmets hanging on the wall. She tossed one over to me; it was bright red and had a little thunderbolt painted on the side. Carrying our helmets, we walked outside and to the bottom of the steps, where Sophia had parked a little scooter bike that was black and shiny. She straddled the bike and put her hair into a tight ponytail, and I couldn't help but stare at her.

"What are you looking at? Do I look funny with my helmet on?" Sophia asked.

"No, no, you look great!" She blushed a bit and tapped the back of her bike, her hand signaling my spot.

Soon we were off, zipping through the small streets and passing underneath the giant walled opening, across the river and out of the city. We emerged onto the open road, where the wind brushed our smiling faces. I held on loosely to Sophia's hips as she pushed the bike into the open air of Chiang Mai. The world seemed to open up for us. We passed massive open fields and farms and small villages. We stopped off at a roadside stand to get gasoline that was stored in old plastic water bottles. The owners of the little stands smiled politely as I butchered the language while trying my best to use the Thai that Sophia had taught me. Sah wah dee khai and kob-khun ka.

I documented our trip with a few quick pictures of the small markets and villages we passed through. The empty roads seemed to go on forever as the warm Thailand sun beat down on us. When I didn't have it in my hands taking a shot, the camera dangled across my back, and I kept my hands softly tucked around Sophia's hips. I could have stayed like that all day. Then we passed by a large sign that displayed Doi Inthanon National Park.

"Ready to hike?" she shouted.

"Hike!!!!" I yelled, inches from her ear as the wind blew loudly past us.

"Yes! Hike! I have a little surprise for you," she shouted as she slightly turned her head to face me.

All I could think of was my goddamn leg and my goddamn brace. I could walk and keep up with her for short distances. I could sit on a motorbike perfectly fine. But kicking a heavy bag in front of her friends and now going on a mystery hike seemed beyond my capabilities.

"Everything ok?" she yelled. She could probably sense my apprehension as I instinctively tightened my grip around her waist and my gaze turned to the fast-moving ground underneath my feet. I looked down at my legs. Why couldn't I have legs that worked? Legs that could make me run fast and jump high. Legs that would let me leap up this mountain with Sophia. The dirty jeans I wore showed just a sliver of my white brace that kept my foot flexed upwards. My shoes wore almost worn to the bottom layer, as I had walked more in Vietnam than I had walked in years. Calluses had formed underneath my feet, and my legs felt stronger than they ever had. I stared at my legs for a long time. No, these legs won't win any races. No, I will never be a professional athlete. But these legs let me walk with my father. They helped me find my love of photography. They brought me to Asia. They walked across the busy streets in Vietnam. They danced until the sun came up. They helped me make friends from all over the world. And now, right now, these same legs that sat behind a beautiful girl were going to take me hiking.

"Fuck it!" I yelled. She parked the bike and looked at me.

"Excuse me?" She looked at me sadly, as if I was disappointed that she had taken me here.

"Let's do it. I may be slow, but I am going to do it."

"Are you sure?" Sophia said worriedly.

"Yes, one hundred P!"

"One hundred P?"

"Haha. Something Maggie says. It slipped into my vocabulary. It means one hundred percent."

"Ahhhh, ok. Well, slower is better anyway; it gives us more time to enjoy the views. One hundred P!" We both laughed.

The first kilometer of the trail started off flat through a few rolling hills with large oak trees that sprouted up everywhere. The density of the trees left almost no vantage point, and I was able to focus on each step. Sophia walked slowly next to me and talked to me about her home, her small village that pushed against the sharp edges of the Swiss mountains. She told me how her grandfather had built a small cabin deep in the woods with no electricity and no running water. She would spend weeks out there with him during the summer months and hike with him among the giant mountains. After he died, she no longer went to the cabin, but she promised herself that she would return to it the next time she was home. She missed the mountains and the snow and her grandpa. She told me that she came here often to feel the fresh, higher-altitude air. She laughed as she explained that it was Thailand's highest mountain and yet its peak was only 2,600 meters tall. I laughed to myself for a different reason—because 2,600 meters might as well have been Mount Everest for me. I enjoyed listening to her, as it helped me forget the sweat that poured off my face and the growing soreness in my muscles as we inched up those 2,600 meters.

As the gradient began to increase, I could feel my legs burn and quiver with exhaustion. The large oak trees were conspiring against me as they blocked the fresh air I so desperately needed. My lungs felt tight and constricted, and my ribs struggled during each inhale and exhale. I stopped several times, and Sophia waited as I took slow and methodical breaths before starting again. Soon the trees reluctantly opened, and we emerged into open air. Behind us stood dense green trees, and in front of us swept panoramic views of rolling green hills that led down to the roads that we had ridden in on. Above us, the trail continued to rise into a sea of blooming flowers. A parade of wild blues and greens scattered along the side of the mountain and resembled a Monet painting.

The trail continued to march up a collection of steep stairs. You know the runner's high that endurance runners often talk about? The point where, in the middle of a long endurance run, their brain gets a shot of endorphins? They tell you that all the hard work evaporates and they lose all the pain and aches of running and instead float while they run. Well, as I climbed up that mountain, I never got a runner's high and only got more tired, and those runners are full of shit.

This was pure hell, and I felt terrible. Every inch of me wanted to stop and tell her I couldn't go on, but I was determined and took pride in taking as few breaks as possible as I repeated to myself, *One step at a time. One step at a time.* Sophia didn't say much now but would encourage me every time I stopped to take a break.

"Almost there! Only five more minutes."

Five minutes felt like five hours. *Come on, Charlie*, I said to myself, nearly reaching exhaustion. My shoes felt like someone had put lead in them, but I continued to inch upwards anyway, and soon I reached Sophia as she waited up on a bluff. In exhaustion, I put my hands on my knees and breathed deeply just as the Muay Thai fighters had done the previous day. I stared at the ground and at my feet. That was it. I was done. I didn't think I could go any farther.

"Look! We didn't come all the way up here for you to look at your feet!" she said.

Concerned more with my feet than the views, I slowly stood up, and in front of us, tucked away in the sea of green, two small pagodas emerged. They looked like mountain fortresses from a lost time. I stood there and stared in awe at the view. Sophia told me that they had been built for the King and Queen of Thailand.

"Views from the highest peak and the tallest mountains," Sophia said, staring straight out toward the endless view.

"What?" I asked.

"I heard you tell Maggie about your dream. This is it. The highest peak and the tallest mountain."

The view in front of me was just like my dream but only better. Together we sat down and stared for a long time.

"I wish I had brought my landscape lens. This would be a great photograph."

"Sometimes things are better to just be remembered," Sophia said. We sat there for what seemed like forever, not speaking any words but just enjoying each other's company. After a while, Sophia broke the silence:

"This is my favorite spot in Thailand. I have been to the beaches, but they are crowded. I've been to the large temples, and they are crowded too. But when I come here, I only hear the same noises that you would have heard if you had stood here thousands of years ago. The sound of the leaves blowing in the wind. The birds crying to each other. And my own breath. It's nice, no?"

"Absolutely amazing. Thank you for bringing me."

"If I close my eyes, I can almost hear the cowbells from the farms in our village. I used to hate that sound, because it would always wake me up in the morning, but now it's what makes me smile the most."

We looked at each other and smiled, and I felt as if something was pushing me toward her that was out of my control. Our heads drew closer, and our lips touched gently together. Her lips were moist and inviting, and we kissed. I felt her arm reach around my back, and she pulled me closer to her. I put my hands around her waist, and she did the same to me. I could feel her heartbeat as her chest pressed against mine. We kissed and looked at each other and smiled.

I was sure she preferred handsomer men, but I was glad she had made an exception. As she bit her upper lip and I watched a thousand tiny goosebumps gain territory of her skin, for that moment, at least, I was sure of everything.

39

Sleep did not come easy to me that night after Sophia dropped me off and went to work. I replayed our afternoon over and over again in my head. When she finally arrived home, I heard her softly pace around and then go back into her room. I had hoped she would come to me and wake me from my pretend sleep, but that touch never came. I rolled over with my eyes open, and my mind ran wild with insecurities. Did she regret kissing me? Did she really like me? Why had she rushed into her room so quickly?

That night I did not dream of rivers and mountains but stared at the ceiling and thought of Sophia. Ace had warned me about meeting girls on the road. I was sure most other men were more equipped for handling this kind of situation. All I knew was that I was leaving in a few hours to a meditation retreat and all I wanted to do was stay here with Sophia.

In my sleeplessness, the only thing I could do was wait for the sun to slowly emerge into the room where we slept. I watched the sun wage its daily battle with the darkness for space on the floor. I lay there, eyes wide open, watching the illumination creep millimeter by millimeter from the window to the edge of the plants that were positioned perfectly to capture the morning light. I was positioned next to the window on my thin air mattress that had deflated in the night, leaving me pressed against the hard floor by morning. Soon the sun touched my face, and I watched Ace and Maggie wake up as the sun rolled over their faces too. I smiled, and sleep finally fell over me.

Chop Chop Chop. My eyes slowly opened, and I found everyone was up and in the kitchen, talking. Everyone except Sophia. Mia was cutting fruits and vegetables and was again preparing breakfast. The food was ushered into a large blender, and a green liquid was produced. Mia said that it would give us all the energy we needed to complete our journey. I wasn't sure how much energy we needed to sleep on a bus, but I didn't argue because the juice tasted magnificent as it energized my sleepy body.

At the table, Ace discussed our transport and said we had to leave in two hours if we were to make it before sunset. I was hardly able to pay attention because I was wondering what was keeping Sophia from joining us and questions once again flooded my mind. Was she trying to avoid me? Waiting for me to leave so she didn't have to face me in the morning? My heart pumped as conversations blitzed around me, and I tuned most of it out.

When Sophia finally opened her door, I tried to stay calm and not stare. She slowly walked around the kitchen, and I did a terrible job of not staring, and we made eye contact. She smiled at me but quickly turned away to talk to her sister. They talked softly, and I could feel them both stealing glances at me. I tried to occupy myself by cleaning the area around me and getting my bag packed when, out of the corner of my eye, I caught Sophia retreating to her room. *That's it*, I thought. *She doesn't want to see me.* I began to hurriedly stuff the last of my clothes into my backpack, and just as I pulled the top string of it closed, Sophia emerged again from her room. She had a small envelope in her hand, and her camera danced around her neck. Without hesitation, she walked right toward me.

"Would you take a walk with me?" she said in a serious tone.

Ace and Maggie were finishing packing their bags, and I told them I'd be back shortly. Ace smiled at me like a proud father. If only he knew the torment I was putting myself through. Sophia stopped me as soon as we got outside.

"You know what makes a great artist?"

"Ummm, no?" I said, unsure what she was getting at.

"Someone whose art inspires others to be better."

"Ok." I was so confused.

"I hope this doesn't upset you—" That was never a good combination of words to hear someone say to you.

"—but I received a message from Mr. Jake last night while I was working at the hostel."

I had completely forgotten about my film, as thoughts of Sophia had occupied every square inch of my mind. "He is not able to develop my photos?" I asked sadly, as if things could not get any worse in my mind.

"No no no. The complete opposite. He finished early, so I rushed over last night to pick them up so we wouldn't have to rush this morning," Sophia said.

"Why would this upset me? Where are they?" I was getting anxious and confused. Had Mr. Jake told her they weren't any good?

"Because I looked at them."

"Oh... ," I said. I was protective of my photographs and was self-conscious of people looking at them, especially if I hadn't seen them first.

"I don't want you to be upset," she said, "but Mr. Jake praised them, and he never says that to anyone. I rushed home to show you, but you were already asleep." If only she knew. "I went into my room, and this package stared at me, almost begging me to view them. See, I would do no good at meditation, and unlike you, my mind races off in too many directions." Again, if only she knew.

"Despite my best efforts to leave them be, I broke down and looked through them, and, Charlie, these are amazing! You are amazing!"

"Can I see them?" I was anxious to see them.

"Oh yes. Sorry. Of course." She handed them over to me. "I'm sorry. I understand if you are mad. I shouldn't have done that, but listen, I have never been to Vietnam, and these photographs put me there. Your photography captures people and feelings in a way that I could never do. I was mesmerized by them, and I'm inspired by them. That's why I have my camera today. You made me want to be better behind my own lens."

I hurriedly scanned through them as we sat down on the street out-side Mia's apartment. There were the women cooking noodles on the streets. The men singing karaoke in the garages. Ace making drinks. The empty bottles of beer scattered across small tables at Z's. Assorted hands holding playing cards. Maggie reading on a park bench. Mhi making chai teas. They were all there. The best month of my life, in eight rolls of film.

"Are you mad?" Sophia asked.

"No, I'm just happy you like them." Then, without talking, we got up and walked. We walked several streets in silence, neither of us sure of where we were going, or what to say.

Sophia finally broke the silence and blurted out, "I don't want to make this a big deal. I enjoyed spending time with you, but you are trav-eling, and I know how backpackers are. So I want this to be simple."

"I like spending time with you too. And I'm not really a backpacker...," I began.

"Let me finish, please." She cut me off. "I'm going to be honest. I think you are great and honest and someone who I want to get to know more, but I also think you are a talented photographer who needs to show his work. My sister is organizing an art show here in Chiang Mai, and we want to invite you to have an exhibit in the show. I think you need to be in it. And if you come back and we still have a connection, then I'll be happy with that too." She handed me a flyer. Printed on it were the names of several artists, including Mia and Sophia, as well as Mr. Jake.

"I wan—" I started to say.

"Sorry to cut you off, but I don't want an answer from you now. Go to your retreat, and if you want to come back, you know where to find us." She smiled and kissed me on the cheek before she turned and briskly walked away. I stood there and watched as she disappeared down a small alleyway.

40

Ace had his hands crossed over his chest and looked as if he were sleeping, and Maggie had her large sunglasses on with her head buried in the Thich Nhat Hanh book. All of our bags were pushed to the edge of the sidewalk, leaning against Mia's apartment. Without looking up, Ace mumbled, "About time, Romeo," a sly smile emerging on his face as he peered up at me with one eye; the other one stayed closed, trying to get a few more moments of rest.

"Sorry, I didn't mean to keep you waiting. I guess I lost track of time."

"It's okay, babe. It gave me time to read. Good stuff in here." Maggie lifted her head from the book and smiled at me, that big smile that always made me feel better.

"Well, mate, you just finished your first travel romance," Ace said as he rolled a cigarette. "They start fast and end even faster. You don't look too worse for wear." I didn't tell them about the conversation Sophia and I had just had. About the art exhibit. About coming back here and showing my work. I just nodded and grabbed my backpack, and we were off.

We walked in our usual order—Ace in the front leading, then Maggie strolling comfortably behind him and then me a full two or three lengths behind her—so I couldn't quite hear what Ace was saying. I assumed he was telling a story, probably one I'd heard before. Again, my thoughts floated off, thinking about what I was going to do. Would I agree to go with Ace to Myanmar or come back for the art exhibit and see Sophia again? Who would I choose, between the person who had befriended me when I couldn't even cross the street and Sophia, who believed in my work and whose lips I could still taste? I would have to say no to someone.

Far ahead of me, as I drifted in and out of my own thoughts, Ace and Maggie continued walking and talking. I was no longer within earshot of them and was unable to hear their conversations. My attention had turned to the awakening city. The morning rush of new tuk-tuk drivers had now begun, and their vehicles were pumping through the city. The drivers were constantly pulling alongside us, asking if we needed rides, before Ace waved them off. The lawnmower engines rattled as they accelerated away. I assumed we must be close to the bus station. I hurriedly caught up with Maggie.

"Where is this bus station?" I asked out of breath.

"Bus station?" she asked, looking confused with my question.

"Yes. The bus station that will take us to Pai. Don't tell me Ace never sorted out a bus booking?"

"Charlie, we aren't taking a bus to Pai. Ace has been talking nonstop about how we are getting there." I guessed that I'd been more tuned out than I had thought.

"How are we getting there?" Up ahead, I could see that Ace had stopped and was unloading his bag at a place that was definitely not a bus station. He was smiling and laughing with an older Thai gentleman whose fingers were full of black grease stains that contrasted with his thinning white hair.

"What time does the bus leave, Ace?" I called to him, still unsure of what was happening.

"Bus? Mate, we aren't taking a bus." And just as he said that, I looked around and realized what this place actually was. Motorbikes lined the outside of the small shop, and small helmets dangled from the handle-bars.

"I was here negotiating yesterday, and we got the best deal in Thai-land. It's cheaper than a bus and much more fun."

The small man with the dirty hands smiled and said, "You know how to ride? Lots of turns to Pai." Ace responded quickly, answering for all of us:

"We are all experienced in motorbike riding." He made a vroom vroom noise and leaned low to one side, holding two imaginary han-dlebars as he mimicked racing on a track. "Charlie here was a semi-pro cyclist back home. These little bikes will be easy to handle for him."

The small man was counting the money and hardly paying attention to the stories Ace was fabricating as he handed over the three keys. Ace quickly swiped them, and we walked over to the bikes. He tossed us each a key and then lugged our bags back to the man and signed a form. Ace explained how the bags would be driven by van and we would pick them up in Pai.

"First class all the way!" Ace proclaimed, beaming, as he excitedly mounted his bike.

I had been a passive passenger on one with Sophia, but driving one to Pai was completely different, and I was starting to get nervous.

"Ace, I've never driven a motorbike before. Should I have a quick lesson or something beforehand? How do I drive?" I whispered.

"Like I said back in Vietnam. Carefully. Very carefully," Ace respond-ed.

Maggie seemed confident in her skills as she quickly straddled her bike and put on her black helmet. "Charlie, you got this. We will take it easy until you feel comfortable," she said.

"We must move if we want to reach Pai before dark, so let's goooooooooo!" Ace turned on his bike and sped off quickly as he let out a "Wooo hooooo!" He charged off the sidewalk with a sudden burst of speed. His legs flew wildly out from underneath him, and his bike bounced around from side to side as he tried to get control of it. He had to swerve quickly to avoid a tuk-tuk as the driver honked his horn and screamed at him. Ace continued to bounce unevenly down the street but eventually balanced himself and then finally stopped, miraculously unharmed, halfway down the road.

I looked back at the man who had just rented us the bikes, and he calmly shook his head at this sight that was probably all too common for him. Then, just as quickly, he ignored us and went back to sitting behind his little desk.

"You want to know how to ride?" Maggie looked at me. "Do the opposite of him." She turned on her bike and slowly walked it off the curb. Then, hopping back on it, she sped carefully down the street to where Ace was stopped. I assumed the position on the bike, put my key in the ignition and turned it to the right. The small engine on the bike turned over, and I felt a small vibration through my sit bones that traveled up my chest, into my arms and down to my hands that cradled the handlebars. It felt as if life was shooting up into my bones. I slowly walked my bike onto the street and watched for traffic. I was glad we were in Chiang Mai with empty streets and not in Ho Chi Minh City. I turned my wrist and lifted my right hand back slowly. The bike jumped forward, and my head swung back, not anticipating the force of this little machine. I slammed on the brakes, almost falling off, but I soon balanced myself and turned my hand softly again. This time I was prepared, and off I went, piloting the bike slowly down the road until I came to a smooth stop next to Maggie and Ace.

We sat on our bikes at the corner, and we all looked at each other with big smiles. Ace said we were now the hardest and fastest bike gang in Southeast Asia. We all circled around and put our hands out for a little handshake. Ace talked quickly about the route and that we should be careful after his almost disastrous start.

"These bikes have a little more jump than the bike I rode in India," Ace said.

"Oh, Ace. Please tell us about it?" Maggie said, looking earnest.

"I was down in Fort Kochi and... ," but before Ace could finish his story, Maggie throttled her bike and took off laughing. I also laughed and followed suit, but this time my takeoff was smooth, and just like that we were on the road. Ace yelled something incomprehensible as Maggie and I pulled away, smiling at each other.

The road to Pai was long and seemed to be modeled after cooked spaghetti. It twisted and turned over the hills of Northern Thailand as it took us on a four-hour ride that hooked and curved around 762 turns over 200 kilometers. Shortly after leaving the city of Chiang Mai, we were on the open road, and soon we began ascending and turning our way toward Pai. Marvelous and expansive views of the Thailand landscape had us stopping and smiling at each other as we took several breaks to document our trip. We raced past the dense forest with the lush green trees, and then we elevated above the trees where the sun could reach our faces. Large buses filled with travelers passed us often, but we felt like we were on our own adventure with our motorbike gang.

It felt great to be in control of the machine below me. Miles were vanishing behind us as we zoomed up and up. On the bike, I didn't think about my leg. I was bursting ahead of Maggie and Ace and enjoyed setting the pace as we ticked off mile after mile on Route 1095 toward Pai. I took each turn with a light touch of the brake and throttled quickly out of it as fast as I could. We escalated to new heights, and it felt as if we were going to touch the big fluffy clouds that moved slowly overhead.

We stopped at a local street-side restaurant to eat lunch and fill our tanks. Ace enjoyed a little nap in the warm sun during our short rest, and Maggie tried to ask me about Sophia, but I changed the topic quickly, and soon she stopped asking. I was looking forward to getting back on the bike and feeling the ground move underneath me. Once our break was over, we moved quickly and passed road signs that signaled how many kilometers away from Pai we were. Quickly the number decreased, and after nearly four hours of driving, we were now finally only minutes away from Pai. Maggie was tired and Ace was hungry, but I could have continued on forever. The feeling of speed and mobility was intoxicating, and I wanted to keep drinking it in. On the bike, I was on an even playing field.

Soon we were riding into the small streets of Pai. We passed several signs for hostels, and everyone in town seemed to be a backpacker. Everywhere you looked, you saw backpackers on motorbikes, backpackers walking the street or backpackers shuffling out of restaurants and bars. We stopped at the Aya bus station, where we would be able to get our bags and a truck from the retreat would pick us up.

Now on this feet again and unable to sit still, Ace immediately raced off down the street to one of the several 7-11 stores that seemed to have taken over the town. Maggie and I sat on our bags to rest and wait for someone from the meditation retreat to pick us up. We didn't know who would be picking us up, but I secretly anticipated a man in an orange robe to quietly summon us to our zen weekend.

As we rested, I could feel my energy level plummeting. Gone was the adrenaline of the bike ride, and my face was now feeling the effects of both sunburn and windburn from it. Soon my eyes grew heavy in the afternoon warmth of Pai. Trying to stay awake, I leaned over to Maggie, who was lying peacefully on her large bag with her sun hat covering her face.

"This town doesn't seem so bad," I said.

She replied from underneath her large hat, "Don't let Ace's travel snobbiness ruin you. I've heard only amazing things about this place. We are going to have a great time." I nodded as I watched the streets move in front of me and tried not to let Ace's comments about Pai seep into my brain.

The warm sun began fading quickly as an early evening breeze began settling in. Reaching for my bag, I pulled out a hoodie that was coming in handy here in Northern Thailand. Maggie was now asleep, despite the chaos of the station. I stayed up and awaited our host's arrival. To stay awake, I watched the action on the streets in front of me. A night market was being set up, and small tables were being ushered in and placed on the streets. The brick and mortar shops buzzed with foot traffic from backpackers buying whatever Pai essentials they needed. Assorted elephant pants, colorful poncho shirts and beaded bracelets were all for sale. In front of us, a guy was sitting with a sign that read, "Dreadlocks Here" as he and three dreadlocked friends sat and smoked cigarettes.

"Man, this town is the worst." Ace returned with three warm cups of cheap ramen from the 7-11. "Now you see what full Pai is." He passed the ramen over to Maggie and me. Trying not to get him going, I ignored him and asked Maggie what time our meditation pickup was.

"Now," Maggie called out from underneath her hat, showing no interest in the ramen or in conversation with me.

Thirty minutes passed, and we were still sitting there. The stillness made us tired, and eventually my eyes became so sleepy that I decided to doze off for a few minutes, but just at that moment, I heard a woman yell out, "Meditation with Bhud!" My eyes sprung open, and in front of us stood a small woman. Despite her size, her body exuded strength. Her toned arms were decorated with several tattoos, and she wore a cut-up sweatshirt that hung over one shoulder, revealing a white tank top underneath. Her hair was pulled up that revealed an undercut hairstyle. Full of energy, she was good-looking and had kind eyes, with the type of face that made it hard to guess her age, and her movements were child-like as she jumped out of her little blue truck and hopped around the station, looking for people going to the retreat. As she darted around the Aya station, she reminded me of one of those old mechanical toys you wound up. She was definitely not the orange-robed monk I had been expecting.

"Meditation Retreat!" she continued to yell as she raced around with an excited energy. We all looked at each other. Maggie and I liked her right away. I think Ace had his reservations.

We sat up and told her we were going to the retreat, and she jumped over our bags and hugged us with big, warm and loving hugs as if we had been lifelong friends. It felt good, and we all laughed with her.

"Ok ok, let's go, let's go. I'm late. So sorry. Hop in the back of the truck, and we will get you there soon," she told us, her eyes wide and friendly to go with a happy and earnest smile. We all heaved our bags up onto the bed of the little blue pickup truck and sat on the benches installed around the edges. She got into the front seat and, before she drove, turned around and looked at us with a big smile through the little hole in the partition and yelled back, "My name is Bhud, and I will be your guide for the next three days. Woooo hooo!!!" as she roared her truck down the street.

41

The clothes Ace had brought with him one year ago were now wearing thin. If they weren't decorated with stains or pricked with holes, they seemed to emit a permanent smell that revolted Caroline. Soon, Caroline had had enough of his style. It was time for him to go shopping and dress less like a backpacker and more like the permanent resident that he had become with her at Rue Lamarck. Just like that, gone were the tattered shorts and dirty tank tops. Now he wore new jeans and a few sweaters that kept him warm in the cooling temperatures as fall rolled into winter. He felt older and sophisticated as he stared at himself in the mirror. He looked handsome, and Caroline told him so. When he looked at Caroline and they both smiled at each other without talking, they both knew that Paris might become home.

Along with his new clothes, a new confidence grew in him, especially in his writing, and he thought for the first time that he might be good at something other than being able to play a sport. That week, with Caroline sleeping and breathing softly next to him, Ace opened his little notebook and wrote a short declaration.

On top of an otherwise blank page, he stared at the fresh new words he had just penned. At that moment he had declared himself a writer, and he was sure that he would become a good one and that writing was where his future was. Writing and being with Caroline. In fact, Ace had begun working on a novel. He didn't know how it started, but word by word and paragraph by paragraph, characters were invented, and a story had developed. He toiled over each sentence, but he enjoyed the struggle that came with the new project.

It was easy for him to lock himself away at Café Lavender and write in the warm and pleasant space. He would write words as they came and would take periodic breaks when they didn't. He would also sit near the window and watch as the weather changed. Every afternoon, he knew that once the streets grew quiet and he could no longer make out the swirling leaves in the darkened street, he would be done with his words, and he would return to the flat where he would join Caroline for the rest of the evening.

On the weekends he would not write. The weekends were for Caroline and him. One day, they sat like tourists at a café that faced Notre Dame. They drank champagne and watched the boats full of eager tourists float up and down the Seine River. It was an unusually fine day in the middle of winter, with only a hint of dark afternoon clouds that floated well off in the distance. A light breeze passed between them that made them keep their jackets on, but it was not strong enough to make them cold.

"What a beautiful day. Aren't we lucky, Ace?" Caroline said as she took a sip of champagne.

"We are lucky, for at least a moment, but it looks like a storm is coming soon," Ace said for some reason, as he fixated on the dark clouds in the distance.

"That's unlike you to be negative about the weather, and those clouds look too far away to bother us. Let's just enjoy this wonderful afternoon together."

They talked and made each other laugh as lost tourists strolled back and forth searching for a café or a street to cure their Parisian appetite. They always enjoyed being in places like this where most locals would shudder with disgust and mock you for spending your time.

The afternoon moved forward, and they continued to drink champagne. The sun began to set over the city, and soon the sky was magically painted with a variety of oranges, yellows and pinks. The champagne was delightful, despite being overpriced, and they held each other's hand across the small table. Caroline looked toward the beautiful sunset and smiled. Ace smiled a bit pensively as he stared at the approaching clouds, but being in a general state of happiness, he shook off any fears of an upcoming storm.

"I think I know why I like this place," Ace proclaimed.

"Oh yeah? Why is that?" Caroline said, smiling, still looking over Ace's shoulder at the sunset.

"It's full of tourists!"

"Spot-on observation there, my love, but that can't be why you like it," she said, confused.

"Why not?" Ace asked.

"Everyone hates things that are too touristy."

"And yet why do we always find ourselves here?"

"The views aren't bad and the company is ok," she said, smiling, thinking she was being funny.

"Well, tourists aren't jaded like your friends who sit around and drink at hipster bars and complain and critique everything until there is nothing to like anymore. Here everyone is fresh and new to Paris and in love with every moment. They are seeing Paris for the first time, and it's wonderful. Everyone is happy and smiling. Just look around." It was true. Everyone was happy. Couples on honeymoons. Families on vacation. Men. Women. Children. Everyone seemed to be loving every moment of this magical city.

"Oh, there it is. You Americans with your optimism—or maybe it's because we've had a bottle of wine."

"I'm serious!" Ace said.

"I know you are, and I'm happy you are happy. But maybe because I've had a bottle of wine I'm going to say it: I think there is something different about you, my love." She paused and stared at him with a knowing smile. "Maybe it's those morning walks?"

Ace hadn't told her about his writing, but obviously she had noticed, and she was too smart to think that he spent those morning hours searching for a bakery in Paris. He knew now was the right time to tell her. "I've wanted to tell you, and now seems like a good time... I've been writing." The words squeaked out, lacking any form of confidence. It was the first time he had told anyone about his writing, and the way he said it made it sound as if it were some type of disease he had caught.

"Writing?" She looked at him with a large grin.

"Little short stories and now maybe a novel. To be honest, I only started because of your photographs. They inspired my first few stories, and now I almost have a full notebook of words. I don't know if it's any good, but I don't care. Like your photography, I'm writing for me."

"My photographs inspired you, and you weren't just up early and being nice and buying me fresh bread from the bakery? That's a lot to digest!" They both laughed. "That's wonderful, Ace. Truly wonderful. Maybe one day you will let me read these stories." She reached her hands out to assure him that she was proud and held his hands tightly. Despite the warmth of the afternoon, her hands felt clammy and cold.

"Are you ok?" He looked up at her, and her face looked ghost white, as if the blood had drained out of her body.

"Sorry, I don't know if it's the wine, but I'm not feeling too good. I don't want to ruin this moment. I'd really like to stay and watch this sunset," she said as she looked like at any moment she could fall asleep.

They didn't make it to the end of the sunset and quickly took a taxi home. Just as they got back to the apartment, the warm afternoon disappeared and a cold, heavy rain started. Those distant dark clouds had moved quicker than expected, and the city grew cold and dark.

42

The next day Caroline didn't get out of bed, and the day after that the same. Soon she was missing more classes and rarely picking up her camera. She couldn't seem to shake a high fever and daily chills. She wouldn't complain and would always say, "It's just the flu. Give it a few days, and I'll be okay."

But she wasn't okay, and the fever continued, and she began to have little energy to do anything. She stopped going into the darkroom, and no new photographs were being produced. Ace would watch her sleep most of the day, something he used to love to do, but now his heart hurt as he watched her. Her usual self would have been hopping about with energy, but now she always felt sluggish, and simple activities were becoming exhausting. They stopped traveling away from home, and most walks would end in her needing a taxi home. They no longer met up with friends for drinks and hadn't made love in weeks.

One day turned into a week, and a week turned into a month, and she was still sick. Ace continued with his morning routine of walking and writing, but he was no longer able to focus. His mind began to wander, and writing became difficult. Instead of enjoying the difficult process, as he had been, he grew frustrated with it. His mind always drifted to Caroline, and he usually went home before he was able to produce any meaningful words. Each day he still returned to the apartment with a fresh loaf of bread and cooked breakfast, but now Caroline rarely rose, and when Ace would bring her food in bed, she only ate small bites. Like her appetite, his writing slowed down and eventually stopped, as he could no longer concentrate. He grew angrier and more frustrated because his writing no longer brought him so much joy. His notebook and pen soon found themselves untouched for days. He even began to get impatient with Caroline and her lack of urgency to see a doctor.

"I think you need to see someone. Should we go to the hospital?" Ace pleaded.

"I don't think I do. I'm feeling better," she repeated to him day after day, despite not showing any signs of improvement. The only place that was close enough for them to still walk to was Café Lavender. Caroline's wit and charm were still evident as she talked to the young girls working behind the counter, but Ace could tell that even they were worried about her. She and Ace would sit in the small, dark café, where she would drink water and he would try to share a croissant, and she would nibble at it as she stared out the window. The only thing she seemed to enjoy was smelling the lavender flowers that she had recently planted in the café.

"They were my mom's favorite flowers. Well, that's what my grandparents used to tell me, and when I smell them, I sometimes think I can remember her."

"They have a wonderful scent," Ace agreed.

"They do, don't they?" She took a big inhale and then coughed weakly into her scarf.

"Are you ok?"

"Oh yes, I'm fine. Now, about this secret of yours. Tell me more. I want to know about this book. What is it about? An American traveler falling in love in Paris?" She smiled.

Ace shook his head. "Haven't made much progress on it."

"Yes, I've noticed you haven't been going out as much. I hope that is not on account of me?"

"No. I just have nothing to write about. Maybe it was a fleeting thing and I was never actually good at it. It's ok. I think I'm done with it now. It was just a dumb hobby."

"Nonsense!" Her voice rose to a level he hadn't heard in a while, and she must have realized it, too, as she immediately talked much softer.

"I saw how happy you were when you were writing. You would wear that smile on your face when you returned each day, and I loved that smile. I knew you were doing something you truly loved, and now I see less of that smile. You need to keep writing, Ace. You will find your words again." They sat for a while as Caroline positioned her chair in the late afternoon sun that peeked into the café at this time every day.

"Before we go back home, I want you to promise you will share your writing with me. You can read me your stories as I rest on your lap. Maybe that will re-spark you?" Caroline said.

"Are you sure you want to hear them? They are probably not very good."

"I couldn't think of anything I would rather hear."

Ace knew he had no choice in the matter but thought he might as well try to bargain with the only chip he had. "Ok. If I share the stories with you, you have to promise me you will go see a doctor." Surprisingly, she agreed, and she smiled as the sun hit her perfectly. She still had the most gorgeous smile he had ever seen.

That evening they sat at home on the couch in the fading sunlight from the day. He nervously rummaged through his notebook that was now filled with his chicken scratch writing. He had not spent much time reviewing or editing his words and told her that as a disclaimer. The thought of reading them out loud to someone made his mouth dry; then he looked at her.

She was lying down, her face kissed by the sunlight that peeked through the curtains as she pulled a small blanket over her body. With her hair pulled back in her usual ponytail, she looked like an angel. He lifted her head and placed it on his lap as he sat next to her, and she smiled up at him with a look of confidence that he knew his own face did not have. He could feel his pulse pump as he found a few stories that he liked the most. But he couldn't quite get started.

She looked up at him and said, "I love you, Ace. Now spit it out!"

Her humor always put him at ease, and he began reading. As the words rolled out, Caroline closed her eyes. He liked to think she was imagining the story in her mind, but he didn't ask if she was and simply continued reading.

He read three different stories. The more he read, the more confident he became, because he thought they were good stories. They all felt like someone else's words, but yet they were right there in his notebook, written in his handwriting. When he finished, the sun was gone from the room and the lights on the street had just turned on. Caroline opened her eyes and stared at Ace. For a long time, she didn't say anything. Then he saw a small tear run down from her eye and roll down her cheek. "Those were beautiful, Ace. Are those stories also based on my photographs?"

"Yes. Yes they are," Ace said.

"Ace, you brought my photos to life."

"I think they already had that quality. I just wanted to add to them."

"That was amazing. Simply perfect. You are a fine writer, my love. I hope you can continue and stop worrying about me. But may I ask you something?"

"Sure."

"Why are they all so sad?" Ace wasn't sure. Yet it was true. All of his stories had sad endings. Death. Breakups. Abandonment. "Not all great art has to come from suffering. I want you to one day write a story with a happy ending. I would like that very much," Caroline said.

"I promise." He bent down and kissed her lips. They were dry. "Are you thirsty?" he asked.

"Yes, I am. It seems these silly tears have dehydrated me. Could I bother you for a drink of water?" Ace laid her head down and went to get a glass of water, and when he returned, she was sleeping silently underneath the glow of the streetlight.

43

Five days later, she was leaving.

"Are you sure you have to leave Paris? I'm sure there are great doctors here that will be able to sort you out," Ace asked, but Caroline was persistent.

"I'm going back to Sweden and will see a doctor there. I'm overdue for a visit, and I think it's important that I see my father."

"Like you said, it's probably not that serious. You probably only need antibiotics. I don't think you need to go home." Ace knew that whatever was happening was serious, but the thought of her leaving tore him apart.

"Are you also a doctor now? I will only be gone a few days, and I haven't been home for ages. It will be nice to see my father, and then I'll come right back to you. Then I promise I will have more appetite for your breakfasts, and you can carry on writing again without worrying about me."

The next day, Ace carried her small bag down the narrow stairs, and Caroline followed closely behind. It was early in the morning when her energy was the highest. He hoped it would maintain during her journey home.

The streets were quiet as the dark sky rumbled and threatened to rain at any moment. Ace waved a taxi down as they stood on Rue Lamarck. They held hands as they both hurried into the taxi. A storm looked imminent as the cab drove off. Ace watched out the taxi window as the wind blew with a force that swayed the trees back and forth, ripping off the last remaining brown and red leaves that still hung on from the fall, leaving the branches completely devoid of visible life. Ace followed the leaves as they floated gracefully away from the trees and watched them turn over in circles. He fixated on one twirling leaf and followed it as it soared up high but just as quickly fell to a silent stillness on the wet pavement, ending its beautiful dance just as the taxi rolled over it.

The streets were deserted because the approaching storm kept people indoors, so the short trip from Montmartre to Gare du Nord was even shorter than usual. As they exited the taxi, Ace's grip on Caroline's hand tightened. They walked slowly from the taxi to the terminal and did not rush despite the now steady rain that began to fall.

"I think you should change clothes before getting onto the train. I don't want you to catch a cold," Ace said.

"I think it's too late for that." She looked up at him, and water covered her face, but he could see that most of the water had come from her eyes, not the rain. She wiped them quickly. "I should get on board."

"Yes, I think so too." They both tried to avoid sounding too melodramatic. "Wait—before you leave, I want to give you something." Ace pulled out from his belt loop the black notebook that included the three stories he had read to Caroline and handed them to her.

"I can't, Ace."

"You can't have them! I want them back!" Ace quipped. "I just want you to read them...if you can decipher my writing."

"I think I've learned how to read Ace writing by now. Thank you, my love. This will be a perfect way for me to have you with me until we see each other again." She threw her arms around him and hugged him tightly, and they embraced with their wet bodies, pulling them together. "I will see you soon, my love. I can't wait to read your stories. I love you."

"I love you too." They kissed, and for a moment the skies cleared and everything was the way it was supposed to be, but then she was gone, and the train pulled away from the station, leaving only the resuming rain.

He decided to walk home despite the rain, which was now coming down in sheets. The sky above him shook with anger, and the rain fell heavy on his already rain-soaked jacket. He walked slowly and was distraught. He was alone, and his mind raced. Should he have let Caroline leave? Should he have gone with her? Should she have seen a doctor sooner? His thoughts drifted with anger and sadness, and soon he was inside the only place he felt comfortable without Caroline.

"Ah mate, long time no see!" The Australian bartender was still there. "Lucky you caught me—I'm leaving in a few days to South America." He looked down at Ace's sad body, which was wet and shivering. "Mate, you look absolutely frigid, and where is that beautiful missus of yours?"

"On holiday," Ace mumbled.

"Ahh, so while the missus is away, you can grace us lowly backpackers again?"

"Can I get a shot and a beer, please?"

He usually drank only when he was happy and wanted to have a laugh. Now he was drinking to forget. But the worst part of drinking to forget is that you never do, and the more quickly the drinks consume you and the drunken state gets deeper and more established, the more you remember the things you wanted most to forget. Finally, your only option is to keep drinking until you no longer remember anything at all. Until the sadness washes over you and you become drunk and sloppy.

That night after several attempts at stumbling up the stairs, he managed to make it into bed, and there he lay drunk with no thoughts.

44

The next few days were slow and painful, and the rain continued to thrash the city. Ace's only activity was staring outside for hours, hoping he would see Caroline walking up the rain-soaked street.

He would often daydream as he watched the rain fall heavy and fast. He would visualize Caroline walking up the small hill, and she'd be soaking wet. She never used an umbrella, as she liked to feel the rain and it was always her favorite time to take photographs. She would say how the rain-soaked landscape made her photographs better. Without showering, let alone drying off, she would hurry into the darkroom and hours later exit with new photographs. They would then cook dinner together and make love in the kitchen and eventually fall asleep on the couch with a Coltrane record playing in sync with the raindrops that fell on the roof.

The vivid daydream almost convinced him that she had just gone for a walk and she would return soon, but she never did, and nothing happened besides the rain that kept falling and the streets that stayed empty.

Even the plants, so lush and green due to Caroline's diligence, began to droop and fade in the quietness of the apartment. Ace hated quiet. It made him think too much. His mind would wander to dark places. He needed to leave that silence, and quickly. The only place that he felt he could go was the familiar territory of the hostel bar.

He walked in drenched, and the bar was crowded with drunk travelers. A sign above the bar written in fresh chalk read *HALF OFF UNTIL THE RAIN STOPS*. Ace sidled up to the bar to order.

"This rain is crazy!" he said to the Australian bartender, shaking the wetness off himself.

"I haven't seen this much rain since traveling through Southeast Asia," the bartender replied.

Ace shrugged. "Haven't been. Can I get a Kronenbourg and a shot of whiskey, mate?"

"Half off, so you can order whatever you want!" He looked around and whispered, "And because it's my last day, these two are on the house!" He slid over the beer and whiskey.

"South America, right?"

"Yeah, flying into Buenos Aires tomorrow."

"Thanks for the drink. Safe travels! And cheers, my old friend." They clinked glasses, and Ace swallowed the brown liquor. It felt warm and satisfied him for a moment.

The bar was crowded, and he sat alone as the noise level soared. *Any drink deal will make backpackers show up*, he thought. He drank his beer and thought of Caroline until he was well on his way to being drunk enough to sleep. Soon, the bar was about to burst and was buzzing with intoxicated travelers. Ace was about to walk out when the Australian bartender yelled him over to the bar.

"Ace! Mate! Ace!" Ace made his way back through the crowd.

"What is it?" Ace questioned.

"I need a favor. Would you be willing to take over for me at the pub crawl tonight?"

"What?" Ace asked, puzzled.

"It's my last night; I need to say good-bye to a girl. My Paris amour."

"Oh, you finally found her?! Does that mean you speak French?"

"Oui, just like you, mate."

"Dude, then why are you leaving for South America?"

"I haven't learned Spanish yet!"

Ace couldn't help but laugh. It was the first time he had laughed since Caroline had left, and it felt good. "What do I have to do?"

"Just take these lovely newbies to these bars here." He pointed to piece of paper scattered with doodles and drawings that also contained a list of bars. "Each place will give drink specials if you are part of the pub crawl—and that's it. Nothing better to do in the rain than drink, right?"

Ace took a look at the list. He knew where all the bars were, so he agreed. He didn't want to go back to that lonely apartment. He folded the piece of paper and put it in his back pocket and took another shot of whiskey.

"Thanks heaps, Ace! I owe you one!"

"You are welcome, Willy. Maybe I'll see you in South America and you can buy me a drink."

"Do it, mate! Would love for ya to join." Ace shrugged, and William rushed out into the pouring rain.

The night pushed on and the rain didn't stop, and neither did the drinks. He joined the backpackers' party and pub crawl. Here no one knew Caroline or asked about his past, and in his drunkenness he began to give out advice to all the eager backpackers, who seemed to hang on his every word. Telling them all the best places to go in Paris. What bars to go to. What museums to go to. He liked the attention that the women gave him as they all flocked around him to hear his tales of living in Paris, and the men enjoyed his humor and crass jokes. Mostly, though, Ace was just trying to get drunk enough so he could fall asleep, and after a long night, he succeeded.

He slept most of the next day. His head pounded from the alcohol, his skin was sweating and his body smelled. When he finally got out of bed, he shuffled around the apartment. It was a sad apartment with Caroline no longer there, and its stillness made him shiver. The only thing he wanted to do was to look at her photographs that would still make him smile. He took a big stack of photographs and shuffled through them, and soon the afternoon turned to evening. He was still slowly working his way through the hundreds of prints when he heard the telephone ring. He leaped off the couch and picked up the phone.

"Caroline?!"

45

I was up early. Early enough that I had beaten the sunrise and I laid underneath the warmth of the blanket, avoiding the cold Pai air. Eventually, I watched a hint of light come through the small windows in our three-bedroom dorm and reluctantly pulled myself out of my blanket cocoon.

Ace and Maggie were still asleep, so I walked lightly around the room, careful not to wake them. I put on my sweatpants, a sweater and a beanie and emerged into the cold, brisk morning.

We were staying at a simple housing complex with several small rooms about 20 minutes outside of the town of Pai. I walked to the retreat space, which was a short walk down a gravel road, and into a small open space that consisted of an open-air dining area with an adjacent kitchen. Next to that was a barn-like structure with an A-frame roof with no walls that led up to a garden of lush green grass and an assortment of flowers. Light had just begun to peek above the horizon over the hills behind the little plot of land in the countryside of Pai.

From here, Pai seemed untouched. There were no 7-11s and no souvenir shops, just endless miles of pristine country landscape with rolling green hills and green trees and a few small houses that led to small dirt roads.

The brisk air caused me to shovel my hands deep into my thin sweater. My bones seemed to have forgotten what cold air felt like as I shivered uncontrollably. A few people were gathering now, but an awkward silence hung over us. We had been told the day before that the mornings were to be silent and that we should be mindful of our surroundings and of our actions. I didn't really know what that meant, so I just walked in circles on this cold morning, trying to warm my body.

Near the kitchen, a small congregation of people crowded around the warm tea that was being served. It wasn't just me who was not accustomed to cold mornings, and we all found refuge in the warmth of the tea. We had all met briefly the night before as Bhud explained the itinerary for the weekend. Morning silence. Morning meditation. Mindfulness philosophy. Evening meditation. Evening silence. Sleep.

I poured myself a large cup of hot ginger tea with a teaspoon of honey. The hot tea felt great in my hands and felt even better as I drank it and it thawed my body. I made eye contact with a few people, and we awkwardly smiled at each other before returning our nervous gaze to the ground.

The barn-like structure was already prepared for us, and several pillows and blankets had been meticulously laid out. In the garden there were a few uninhabited benches that overlooked the Pai valley. I sipped my hot tea and took a seat on one of them. The low fog covered the valley below us and reminded me of the spot where Sophia and I had sat just a few days earlier.

Maggie soon appeared, and she too looked cold. She wrapped her arms around herself as she waited her turn to warm herself with a cup of tea. She spotted me and walked over as she took a big sip and shivered. I glanced around, and I guess she knew what I was thinking. She gave the sleeping sign and shrugged. Ace was not one for an early morning or silence, and I began to doubt if he would show up at all.

Bhud was now present, and she was walking around in a large puffy jacket, black yoga pants and colorful, thick socks and giving everyone a morning hug. Her embrace felt warm and honest. As she pulled away, she looked into our eyes and whispered, "Thank you for being here with me." We all migrated toward the large empty room with yoga mats. There was still no sign of Ace. Maggie sat to the left of me, and next to me I held a space for Ace, if he ever showed up.

"Please feel free to wrap yourself with the blankets and sit on the pillows," Bhud said quietly. "I want you to get as comfortable as possible, as we will shortly go into our first meditation practice together." She was smiling at all the anxious bodies around her awaiting further instructions, when Ace finally emerged.

"Bloody cold out here!" he yelled as he stomped his way through the room. Everyone gave him a sharp glance, but Bhud just smiled.

"Remember, Ace, we will be quiet in the mornings, as it helps us get in the right mindset to promote mindfulness," Bhud said again in a calm nurturing voice.

"Oh yes. I'm ready for it! Oh shit. Sorry." He made a zipper motion across his mouth and looked at me, making a face. Bhud smiled as she sat in a cross-legged position on her mat and closed her eyes. I tried to twist my legs like hers, but my body said no. I was already uncomfortable.

46

Inhale... one, two, three, four.

Hold... one, two, three, four, five, six.

Exhale... one, two, three, four, five, six, seven, eight.

Again.

Inhale... one, two, three, four.

Hold... one, two, three, four, five, six.

Exhale... one, two, three, four, five, six, seven, eight.

Bhud was leading us through our first meditation practice with only counting as our guidance. I had been expecting her to tell us exactly how to meditate so that I'd look like the monks I had seen in Chiang Mai, but instead she simply counted breaths.

I sat up with several pillows stacked underneath me because I knew from earlier defeats that sitting on the ground was a losing battle. I wanted to focus on my breath and try to let go of my thoughts, just like I had read in my book. Maggie was breathing peacefully next to me, but I could feel that Ace was struggling. I could hear him groan with frustration as he shuffled around and switched positions. Though he wasn't saying any words, he was still the loudest person in the room. I was also having difficulty, and I opened my eyes several times, especially as my mind wandered to Ace and Sophia and the decision I would soon have to make.

The thirty minutes slowly clicked away. Then a gentle echo of a singing bowl sounded, and we were instructed to open our eyes. Still sitting cross-legged in front of us and smiling, Bhud looked every person in the eye.

"Congratulations! You have finished your first meditation. How many people found that difficult?" Almost everyone raised their hands. "That's good. That's ok. If you were uncomfortable, that's ok. If you are having a hard time focusing, that's ok. We are all getting used to being uncomfortable. This weekend is all about doing things that will make us uncomfortable. What I want you to try to do is not resist when you are uncomfortable or to get frustrated with yourself. What we are doing seems simple, right? But each of you raised your hands, saying it was not so simple. All we are doing is sitting. Should be easy, right? But why is it not? Because we have wild monkey minds. Our little smart brains are always on, always thinking about something. That one night five years ago, or maybe where am I going after I finish with this crazy person here in Pai." We all laughed, and Bhud let out a loud chuckle that was so honest that it made everyone else smile. "Ok, now everyone go eat and drink more tea! Woo hoo!" she shouted.

We all shuffled up to the kitchen area, hoping to sit down to a warm breakfast, but what we got instead was cold vegetarian soup. I dived in, and it wasn't half bad. I looked over at Ace, and he made a face of disgust as he poured a spoonful out over the bowl and made a mocking prayer salute, but even he was hungry and eventually shoveled spoonful after spoonful into his mouth. He may have even enjoyed it, as he scraped the empty bowl until it was all gone. Bhud then called us back down to our meditation area, and we were soon back on our pillows with our blankets wrapped around our cold but warming bodies.

"As you may already have noticed, this isn't your classic meditation retreat, and I'm not your classic meditation teacher. We are not in a Buddhist temple. There will be no chanting and no talking of religion or spiritual ideology. This retreat is here for you to learn about yourself through silence and through laughter. I want all of us to regain a connection to our body and to our life force—our breath! I want you to leave here not becoming a different person or completely changing your lifestyle but, rather, being able to improve your ability to react to daily experiences and to appreciate the world around us that is so beautiful and special. And, don't worry, we will not only do silent meditation but several forms of meditation. Like life, meditation doesn't have a rule book. You don't have to be in the Himalayas in Nepal or in a silent room. It can be done anywhere at any time. Now, let's dance!" We all looked around silently, feeling confused, but Bhud was serious, and she kicked and threw our pillows and blankets out of the way and turned on music. She began to sway her hips rhythmically to the music. Everyone else stood still.

"Come on, people. Move! This is to release all that energy you have stored up in your body. If you are nervous or thinking too much, you can't meditate. We aren't here dancing to look cool but to find that inner child inside of us that is happy and free." Bhud jumped up and down and did somersaults and rolled on the ground as she smiled and laughed. We slowly joined in and moved rigidly at first, but soon we were all moving whimsically and shaking our arms to the steady drumbeat. Bhud was laughing and making playful faces at everyone. She truly did move like a child; her happiness was contagious, and we all began to buy in.

We were all beginning to sweat when Bhud turned down the music and our bodies slowly stopped swaying. "Everyone now find a comfortable spot to sit. Now that we have found our body, let's find our breath again." We sat down again as Bhud counted our breaths, and soon we were once again sitting in silence. It was much more calming and relaxing this time, and I felt more at ease. Even Ace was not shuffling around as much, and quickly the thirty minutes were over.

"Wow, she is crazy!" Ace said immediately as we returned to our room for a break.

"Yes, but in the best way possible. I love her," Maggie responded.

"Yeah, I like her too," I added.

Ace shrugged. "Yeah, I like her too, but I don't think this meditation thing is for me. I will be glad to leave and soon be in Myanmar. Right, Charlie?" I looked at him and nodded but didn't say anything at least not about going back to Chiang Mai.

The afternoon session started with us eating a light vegetarian meal that consisted of spring rolls that we helped construct and a fruit smoothie that was prepared beautifully by the two women cooks. We all thanked them as we ate in the warm sun. Bhud walked by smiling and seemingly glowing. She was now wearing a tank top and a ripped sweater that hung to one side of her body, exposing her right shoulder and giving us a peek at another tattoo. We silently gathered in the open-air A-frame and watched her circle us in silence before presenting us with a question.

"How many of you are backpacking?" Bhud started. Everyone raised their hands. "That is a great way to see the world, no?" We nodded our heads in agreement. "More and more people are flying all around this little planet, and we are connected now more than ever. We all have access to computers and to the Internet. We have our little phones that we hold so close to our bodies, and yet with all this new technology and all this wealth that allows us to do such great things, why are so many people miserable?" Everyone seemed to agree, as I saw people silently nodding their heads.

"I receive lovely emails from people who have visited me here in Pai. They will say such nice things about me and about our little retreat and how happy they were when they were here. Here they could meditate and be mindful. Here was their paradise. Now that they are back home, they are bored and have post-travel depression. They tell me about little pet peeves that make them angry, and they tell me how they would love to come back here to Pai to once again find happiness." She walked around the room, and all our eyes followed.

"What is this 'bored'? What is this 'pet peeves'? Why do you have to be here to find happiness? Help me understand it. Can someone share so maybe we can answer this question for me? Pet peeves, anyone?"

"Bad drivers!" someone yelled out. There were a few chuckles.

"England rain!" someone else yelled out, and everyone laughed.

"Elephant pants!" Ace yelled out, and a few people awkwardly laughed. Nearly everyone except the three of us was wearing some sort of elephant-style pants. Maggie shot him a look that could have burned a hole in him.

Bhud continued on quickly, "Why do we let weather bother us?

Shouldn't we be happy if it rains and the water feeds the plants and animals and gives us water to drink too? Bad weather? In winter a tree loses dead leaves only to grow new life and new energy when the weather warms up. Isn't that circle of life amazing? Elephant pants? Why should other people's clothes bother us? Who does it really hurt? Bad drivers? Well, I'm no great driver, so please don't hate me." Everyone let out a chuckle. I looked over at Maggie, and she still seemed upset with Ace's comment.

"Why get upset with things you cannot control? Yes? You understand? So many little things we let bother us, and those little things add up to big things, and soon we are angry at everything. That doesn't make sense. Why do we allow it to affect us? Can we change our way of thinking and let go of the things that are out of our control?" she continued.

"And why do you think everyone gets bored? Because they are no longer traveling? I know I said this isn't a Buddhist retreat, but Buddha sat underneath the bodhi tree for 49 days! He did not travel. He wasn't getting passport stamps. He wasn't posting on Instagram. He just sat underneath one tree, and during those 49 days—nearly seven weeks—he found nirvana, or complete happiness. Now, I know we aren't Buddha, but why can't we find happiness in the stillness of life? Can we find it in the mundane acts of waking up every morning and finding happiness on our walk to work? How about eating dinner with our friends, or better yet, eating alone? Enjoying our alone time to laugh and breathe. For our next meditation, I want each of you to walk around these beautiful grounds by yourself and find your own bodhi tree and sit with your eyes open or closed, but focus on being calm and enjoying the simple pleasures in life as you breathe mindfully. Now, go and have fun!" Everyone scattered off.

I walked about the openness of the land and found a flat rock underneath a small palm tree. It was shaded and looked out onto the valley below. We hadn't been instructed on how long we were supposed to sit, so I just sat and watched. I watched the clouds gather and fade away as they passed the deep valley. I watched thousands of blades of green grass curl and straighten in the wind. I watched the tiny ants make their way across the grass to get food. I watched the soft, brown dirt give the plants life. I thought of Sophia and my photographs, and the opportunity to present my work, and I thought of Ace and how helpful he had been to me when I first arrived. But, mostly, I thought about my dad. I thought about everything he had taught me. His words resonated with me, as did his life and what he had hoped for me. At that moment, I knew the answer to the question that stirred in my head. Why does everything seem so simple when you have the right answer? I wasn't going to say no to anyone. I was going to say yes to me.

When I got back to our room, Ace and Maggie were already there. Maggie was reading, and Ace sat alone next to a mound of cigarettes that were perfectly rolled. The tobacco case he had brought with him now sat empty next to him on his bed, and stringy pieces of tobacco hung from his fingers. His eyes were big and blank. He seemed to be in a daze. It was a familiar stare I was used to seeing late at night when he had had too many drinks, but this was different. This was the first time I'd seen those eyes when he was sober.

"How was your session, Ace?" I asked, trying to pull him out of his trance.

Maggie put down the book and yelled, "This asshole has been here the whole time!"

Ace blinked and shot her a look. "Yeah, I know. I'm the asshole. Sorry, I just think this silence and meditation thing is not for me. I might not make it to tonight's session," he said firmly, but his tone was devoid of any of the passion that Ace usually talked with.

"I still can't believe you brought up the elephant pants!" Maggie chimed in again. "That was just mean; you know that everyone there was wearing them. Maybe you should skip tonight and go back into town so you can get drunk and impress the travelers there with your stories."

"I was just joking," Ace said.

"You weren't just joking. You were trying to prove you are better than everyone else. You can call me young, but I'm not immature." Maggie tossed her book down and walked out. Ace returned to his empty bag of tobacco and tried desperately to gather enough tobacco for one more cigarette.

"Ace, we need to talk," I said to him, ending his fruitless attempts at gathering tobacco.

"Are you mad at me too?" he asked pensively.

"No. Not mad. I just wanted to tell you that I can't go with you to

Myanmar. I'm going back to Chiang Mai after we finish here."

"Going back to see Sophia, huh?" he said, never once looking in my direction.

"Not just that. But guess what? She was able to get my films developed, and she thought they were good. And so did Mia, and they invited me to present them at a show they are hosting. Here—take a look!" I pulled out the envelope that held my developed prints. Ace barely acknowledged the envelope that I waved in his face. He didn't even try to convince me not to go or say that I was breaking some travel rule. He just stared past me as I held up my photographs. "You can come back with me. I'd love to have you there to support me. I know Mia wouldn't mind either. Maybe you can bartend the show?"

"HA HA. Bartend your event?! Is that all I am to you? Some bloody bartender? And now you think you are some big shot, having some shit event with flashpackers!"

"No, of course not, Ace. I didn't mean that. I just meant... You don't have to go off again, alone. I thought you would be happy for me."

"Because you are going to have an art show in front of stupid expats and flashpackers?" Ace said.

"At least I'm trying! And I'm proud of my work. Maybe it will be a shit show, or whatever you want to call it, but I'm happy that someone likes my photographs, and I'm excited to show off my work. I thought you would be excited for me too."

"Yeah—sorry, mate. Not my audience, Charlie."

"I don't care if a flashpacker or Instagram traveler with the brightest pair of elephant pants likes my work. At least I'm doing it. And I'm taking a chance. I can't believe you, Ace. I've held my tongue for so long because I looked up to you and thought you were better than this. For some reason, you can inspire everyone you touch. Look at William, look at Mia, and now look at me! But you can't inspire yourself. I thought you were more than the selfish person everyone from your past makes you out to be. I know if you could forget all that stuff in your head, you might be able to write again. But it looks like you are just going to run away like you always do."

"You don't know anything about my writing, or anything about me. I'm tired of this place. I'm outta here."

"What?! Where are you going?"

Ace stood up and walked out. Leaving behind his backpack and a mountain of perfectly rolled cigarettes.

47

I waited for an hour for him to come back. Waited for the door to swing open and for him to spring back in with that big, booming voice. But the only thing that occupied the room was a silence that hung on me like a weight.

When I finally left to have dinner, I half expected Ace to reappear in his normal fashion, but he never showed.

At dinner, I told Maggie about the argument between Ace and myself.

"Good for you Charlie," Maggie whispered, "Don't worry, he will be fine. He needed to hear it from you. Everyone gives him a free pass, including myself. He needed a good friend to call him on his shit." I nodded but still couldn't shake a feeling of anticipated sadness, as if I knew something bad was going to happen. After dinner, my head spun as we formed a tight circle in the center of the room and began our nightly meditation session. I kept a steady lookout for Ace as Bhud began.

"This is called laughing meditation. It's time to let go of the control we desperately want. We want to control every little thing—part of our own lives and sometimes other people's lives too—but life can't be controlled. Sometimes we make good decisions and choices, and sometimes we make bad choices or maybe we say the wrong thing. No matter if it turns out good or bad, we have to acknowledge it happened and let it go. We can't get too high on victories or too down with defeats. Everyone who has thoughts that you can't control, take a step in closer to the circle." We all moved in. "It's now time to laugh these thoughts away."

We looked around confused, because we didn't know what on earth she was talking about, and then out of nowhere Bhud let out a crackle of a laugh:

"HAHAHAHAHAHAHAHAHA!" She smiled at us all and dived into another one: "HAHAHAHAHAHAHAHAHA!" And another: "HAHAHAHAHAHAHAHAHA!"

Slightly taken aback, all of us smiled and laughed a bit, thinking it was a joke, but she continued, "HAHAHAHAHA!" Big belly laugh after big belly laugh. Soon someone behind joined her and let out their own laugh, and Bhud smiled a pointed smile. "That's it; let it out." Then another person laughed, and I turned and saw Maggie laugh. Then, as if it were a virus spreading, I caught it too and laughed. I let out a wallop of a laugh that even surprised me.

Soon we were all laughing almost uncontrollably. My body was no longer mine. I was laughing and giggling without trying. There were 15 adults in a circle laughing as loud as we could. We continued for several minutes until my side ached and I had tears streaming down my face, but I continued to laugh because I couldn't stop. It was magical. No one cared about what we looked like or how we were acting or why we were even laughing.

Then Bhud lifted her hand in the air and slowly brought it down. The laughter quietened down, and she began to lower herself to the ground. We followed her movements and formed a large circle. There was complete silence, and I fell into a peaceful meditation.

Bhud then rose and whispered, "Remember, try not to control you or anyone else. Sometimes we just need to laugh with people."

After the meditation, I felt a weight was lifted off me, as if the fight I had had with Ace hadn't even happened. That ominous feeling that I had been carrying around was no longer rattling in my brain. I no longer felt like I had to apologize to Ace. I had said my peace, and I was content with that, and I was going to let it go and talk to Ace in a calmer manner. Ace had to be back in the room by now. With my head clear, I rushed back to the room. I was looking forward to going back to my room and finding Ace rolling cigarettes, but he wasn't there. The only thing that was moved was the manilla folder that now rested back on my bed.

48

His backpack sat there all night. Every time I opened my eyes, expecting him to be there, all I saw was his old, tattered backpack. Several holes had worn through the edges, and the shoulder and waist straps where soft padding had resided were all but worn down to nothing. The color of the pack, once a bright blue, was now faded into a sun-bleached blue that showed a mixture of dirt and stains. Unlike the fresh new backpacks of most people whom you meet at a hostel, Ace's told a different story. It wasn't always a pretty story, but it was a story all its own. The places his backpack had gone. The things it had seen. There was something about that bag, the way it was worn down by time and abuse but somehow still shone in the darkness.

"Where could he have gone without his backpack?" Maggie said, now a bit worried, as Ace had not come back. "He would never just leave his bag behind." Then we rattled off our favorite Ace anecdotes and smiled as we both missed him. He wasn't just a person or a fellow backpacker. He was our friend.

That morning, Maggie and I silently walked on the gravel road down to the retreat space. Once again, everyone was crowded around the tea. I drank my tea and waited for Ace to make one more grand appearance, but only the distant cows were making noises this morning. Maggie and I walked around the A-frame to a bench that overlooked the valley when we saw him. My mouth dropped, and I couldn't believe it.

Sitting alone off into the distance was a person covered in a blanket. We both knew it was Ace, as his wide shoulders were unmistakable, even with the thick blanket wrapped around him. I ran up to him and looked at him. His eyes were bright blue. I had never noticed that he had blue eyes; now they were almost sparkling. He didn't say a word, but he smiled and gave me a hug. He engulfed me with his large arms, and I began to cry. I don't know why, but I cried, and only Bhud's voice pulled me away from him as we returned to the A-frame for our last meditation.

"What a wonderful weekend. I want to thank everyone who partic-ipated with me. This has been a short retreat, but hopefully you learned something, and maybe you will take something home with you or wher-ever your life leads you next. Now, let's finish off the same way we started with our last meditation."

The singing bowl once again ended our session, and when we had finished, Bhud walked around and hugged everyone. This time, unlike the first day, the hug was reciprocated from every participant, accompa-nied by love and praise for the wonderful weekend. When she came to Ace, she pointed her finger at him and smiled, and they embraced. Ace whispered something in her ear, and they hugged again. Soon everyone scattered either to take a photo with Bhud or to gather their stuff to leave. I just watched Ace as he strolled gracefully toward me.

"You know what, Charlie? I hate silence. I hate the way I feel in it. I hate the way all the memories I don't want to think about seep into my head when it's quiet. Silence makes me go to places I don't want to go. Back to everyone I disappointed. To everyone I let down. Most people don't last around me long enough to call me out like you did. Backpack-ing was my shield, a way for me to avoid not getting too close to anyone. And if anyone gets too close I'd run and I had all intentions of running last night. I went back into town. I went to a bar. It was full of people

I didn't know and no one knew me. It was perfect. I sat there for hours with a beer that I couldn't bring myself to drink it. You know why?"

"They only had Budweiser?" I smirked.

"When did you become so funny mate?" he said shaking his head. "I thought about you and how you much you reminded me of someone I used to know and both of you were stuck in my head. I dropped the beer and walked back here. Took me ages, and just as the sun was beginning to rise I arrived back here and was making my way back to the room, when I ran into Bhud. She didn't ask me anything. She just looked at me. She stared at me, and then she hugged me. She hugged me long and hard, and I don't know what happened, but I began to talk. I talked about my regrets, all the people I've hurt, how I've been wasting my life away. I talked until I couldn't talk anymore, and she stood there listening. No judgment. No interjections. Just listening. When I had talked myself into a silence, she whispered, '*You will only be able to get over your past if you forgive yourself now.*' After that, I just sat here, in the silence of the morning, and finished watching this beautiful valley wake up."

"And have you forgiven yourself?" I said cheerfully, still happy to see him.

"It's not that easy. I have to go back somewhere first and finally tell someone I'm sorry. Then maybe I'll finish forgiving myself. But first I have to say sorry to you, and thank you for being a friend. A true friend. It's something that I haven't had in a long time."

"I'm sorry too, Ace. And back? Back where? No Uzbekistan?"

"Haha. No, that trip will have to wait. And one more thing. Why didn't you tell me your photographs were so good? If I'd have known how good they were, I would have had a friend develop them." He winked as he lightly hit my shoulder.

"Haha thanks! Wait... but you haven't seen them."

"I may have snuck a peek when you crazy hyenas were laughing. What the fuck was that?"

"Long story. And why is everyone looking at my photographs without telling me!" We both laughed.

"I'm excited about your show. I think your future will be bright after the event."

"You are going to come—right, Ace? You are coming back to Chiang Mai?"

"I can't. I'm flying to Paris."

"Ohh Paris, that's great." I said trying to sound happy but was sad he was missing my show.

"Nah, only kidding. Yes... of course I'm coming to Chiang Mai! I wouldn't miss it. Not every day you get to see a legend's first show." He held his hand out for a handshake.

"Thanks, Ace. That means a lot." I pushed his hand away and threw myself at him embracing him with another big hug as he engulfed me with his arms.

"Now where is Maggie? I owe her an apology or ten." She was standing off to the side stealing glances our way. I could tell she was happy to see him. He walked toward Maggie. They talked for a while, and at the end they shared a hug and then walked over to me, both of them smiling. The three of us stood there grinning at absolutely nothing, but all of us completely happy.

"Oh no. I think we went... ," I started to say.

"Don't you say it," Maggie said.

"Full Fucking Pai!" Ace yelled.

49

He walked up Boulevard de Magenta toward Montmartre. He took a deep breath in, and the spring air smelled the same as it had years ago. He knew the flowers in the Luxembourg Garden would be blooming and people would be gathering in front of the Eiffel Tower drinking wine and the young travelers in the hostels would be spending their evenings drunk and carefree. He didn't need to go to those places or see those things because he already knew them to be true. Paris never changed; only you did.

He read the signs and words on the shop windows. He was a bit rusty with his French, but as he repeated them to himself like he had done years ago, he felt the magic of the language reappear in his mouth. It had been a few days since he had gathered up his belongings and left Chiang Mai and flown to Europe.

He was wearing new blue jeans and sneakers and a light-gray wool sweater that he had bought in a boutique store just outside of Gare du

Nord. As he stared at himself in the dressing room mirror, he couldn't help but smile, and he walked out of the store, leaving behind a small pile of dirty clothes in the dressing room.

The cold air felt refreshing and comfortable as he walked slowly away from Gare du Nord. He walked up Boulevard de Magenta toward Montmartre. Men in cheap suits waited outside stores that lined the streets and attempted to draw him in, but after years abroad, he was immune to storefront hagglers. He would answer them in French, and they would no longer think he was a tourist and would stop their pursuit.

He passed a few Metro signs, and a tinge of nostalgia came over his body as he fondly remembered how beautiful he thought those signs were when he first arrived in Paris all those years ago. He hadn't placed a step in this city for nearly a decade, but his feet knew exactly where to go. He marched past Rue de Garreau and passed the On the Road pub. He glanced in and saw four young boys at the bar obviously filled with the excitement of being in Paris and celebrating by doing shots of cheap liquor.

Then he turned to the right and saw those long, white stairs that led up the hill to the white, towering building in the sky. It was mid-afternoon, and tourists had already been gathering for hours. He smiled as he passed families and couples and some backpackers as they hurried up to the beautiful church. That afternoon he finally walked up those stairs himself. Surrounded by selfie sticks and Instagram poses he smiled and enjoyed the view.

He then walked up past the Montmartre Cemetery and pushed up the hill. As the hill ascended, the tourists decreased, and then he stood directly across from it.

It was still there, as he knew it would be. The only differences were the ivy plants that had once been small and confined and had now overgrown the café. They marched out of the front window and crawled up the side of the bricks and disappeared over the edge of the small building—Café Lavender.

He closed his eyes and tried to breathe deeply to get his mind under control. Five breaths. Ten breaths. Still, his heart raced. More deep breaths. He lost count. Who knows how long he was there, but somehow he was able to get control. He walked across the quiet street and pushed open the door.

The café was dark, with only one young couple inside. They sat across from each other, enjoying an afternoon coffee. Behind the counter, an old man sat drinking from a large cup and looking out the window. Ace sat down in the chair closest to the door, and from the moment he walked in he could tell something was different. It wasn't the smell. With each inhale he breathed in that same smell. In each corner hung a lavender plant, and he turned his head and put his nose near one of the blooming purple flowers. The smell filled his nose and tickled his senses. It was intoxicating. It smelled like her. He closed his eyes, and it was like having her next to him in bed.

He continued to move his gaze across the room. The café reminded him of the apartment they had once shared: small and cluttered, yet still peaceful, organized chaos. The old man working behind the bar didn't even notice him walk in as he continued to stare out the window.

His eyes made the rounds on the room. Still there, hung on the otherwise empty walls, were small, black-and-white photographs just like before, but something was different. He looked more closely and saw that the images were different than they had been and that something new hung below each of the photographs. He stood up from the chair, walked over and stared at the first one. Then he rushed over to the second one, and the third, and the fourth and fifth, and finally he ended his race around the room at a small plaque beside the last photograph:

I never wanted these photographs to be in a museum
They belong to people like the ones in this café
To the people of Paris
These photographs were a part of me as they were a part of
the strangers whose moments I captured
And they were my own little secrets
They were hidden away until someone whom I love dearly
brought them to life
Inspired by them, he discovered his voice, and that would
change my perception of my own work
I'm forever grateful for his words, as he gave me the
courage to present a collection of my photographs with his
accompanying short stories
He was my love, and I am forever indebted to him for

helping me find my voice
These are ours as much as they are yours

—C.S.

Below each photograph displayed in frames were Ace's original short stories. He hadn't read them in years and thought they had been lost forever. He rushed back to the first one and stared at her small insignia in the right-hand corner, and then he slowly mouthed the words of his own writing before turning back to her image.

His legs began to feel shaky as he stood there staring at the wall, and before he knew it, small tears streamed down his face. He put his arm on the wall to brace himself, because he felt as if he could collapse at any moment. He forgot about the couple behind him and made no attempt to hide what was now pouring out of him. He sat there crying loudly, and then he knelt down, his forehead softly making contact with the wall. As he sobbed, he felt a hand on his shoulder.

"I'm sorry, sir," Ace mumbled. "I'm ok." The man said nothing but lifted him up and walked him over to the bar. Ace sat on the barstool. He was shaking, and the old man gave him a large glass of water and tissues. He drank the water quickly, then wiped his tears with the tissue, not once looking at the old man.

"I think I will need something stronger than that." Ace pointed at the empty water glass.

"Me too," the old man said. Ace then looked at the old man: his face calm and gentle, with wrinkles covering every inch, his pure-white hair sprouting sparsely on his head. Everything about his face was old and tired except for his eyes. His eyes were dark black and youthful and vibrant. Ace immediately knew who he was.

"Hello, Ace. You are as handsome as Caroline said you would be." Ace couldn't believe it. It was Caroline's father.

Without thinking, Ace blurted out, "I'm so sorry for not coming to—"

"I'm going to stop you right there. We aren't going to spend our first time meeting apologizing for a past we can't change. Caroline loved you more than anything, so I know you are a good man with a good heart. She was a wonderful judge of character, so I won't take any apology from you, ok?" Ace nodded. His eyes were drying now, and his legs felt steady with the help from the barstool.

"I think I will close early today so you and I can talk properly." The old man walked over, locked the door and closed the blinds.

"Whiskey?" he asked.

"Please," Ace said.

Caroline's father then reached for a bottle underneath the bar and poured two small glasses. They said a toast about a new future, and they began to rapidly fall into a conversation about Caroline. Her father was easy to talk to, and they laughed as they each shared memories of her. Her father recalled how when Caroline became really sick, she had told him that she wanted to show her work. Immediately he sent her work to small galleries. They all responded with a resounding yes. She was too sick to travel, but soon her art was hanging all over the city. He went to many of the openings, and people raved about her work, and many courted him and attempted to purchase pieces but, under her strict orders, none were for sale. He would return to Caroline quickly after such outings, and she was pleased with the response but was getting sicker each day. On one of her last days, she handed him five photographs and five pages of written words.

"These were her photographs and your words. She told me how you gave her the courage to show her work and that she wanted to thank you for sharing your words with her. Her last instructions to me were that they were to be hung here in Café Lavender. She knew this was the place you would return to, and she hoped you would like the display."

"I'm in awe of it." They were both in tears now. They had talked so much that they hadn't even taken a sip of their whiskey. The brown liquid sat untouched in the dim light that hung over the bar. The day had disappeared, and the streets were now dark.

"It's been wonderful to meet you, my son. You are special, and I can see why my daughter loved you. Please meet me here tomorrow. I would like to take you to the galleries where some of her other photographs are still on display."

"It would be an honor," Ace said.

"Now, I'm not much of a drinker, so please have my whiskey, and here are the keys to the café. I want you to stay as long as you like."

"Are you sure?" Ace replied as Caroline's father slid over a large silver key.

"Yes, I'm old and I'm tired and I want to sleep, and I want you to close up so I don't have to. See you tomorrow, Ace."

Ace was now alone in the darkness of the café. He stared into the glasses full of whiskey that sat in front of him. The brown liquor was good and strong, and he could smell its sweet aroma as he took a deep inhale in. He took one more lap around the room, his fingers rolling along the photographs. He felt the power of her work, and he could see the images through his closed eyes. As he got to the last photograph, he slowly opened his eyes and stared at the small plaque that was placed adjacent to it. His fingers slid down the wall as he read and reread her words. The thought of her and of Paris, and of his running away, used to haunt him with regrets and pain. But as he read her thoughts and love toward him, nothing but hope and pride filled his body, and he whispered, "Merci, mon amour."

He turned and went back to his seat at the bar where the whiskey waited. He reached for his glass and slowly pushed it aside and out of reach. He reached behind him and pulled out a black and weathered notebook that was blank. He opened it and turned to the first page and began to write:

> *It was just past one p.m. The sun was hot, and I was hungover. My room smelled of alcohol and sweat. How many days in a row now have I been drunk? Too many.*
>
> *A beautiful young and vibrant woman slept next to me, and I already felt bad about breaking her heart. I hadn't done it yet, but I knew I was going to.*
>
> *"I need a smoke," I whispered to her.*
>
> *Outside, the city moved like it always had... fast.*
>
> *My fingers twirled around paper and tobacco. I licked each side and stood staring at the perfect cigarette. Young backpackers paced back and forth, each smile bigger than the last. Everyone was carefree and happy, while I was worse than depressed. I barely existed. No one knew me beyond what I showed them, and I showed them nothing. I continued to stare at my cigarette and dangled it loosely to let tobacco settle into its new home, when I saw some-*

thing. I don't know how or why this person stood out. I've been on this backpacker road for so long and have seen thousands of new arrivals come in and out of buses, but I had never seen anyone this lost. He stood there across the Phạm Ngũ Lão Street. Frozen. Like someone had magically placed him there without any warning. But there was something about him. Something that made me feel something I hadn't felt in years. Someone once told me the best qualities people can have are that they are lost and learning. This person was indisputably lost, and something drove me to find out if he wanted to learn.

I tucked my cigarette behind my ear and jogged across the street. He was skinny. His bag nearly doubled him in size. His eyes were wide, and his face was sweating from the heat and the ridiculous sweater he was wearing. He wore jeans too big for him that covered his ankles, but still I noticed that his right one bulged out in an unnatural way.

"Hey kid!" His eyes didn't blink. I hope I'm right about you. "Hey kid!" I said again.

"Oh sorry. Do you know where The Sun Always Rises Backpackers is?" he asked in an almost whisper.

"Do I? I work there. I'm Ace." I stuck my hand out.

"I'm Charlie." We shook hands.

ACKNOWLEDGMENTS

To everyone who reads this book. Thank you.

To my Mom who I'm eternally grateful to for reading an early draft of this book. That rough and poorly structured book was a mess and you helped make it less of a mess.

To my Dad, who shares my love for Ernest Hemingway. Without your copy of *The Sun Also Rises* this book would not be possible.

To Chris the real artist in our family that I looked up to growing up. You are, and will always be, my hero.

And to all my beta readers: Jasmine, Melissa, and Ryan your insights and critiques made this a better book. Much love to you all.

My book editor whos feedback gave me the confidence that this was a book people might enjoy.

To Hortense who helped me with French translations. Your time and guidance was much appreciated.

To Bruno, Jon and Kristina. Thank you for visually bringing my ideas to life.

To all the friends I've made staying at backpacker hostels around the world. Keep exploring.

The books that I found inspiration in for this novel. *Prague*, *The Sun Also Rises*, *A Moveable Feast*, *On the Road*, *Dharma Bums*, *Savage Detectives*, *Super Sad True Love Story*, *A Gentleman in Moscow*, *Burmese Days*.

To the bands and musicians whos songs and words helped with the themes of this book. The Menzingers, Jena Berlin, Restorations, The Lawrence Arms, The Clash, Jawbreaker, The Replacements, The Gaslight Anthem, The National, Chet Baker, Sydney Bechet, Miles Davis.

And lastly, to Anneka. You have been a guiding voice in all of this. Your feedback and open ears were so important in all stages of this book. Thank you for being patient with me over the last two years, for listening to my constant insecurities, and being a soundboard for my thoughts.

Jeffrey Eng was born in San Jose, California. He received his Bachelor's degree from California State University, Long Beach, and has a Doctorate degree from Drexel University in Philadelphia. He has written several blogs and short stories while backpacking across six continents and 50+ countries. Jeffrey is the author of *Never Go Full Pai*, his debut novel. He currently lives in Oakland, California.